A Cajun
Christmas
Killing

Also by Ellen Byron

Body on the Bayou

Plantation Shudders

A Cajun Christmas Killing

A Cajun Country Mystery

Ellen Byron

CROOKED
LANE

NEW YORK

Copyright © 2017 by Ellen Byron

Published in the United States by Crooked Lane Books, an imprint of The Quick Brown Fox & Company LLC.

Crooked Lane Books and its logo are trademarks of The Quick Brown Fox & Company LLC.

Library of Congress Catalog-in-Publication data available upon request.

ISBN (hardcover): 978-1-68331-305-2
ISBN (ePub): 978-1-68331-306-9
ISBN (ePDF): 978-1-68331-308-3

Cover illustration by Stephen Gardner
Book design by Jennifer Canzone

Printed in the United States.

www.crookedlanebooks.com

Crooked Lane Books
34 West 27th St., 10th Floor
New York, NY 10001

First edition: October 2017

10 9 8 7 6 5 4 3 2 1

Dedicated to my three Louisiana Ladies: Charlotte Waguespack Allen, Jan Gilbert, and Gaynell Bourgeois Moore. Thank you for your priceless friendship and constant inspiration.

Chapter One

For Maggie Crozat, there was nowhere lovelier than Pelican, Louisiana, during the holidays. Wrought-iron balconies were threaded with sparkling garlands, and from them dangled colorful Christmas ornaments. Town businesses painted their windows with snowy scenes that delighted the local children, most of whom had never seen real snow thanks to Louisiana's mild winters. In a time-honored tradition, images of pelicans were hidden among the decorations, and anyone who mapped all of them received a prize: a toy pelican for the kids or a pelican-shaped shot glass for the adults. The festive atmosphere brought forth much good cheer among the locals. It also allowed them to ignore the fact that the sleepy Cajun village had been the site of four murders in three months.

Maggie decided to join the collective state of amnesia, even though each of the murders had somehow involved Crozat Plantation Bed and Breakfast, her family's ancestral home turned hostelry. As she drove down the Great River

Road, she took in the bonfires that were in various stages of construction on the Mississippi levee. This was where Pelican's good-natured competitive spirit really manifested itself. In centuries past, the bonfires had served as blazing signposts guiding travelers up the river, but they had evolved into a tradition of lighting the way for the Cajun Santa Claus, Papa Noel, on Christmas Eve. Eager participants who vied to create the most ornate structure often began building them right after Thanksgiving. Others didn't care about looks, opting for the honor of loudest bonfire. Maggie couldn't even see one of them under its layers of firecrackers. She noticed that someone else had simply roped together stacks of cane reed, which popped like firecrackers when they blazed.

She slowed down to admire a pirate ship built of combustible logs. Its neighbor was a wooden replica of Belle Vista, one of the area's most ornate plantations. Maggie's own competitive spirit flared up, only to be quashed by a pang of disappointment. In past years her father, Tug Crozat, had gone log for log with Belle Vista's bonfire by erecting a detailed model of Crozat. But this year, Tug had unexpectedly opted for the more standard pyramid structure. He also bowed out of the fireworks display that always accompanied the bonfire's burning. This really surprised Maggie since Tug usually took to it with the glee of a ten-year-old budding pyromaniac. "The whole event's become too much of a dang production," Tug told his family one night as they scrubbed down the kitchen after their guests had gone to bed. Maggie noticed his broad, gently lined face was missing its usual warm smile. "We can't *not* build a bonfire—our guests expect it.

So instead, we're going back to basics. Logs, gasoline, and some matches. Bing, bang, boom. Show's over."

"But—" was all the protest Tug allowed his daughter to get out.

"This is not negotiable," he had snapped in a tone so sharp it had startled Maggie; her mother, Ninette; and her grand-mère.

Maggie parked her 1964 Ford Falcon convertible across the road from Crozat on the shoulder below the levee. As she got out, she waved to the small group of friends and neighbors Tug had assembled to build the bonfire. A handsome, rangy man with black hair and dark eyes grinned and loped down the levee slope to Maggie.

"Hey," Detective Bo Durand said when he reached her. The two shared a chaste kiss. Their relationship was finally public after months of seeing each other on the sly so as not to tick off Bo's cousin and boss at Pelican PD, Police Chief Rufus Durand. Rufus carried a long-standing grudge against the Crozat family. He was currently on leave from the force, a punishment for duking it out with the town mayor over a parking space, but Maggie and Bo were still cautious about public displays of affection.

"Dinner tonight?" Bo asked. "Word on the street is K&B Seafood got in a bushel of Gulf crabs this morning." As he spoke, he wiped his brow with the back of his hand to remove the perspiration threatening to drip onto his high cheekbones. Maggie noted that said perspiration was also making Bo's T-shirt stick to his lean, well-defined torso. She managed to suppress the urge to push him to the ground and have her way with him.

"Dinner would be great," Maggie said. "I'll bring a bib and a hammer."

Bo laughed. "Sexy as the bib look is, I'll order ahead and make sure you don't have to hammer apart your own crab."

"My hero." Maggie glanced up to the top of the levee, where the Crozat pyramid was slowly growing. "How's my dad? He's been acting strange lately. Very tense and short-tempered. Not like himself at all."

Bo hesitated. "He's been okay. But no, he doesn't seem completely himself. He's . . . preoccupied." Maggie frowned, concerned about Tug. "We can talk about it over dinner," Bo said. "I'll text you a pickup time." He kissed Maggie again. This time his lips lingered on hers. Then he pulled away and strode back up the levee.

Maggie took in a deep breath and released it. She walked over to where Gran' was manning a roadside stand stocked with water bottles and homemade baked goods provided by Maggie's mother. The Crozat family sold the holiday treats to curious travelers who stopped to check out the bonfires' progress. Proceeds paid for porta-potties that served revelers who came to watch the bonfires burn on Christmas Eve. Over time, the lighting of the bonfires, like so many Pelican events, had grown from a small affair to a large, raucous party.

"I must say, that Bo Durand has the makings of a romance novel cover boy," Gran' said. She handed her granddaughter the cash box for her sales shift.

"He does, doesn't he? I am a very lucky girl."

"Judging by the way he comes to life when he sees you, I think he'd declare himself the lucky one. And he'd be right."

"Did someone say cover boy?"

Maggie and Gran' turned to see Lee Bertrand, the owner of Pelican's only service station, strike a model pose. He faked a pout when both women burst out laughing. "Oh, come on. You gotta admit, I'm one octogenarian hotty."

"I don't believe such a thing exists," Gran' said. She unconsciously fluffed her soft silver hair, and Maggie smiled. Despite the barbs, her grandmother and Lee shared an affection for each other.

"I'd have to disagree," Lee said. "Because I'm looking at one right now."

Gran' flushed and stammered, much to Maggie's amusement. She rarely saw her grandmother lose her preternatural dignity.

"I wish I could call up my great-greats from their resting places so they could see me flirting with Pelican's dowager queen." Lee crinkled one blue eye in a mischievous wink.

"Is that all I am to you?" Gran' responded, regaining her wit. "Arm candy?"

"'Course not. But it's one heck of a bonus." Lee dropped a dollar on the dessert table, grabbed a coconut pecan pie bar, blew Gran' a kiss, and sauntered back up the levee to where his employees were building a bonfire in the shape of Bertrand's Gas and Auto Repair.

"He smells like sweat and gasoline," Gran' said as she watched him go. "It's surprisingly appealing. Did you know he once wrestled an alligator?"

"Half the guys in Louisiana claim they've wrestled an alligator. If alligators could roll their eyes, they'd be doing it."

"I'm not a fan of the cynicism that bedevils your generation," Gran' said, sighing and shaking her head.

A young man negotiated his way down the steep levee to the Crozats' stand. He was in his early twenties, with boyish features that Maggie guessed would keep him looking younger than his age for years to come. His light-brown hair, held in place with pomade, was styled in a conservative fashion. She had a feeling he hoped the haircut would give him a gravitas that his baby face lacked. "Hey," he said with no trace of the local accent. "Can I get two sweet potato pralines? They're awesome."

"Absolutely." Gran' handed him a couple of plastic-wrapped candies, and he gave her a credit card.

"We take credit cards?" Maggie asked.

"I do, since I downloaded this app and got a cute attachment from the company." Gran' showed Maggie a plastic square plugged into her smartphone. She swiped the credit card and handed it back to her customer, along with the phone so he could sign for the purchase.

"Thanks," he said. He scribbled his name, handed back the phone, and then scarfed down a praline. Then he added to Maggie, "She's so totally cool."

"Yes, she is," Maggie said, looking at her grand-mère with affection.

"I'm Maggie Crozat."

"Oh, sorry. Harrison Fenner."

Maggie shook his extended hand, which was sticky from the praline. "Are you visiting for the holidays?"

"Nope." He opened up his other praline and took a bite. "Here for a job. I work at Belle Vista Plantation Resort and Spa."

Belle Vista. There it was again. Maggie grimaced and then covered her expression with a smile, but Harrison didn't seem to notice. He was looking at the magnificent log edifice being constructed on behalf of his workplace. "I heard Crozat's bonfire usually shows us up big time," he said. "But I guess not this year, huh?"

"Nope. Not this year."

Harrison gave a "what can you do?" shrug, then nodded a good-bye and headed back up the level. Gran' frowned at her granddaughter. "Your jealousy's showing."

"Sorry, but it's frustrating watching Belle Vista step up their game. Their bonfire gets bigger every year. I don't know where they're getting the money, but I know we can't compete with it."

"We can't and we shouldn't. Our goal is to be the best *we* can be. It's not to be someone or something else." Gran' piled Maggie's arms with water bottles. "Before you relieve me, take this water up to our brigade. And don't leave until you see your father take a hearty sip. He's hardly eaten or drunk anything today. I worry he'll become dehydrated."

"Yes, ma'am."

Maggie struggled up the levee with her load, her sneakered feet sinking in grass made marshy by recent rains. She dropped all the bottles but one into a cooler and then walked the single bottle over to Tug, who was on a ladder steadying a row of logs. A flash from the descending sun shone on him, and Maggie noticed new streaks of gray laced into his carrot-red hair. "I brought you some water, Dad."

"Not thirsty," Tug said without looking down.

"You need it," Maggie pressed, concern mixing with annoyance. "You can come down to me, or I'll come up to you." She placed a foot on the ladder.

"Fine," Tug said with a grunt. He made his way down, took the water from Maggie, and chugged a big gulp. "Happy?"

"Yes, and I wish you would stop being so stubborn about—"

Tug suddenly went pale. He staggered for a moment. "Maggie," he gasped.

Then Tug clutched his heart and collapsed to the ground as his daughter unleashed a terrified scream.

Chapter Two

Maggie was in a daze as Bo and the others rushed to Tug's side, but one thing was clear: dating a member of law enforcement had its advantages. An ambulance materialized almost instantaneously. Maggie raced to get her mother, Ninette, from the manor house, and they were transported to the hospital with Tug at light speed. Bo slapped a siren on the roof of his SUV, retrieved Gran', and made his way to the hospital equally fast.

Tug had come out of his faint, but he didn't argue when his family insisted he get thoroughly checked out. "It's probably nothing," he said as he lay in a hospital room waiting for the results from the ER doctor's initial exam.

Ninette squeezed his large hand with her tiny one. She'd been preparing breakfast biscuits for the B and B guests, and Maggie noticed her mother's hands were still spotted with flour. "Maybe," she said to her husband. "But we need to make sure."

"Mom's right, Dad," Maggie said, taking his other hand in hers. "In the meantime, try to relax."

Tug nodded and closed his eyes. Grand-mère reached over and stroked Tug's forehead. "You're from strong stock, son. Remember that."

Jennifer Nyugen, Maggie's high school classmate and the doctor on call, stepped into the room. The first-generation daughter of Vietnamese refugees, Jennifer had attended Tulane University School of Medicine on a full scholarship. Maggie gave silent thanks that Tug had been entrusted to her care.

"How are you feeling, Mr. Crozat?" Jennifer asked. "Any better or worse than when you arrived?"

"A little better."

"Good."

"What do you think is wrong, Jennif—Dr. Jenn—Doctor?" Ninette asked, clutching her husband's hand tighter as she tried to figure out the most appropriate way to address Maggie's childhood friend.

"I've checked his chart, and I don't believe what's happening is life-threatening—"

"Oh, thank God," Maggie blurted out.

"—at the moment," Jennifer continued, and Maggie felt her heart clutch. "Your blood pressure is high, Mr. Crozat, and that concerns me."

"Do you think he had some sort of mild stroke or heart attack?" Gran' asked.

"Possibly. Or it could be extreme stress. We'll have a better idea after we run a few tests. I'll send in a nurse to get them going."

Jennifer left, and Maggie turned her attention back to Tug. "So what aren't you telling us, Dad?"

"Maggie!" Ninette said sharply.

"I'm sorry, Mom, but this is important. You've seen how he's been acting lately. Something's wrong, and if he doesn't tell us, it could end up killing him."

"My goodness, a little less drama, please, Magnolia Marie," Gran' said, shooting her granddaughter a warning look.

"Yes, this is absolutely the wrong time—" Ninette began. But Tug lifted his free hand up to her lips, and she quieted.

"Maggie's right. Something *is* wrong. I've been avoiding bringing it up, but I guess that isn't an option anymore." Tug pulled himself up to a sitting position. "I got some bad news about Crozat."

*

"Why do ER waiting room vending machines only sell soda and water?" Maggie vented, gesturing with the water bottle she'd purchased at the hospital as Bo drove her back to Crozat. "You know what they should sell? Little liquor bottles like you get on an airplane. If there's ever a time you could use a belt of something, it's in the ER."

Tug and Ninette had agreed that Maggie should return to the plantation. "We'll let you know as soon as we hear any news about Dad," Ninette promised as she walked her reluctant daughter to the waiting room. "One of us needs to tend to the guests. Given the current circumstances, we can't afford any dings on travel websites."

Bo cast a wary glance at Maggie as he negotiated his way around a rickety pickup truck carrying a load of cane reed toward the levee. "You keep waving that bottle around the way you are, I'm gonna need to break out the SWAT gear to protect myself."

"Sorry."

Bo took one hand off the steering wheel and placed it on Maggie's knee. "Your dad's gonna be okay."

"I hope so. But it's not just his health that's the problem. He finally told us why he hasn't been himself lately." Maggie winced and pressed the water bottle to her forehead, as if the pressure might stop a blossoming headache. "You know how my dad's a twin? Well, his brother, my uncle Tig, buys historic properties with a group of investors and turns the buildings into boutique hotels. He and my dad always agreed that Crozat should stay in the family and not be part of the Preferred Property Collection—that's the name of his company—but after the murders, they thought Crozat would be better protected if it was part of PPC, so the company bought it with the understanding that absolutely nothing would change. But there's some trouble with Tig's investors. I'm Skyping him to get the ugly details after I check on our guests." Maggie groaned. "I used to think my life was tough when I was a struggling artist dumped by my boyfriend for another woman. Oh, how I miss those days."

Bo nodded sympathetically. "Sometimes I try to remember when life wasn't complicated. And I can't. Any chance y'all could just buy Crozat back from Tig's company?"

Maggie shook her head. "Dad already thought of that. We'd have to buy it back at the price the investors set based on what they consider current market value, and we can't afford it. The proceeds from the original sale are already half out the door. We need them for improvements that will barely keep the place from falling down around us."

Bo made a left and drove slowly down the hard-packed decomposed granite road leading to Crozat Plantation B and B. Branches of centuries-old oak trees intertwined to form a canopy above the road, then split left and right to frame the manor house. The elegant old place was encircled by thirty-two imposing square columns, and galleries wrapped around both floors. Each of the columns was festooned with giant red bows, which was Gran's contribution to the holiday decorating scheme. Maggie and Ninette had made the large wreath that welcomed guests at the front door. Tug had searched resale shops and found two six-foot-high plug-in candles whose lightbulb flames flickered like the real thing; each graced a side of the wide oak front door. Maggie savored the serene image and, always the artist, debated whether oil paint or watercolor might best portray the home's beauty.

Marie Shexnayder, who helped the Crozats with housekeeping, came out of the house onto its wide veranda and waved to Maggie. "Thanks, chère," Maggie said to her boyfriend. She gave him a quick kiss and hopped down to the ground from his SUV. "I'll keep you posted on my dad."

Maggie bounded up the manor house's front steps. Marie had a sour expression on her face, which was unusual for her.

"Uh-oh. I don't like that look," Maggie said. "Which guest is a problem? I hope it's not anyone from the Japanese tour group." The preholiday visitors included a group of eight from Tokyo being shepherded around the region by tour guide Marco Cornetta, who also happened to be Uncle Tig's ex. Crozat had become popular with Japanese tourists for no particular reason Maggie could discern, but she was grateful for it, as well as for Marco, a loyal and entertaining customer. The other guests filling out the preholiday week roster were a family named the O'Days from Ohio and Donald Baxter, a California businessman.

"The Japanese group is fine. Marco took them to see Whitney and Oak Alley. The O'Days took their girls on a swamp tour." Marie pursed her lips. "It's Mr. Baxter."

Maggie wasn't surprised. There was something about Donald Baxter that bothered her. It was the rare male executive who tacked a plantation stay onto his business trip. If he did, the businessman usually explained that his wife had sent him, and he went home laden with souvenir mugs and tea towels. But not Don. Maggie had studied facial expressions and body language in a college portrait painting class, and when Don claimed the need for some R and R after stressful business negotiations in New Orleans, his darting eyes indicated that he was lying.

Marie looked around to make sure she and Maggie were alone. "He complains about everything," she said, keeping her voice low. "And he keeps writing things down on his phone like he's taking notes. I think he may be a travel blogger."

"Oh, that's not good. Sometimes they think they don't have a story if there isn't something to snark about. Do you know where he is?"

"The office. He's all yours. I've run out of nice."

Marie marched off, and Maggie went inside. As she walked down Crozat's wide center hallway, she inhaled the woodsy scent emanating from the gaily decorated pine garlands that draped every doorway. Maggie crossed a threshold into the men's smoking parlor that her family had turned into the B and B's office. Computers and printers rested on heavy walnut furniture that had been in the family for generations. The walls were a dark-forest green, and the intricately carved Cypress molding was painted black. It was the family's tradition to paint this particular room in dark colors; their ancestors had used this technique to hide the accumulation of tobacco stains. The room glowed with color from the lights of several small Christmas trees. A twelve-foot Douglas fir stood bare and majestic in the manor house front parlor, waiting for its ornamentation. Trimming it on Christmas Eve was a Crozat family tradition.

Don Baxter was standing with his arms crossed in front of his wiry chest, staring at a small painting hanging above the office desk. "Nice of you to drop by," he said without looking at Maggie. The man was only a few inches taller than her five-foot-four height, but his body radiated a tensile strength. The only question he asked when checking in was, *Does Crozat have a fitness room with weights?* He wasn't happy when Maggie informed him it didn't.

"I'm so sorry," Maggie said, summoning her sunniest smile. "We had a family emergency."

"And not much of a backup plan," Don said, still staring at the painting. "You advertise a full, hot breakfast. Lukewarm biscuits and cereal do not a full, hot breakfast make."

"Our apologies. You and all the guests will receive a credit on your bills for this morning."

Baxter gave a dismissive grunt. "You're using single-ply toilet paper. I'm not a fan."

Maggie couldn't resist responding, "Of single-ply, or toilet paper in general?" Baxter merely stared at her, a cold look in his eyes. "They were out of two-ply at the store when we shopped the other day," she said. "I'll make sure you have it by this evening."

The businessman nodded and turned his attention back to the artwork. "This painting," he said, gesturing to it, "it's contemporary."

"Yes. Those are our family pets. My boyfriend's son painted it. He's very talented, especially for a seven-year-old."

Don finally turned around, his eyebrows raised. "The artist is seven? Wow." He turned back to the painting. "How much do you want for it?"

Maggie gritted her teeth. "I'm sorry, but it's not for sale."

"Ha. Everything is for sale."

"Not something that has sentimental value to me."

"Even that. It's just a matter of landing on a price. When you decide on yours, let me know."

Don exited the room without looking back, which was fortunate for Maggie because he missed the nasty hand gesture she was making behind his back. She pulled a chair up to the office computer and activated a Skype session. After a blurry few seconds, Uncle Tig appeared on the screen. Although Tig and Tug were identical twins, their lifestyles had sent them down different paths of aging. Tug, with his penchant for outdoor living and Ninette's fine cooking, looked his fifty-seven years. Brother Tig, a self-proclaimed "city boy," didn't. Tig's pale, freckled face was barely lined, and thanks to one of New York's finest colorists, his copper hair didn't sport a single strand of silver.

"Hey, darlin'," he greeted his niece. Tig still retained his accent, despite a thirty-year absence from Louisiana. Maggie was sure this was intentional, having seen her uncle turn on the Cajun charm to seduce the snobbiest Manhattan maître d' into giving them a great table. "Mama called me about Tug," Uncle Tig said, his brow creased with worry. "How is he?"

"I think he's going to be okay. We're waiting to hear from the doctor. Uncle Tig, what's going on with the company?"

Tig dropped his head, as if unable to look his niece in the eye. After a moment, he looked up. "There's a hedge fund manager named Steve Harmon, and he has a company called Harmon Equities. About a year ago, he came calling. Told me how much he respected my dedication to adaptive reuse of historic structures and how impressed he was that I'd turned my passion into profit. He wanted to invest in PPC and help grow it. At first my other investors were resistant. The SEC's got Harmon Equities in its crosshairs and nailed a couple of employees on insider trading. But Harmon insisted his underlings acted without his knowledge."

Tig paused. Maggie could hear the sounds of New York City in the background: horns honking, a distant siren. For a second, she was overwhelmed by longing for her former home. Then she pulled herself out of it. "Uncle Tig . . ." she prompted.

"A few months ago, bad reviews started appearing on some property sites. It didn't take long to realize we were being hit by trolls, but every time we blocked one, another popped up. Our cybersecurity team finally got everything under control, but the damage was done. We lost bookings, had to lay off people. Harmon put the blame on me. He sent letters to all my investors accusing me of incompetence and mismanagement. At first I had their support, but Harmon was relentless, and one by one, they began doubting me."

Tig leaned toward his computer's camera. Maggie could see that his green eyes, so similar to her father's, were flecked with fury. "They're trying to push me out, Maggie. Of the company I loved and nurtured and grew. They're trying to take me down."

"Oh, that's awful." The ramifications of Tig's crisis hit Maggie hard. "And if you go down . . ."

She couldn't bring herself to finish the sentence, so Tig did it for her. "Crozat goes down with me."

Chapter Three

The conversation ended with Tig backtracking from an apocalyptic scenario for Crozat. In an attempt to convince his niece that he would be David to Harmon's Goliath, he strung together a bunch of clichés: "I'm not down for the count. I'm not going down without a fight. It ain't over 'til it's over. It ain't over until the fat lady—"

Maggie was relieved when the Skype connection failed, cutting off Tig's flailing attempt to lessen the gravity of the situation. Panic was useless; what the Crozats needed was a game plan. Maggie thought for a moment and then typed an e-mail to Tig requesting contact information for the general managers of all his properties. If she could organize a show of commitment for Tig from his troops, it might make the PPC investors second-guess their support for the rapacious Steve Harmon.

Maggie pulled her cell phone out of the back pocket of her jeans. When she wasn't pursuing her art career or helping to run Crozat, she worked as a tour guide at Doucet Plantation on the west side of the Mississippi, and she was due there in fifteen minutes. She speed-dialed her coworker and close friend, Gaynell Bourgeois, and explained the crisis. "Any chance you can cover for me today?" she asked. "I need time to try and fix this."

"You know I would." Maggie picked up tension in her friend's voice. "But Tannis is on a tear. She's got some new 'experiential' format for the guides she's 'rolling out' today." Gaynell emphasized the words that their new boss, the proud recipient of a junior college degree in marketing, liked to throw around. "I'm sorry about what's going on with your uncle, but I think you better get here."

Maggie muttered an expletive, thanked her friend, and ended the call. She raced out of the manor house, across the backyard and the graveled parking lot behind it to the shotgun cottage she shared with Gran'. She grabbed her purse and car keys, then jumped into her car and took off for Doucet. In a flurry of ill-conceived last-minute executive actions, Louisiana's outgoing governor had transferred control of several state-run historical sites to private nonprofits. Doucet Plantation, the ancestral home of Maggie's mother, Ninette, was one of those properties. With the change came the new boss: Tannis Greer, a thin, slightly bug-eyed young woman of twenty-eight, four years Maggie's junior, who in her first position of power, operated more as a dictator than a manager. Maggie was not looking forward to Tannis's new "format."

Her cell rang, and Ninette's name flashed on the screen. Maggie pressed a button on her earbud to accept the call. "Hey, chère," her mother said. "I wanted to give you an update. Lee's bringing Gran' home, so she'll look after things while you're at work. Your dad seems to have dodged a heart attack or stroke, but his blood pressure is all out of whack, so they're keeping him here until they get it under control, and I'm going to stay with him. How's everything at Crozat?"

"Fine," Maggie said, keeping her response vague so as not to pile more stress on her already stressed-out mother. "As soon as I'm done at Doucet, I'll go straight home to relieve Gran'. Give Dad a big kiss for me."

Maggie ended the call and parked in the grassy field next to the overseer's cottage, which housed the Doucet employee facilities. She changed into her costume of pale-pink polyester-masquerading-as-silk ball gown and stuffed her thick chestnut hair under a wig bouncing with banana curls. She then hiked up her hoop skirt and rushed into the staff lounge for the morning meeting. She sidled up to Gaynell and her other close friend at Doucet, Ione Savreau, the only African American employee at the plantation. Tannis had replaced her as general manager, but Ione swallowed her pride and stayed on as a tour guide. "I've got a bad feeling about this," Ione muttered as Tannis clicked into the room in black platform high heels. She wore a tailored navy suit and carried a black leather briefcase. Her blonde hair was slicked back into a ponytail, exposing small gold knot earrings. It was the perfect ensemble for a boardroom and couldn't have been less appropriate for the casual, almost ramshackle employees' area.

"I have some superexciting news," Tannis said, her light-brown eyes confirming her excitement by seeming to jut out more than usual. "I'm sure some of you have heard of Living History tours." Tannis articulated each word as if speaking to either a deaf or mentally challenged audience. "It's when you play a character rather than just lead a boring old tour. Well, we here at Doucet will now be embracing that format."

"It's not the worst idea," Gaynell whispered. "I do get bored saying the same old thing all the time." Ione gave a skeptical grunt.

"Since I took a playwriting course at Three C"—Tannis was proud of the nickname she'd given her alma mater, Coastal Community College, and used it frequently, hoping it would catch on—"I took the liberty of writing out individual scripts for each of you after work. Nothing like earning a little overtime pay, huh?" Tannis giggled. Her employees, who'd never seen a dime of overtime pay, didn't. She opened her briefcase and pulled out a stack of papers that she distributed among the tour guides, assigning them their characters as she did so. She reached Maggie's group last. "Maggie, you're the mistress of the house, who must manage the plantation while her husband is at war. And Gaynell, you're her ten-year-old son."

"What?!" Gaynell yelped. "Why am I a boy?"

"Because you're the youngest and smallest guide. Is it a problem?" Tannis's sharp tone indicated it better not be, and Gaynell meekly shook her head no. "Good. New costumes for anyone who requires one are in my office. I've also hired a couple of day players from town to perform adult male roles when we need them, since this staff is female-heavy. I want everyone to memorize their scripts tonight and be ready to go in the morning." Tannis turned to walk away, ignoring the grumbles from her employees.

"You missed me, Tannis," Ione said. "I'd love to know who I get to play."

There was a challenge in Ione's tone, but Tannis was immune to it. "Your costume hasn't arrived yet, so you're assigned to the gift shop until it gets here. Okay, people, time for work. Let's make it another great Doucet day!"

Tannis's peppy sign-off did nothing to invigorate her staff, who shuffled off, clutching their scripts. Maggie, Gaynell, and Ione were the last to leave.

"Are you okay?" Maggie asked Ione.

Ione shook her head. "I've got a bad feeling about this," she repeated.

Maggie and Gaynell exchanged a look. "So do we," Maggie said.

*

Maggie checked her phone throughout the workday, but her uncle had yet to get back to her with the list of his general managers. She did get a text from Marco saying he was shuttling his Japanese tour group to New Orleans for dinner, so not to worry about them. Maggie loved Marco, whom she had known since she was a girl. He never seemed to have a down moment and ended every correspondence with a *"Laissez les bon temps rouler!"*—the ubiquitous Louisiana saying that translated to "Let the good times roll!" Maggie was convinced the sweet man was her uncle's soulmate and wished Tig would come to the same conclusion.

When her day at Doucet finally ended, Maggie headed home to Crozat. As she parked, she saw the O'Day family exiting their rental car. "Hi there," she said, summoning up her best hostess smile. "How was the swamp tour?"

"We saw two gators fighting," Sophie, the younger of the two O'Day girls, piped up. Both hovered around eight or nine and looked so much alike that Maggie was sure they were often mistaken for twins. The whole O'Day family resembled each other in a blandly suburban way. In her time back at Crozat, Maggie had come to realize that there were guests who made an indelible impression and guests she would be hard-pressed to pick out of a lineup a week after their stay. The O'Days fell in the latter camp.

"Wow," Maggie said. "I've seen a lot of gators, but I've never seen them fight."

"It was awesome," Sophie said.

"It was scary," Sophie's older sister, Allison, countered flatly. Maggie pegged her as the daughter who would give her parents a lot of grief when she hit her teens.

"Thank you so much for the discount coupon; it really helped us out," their mother, Lindy, said. "We were wondering if we could have dinner in our room tonight. We downloaded a movie for the girls."

"I'd be happy to. I'll bring it by in about an hour."

Maggie headed into the manor house, where she found Gran' in the B and B office staring at the computer screen. "Your father should be home in the morning."

"That's a relief. Finally, some good news."

"Yes. But this isn't." Gran' motioned to the screen. "We got a bad review on Trippee.com. More than one, I'm afraid."

"What?" Maggie leaned in and read over her grand-mother's shoulder. "'Poor service, charmless rooms, mediocre food.' These are all lies! Trolls hit a bunch of Tig's properties. They must have finally found us."

"I don't believe these are trolls," Gran' said. "In order to post a review on Trippee, there has to be evidence through credit card activity that you've actually been to the establish-ment. These reviews must be from guests, past or present. But the fact that there are several of them and they seem purposely vindictive is certainly a cause for concern. I tried to find a human contact at Trippee but had no luck, so I sent an e-mail alerting them to the problem."

"I'll let Uncle Tig know so his people can get on it too. But we can't tell Dad. Hopefully we can fix it before he ever finds out." Maggie collapsed into a damask-covered antique wingback chair. "If this day gets any more stressful, I may wind up in the hospital bed next to Dad's."

Gran' glanced out one of the floor-to-ceiling windows to the parking area behind the office. "I believe you're about to receive a stress reprieve. Bo and Xander are walking toward the house."

Maggie jumped up and ran out of the room to the back door. She opened it to see Bo and his son heading toward her. Early evening had brought a chill to the air, and both Durands wore leather jackets, Bo's older and more worn than his son's. "Xander didn't want to miss his daily visit with Jas-mine," he said. The Crozats were caring for a brood of pup-pies and kittens until they were old enough to be placed with their adoptive families. Xander had bonded with Jasmine, the smallest pup. The relationship was helping pull the boy out of the shell created by his Asperger's syndrome.

"I think Jasmine would be very upset if Xander didn't show up," Maggie said.

Bo and Xander followed her to a small den the Crozats had turned into home base for the menagerie, which included the mothers of the pups and kitties. A chorus of yips and meows greeted their arrival. Gopher, the family basset hound, added his basso profundo barks to the mix. Xander sat on the floor, and Jasmine leaped into his lap, covering the seven-year-old's small, delicate face with kisses. "We'll leave you two alone," Bo joked.

He and Maggie retreated to the kitchen, where they each downed a beer as she filled him in on the day's unpleasant events. "What can I do to help?" he asked. "With your dad, with the B and B—with anything?"

"The most important thing right now is my dad's health. I want things to stay as normal as possible. I'm thinking we should keep him focused on finishing the bonfire. Maybe you could help with that."

"You got it."

"Thank you." Maggie smiled for what felt like the first time that day.

Bo leaned in toward her, but as they were about to kiss, the kitchen door swung open, revealing Don Baxter. "Just letting you know I won't be here for dinner," he said. "I'm checking out a place in Vacherie that serves real Cajun food."

As opposed to the delicious and totally authentic food my mother serves and you'll be missing, you nimrod, Maggie thought but refrained from saying. Instead she went with, "Thank you for letting me know. Enjoy your dinner."

"Yeah, thanks." Don examined Bo with interest. "You must be the boyfriend."

Maggie sensed Bo tensing up, but he responded politely. "Yes. Bo Durand."

"Don Baxter." Don extended his hand, and Bo shook it. Both men winced slightly as they competed for strongest grip. "Your son's the artist, right? I'm a collector. Not to brag, but I've got an eye for talent, and your son is gifted."

"Thank you."

"I also have a lot of connections in the art world. There hasn't been a prodigy for a while. Your son could generate a lot of heat. You should let me show him around New York."

Maggie could see Bo clenching and unclenching his jaw. "I appreciate the offer, but we'll pass on that," he said, keeping his voice as even as possible.

Don shrugged. "Your call. But you should think about it. By the looks of that jacket you're wearing, money's tight. I get it. Can't be easy supporting a kid with issues on a small-town detective's salary."

Maggie covered her mouth to prevent a gasp from escaping. For a panicked moment, she thought Bo might explode in anger, but he managed to restrain himself. Don left, and the kitchen door swung behind him. As soon as he was gone, Maggie turned to Bo. "I never told him any of that, I swear. You have to believe me."

"I do." Bo frowned. "So the question is, how did he know? And why does he care?"

Maggie had no answer to either question.

Since Xander had school the next day, Bo declined Maggie's invitation to stay for dinner. "Are we good?" she asked, fearing fallout from the encounter with Don Baxter.

Bo responded with a reassuring kiss. "Something's not right with that guy. I'm going to do a little research on him. In the meantime, be careful."

"I will."

Bo and Xander headed out, and Maggie retreated to the office, where Gran' still sat at the computer. "Any more bad reviews?"

"No, but we did get a cancellation."

"Oh, no. I was afraid that would happen."

"At least it's only one. Let's hope it doesn't become a virus that spreads. You got a message from Tig, and it has some attachments."

"Finally."

Gran' stood up, and Maggie replaced her at the computer. She opened Tig's e-mail and downloaded the attachments. One was the promised list of his general managers. The other was a newspaper article.

Gran' peered over Maggie's shoulder. "What's that?"

"A profile of Steve Harmon, the investor who's trying to run Uncle Tig out of his own company. There's a picture of him."

Maggie enlarged the photo, and both she and Gran' stared at the image in disbelief.

"It can't be," Gran' said. "It just can't."

But it was.

Staring back at them with an arrogant, almost mocking grin was B and B guest Don Baxter.

Chapter Four

The two women, both in shock, couldn't take their eyes off the photo. Gran' spoke first. "Why, the miserable son of a—" And Gran', who considered profanity vulgar, used the actual cuss word.

Maggie leapt out of her office chair with such force that it rolled across the room and crashed into a wall. She ran out the back door to where the guests parked their cars. "Hey! *Hey!*" she shouted at Don/Steve, who was about to get into his midsize rental sedan. "Hey, *Steve Harmon!*"

Steve laughed and threw up his hands. "Busted."

"How dare you—"

"I'll finish the sentence for you. How *dare* I check in under an assumed identity? Simple explanation: it's business. I'm a money guy, and right now, my particular passion is for destination properties. I need to scout them before I invest, and if I check in under my real name, I don't get the same service the average guest would, which skews my impression of a property."

"Your tactics are despicable. Trying to put my uncle out of business, trolling on travel websites to slam his properties. And how dare you—and I'm going to finish this sentence *myself*—how dare you slam Crozat on Trippee when we've done everything we can to make you happy here?"

"Whoa. First of all, any review I write is a truthful representation of my guest experience. Second, sorry, but it wasn't me who slammed Crozat on Trippee. But if you continue to harass me, I sure will. Remember, I'm still a guest."

"I don't believe you. And while we're on the subject of harassment, stop trying to destroy my uncle. You want to talk about passion? Without him, who knows how many amazing historical structures would have been demolished. He's a hero."

"He may be a hero, but he's not a businessman. He should stick to preservation and leave running his business to people who know how to do it. Your uncle has parked his butt on a potential gold mine, and if he won't step aside, he needs to be forcibly removed."

Before Maggie could respond, Harmon got in his car and gunned it out of the lot, spraying her with dust from the decomposed granite. Maggie kicked a rock and sent it flying. She paced back and forth, trying to calm herself. Harmon's harsh take on Tig infuriated her. He was the epitome of a heartless businessman, who couldn't comprehend how for her uncle, making money was a bonus and not a goal. Tig's investment group had never complained until the financier insinuated his way into Preferred Properties and upended the status quo.

Gran' appeared in the back doorway. "I heard every-thing," she said. "Any chance there was an oil tanker spill on the road today? He's going fast enough to lose control in a very bad way."

"Afraid not," Maggie said. "I promised the O'Days I'd bring dinner to their room. After that, I'm going to contact all the PPC general managers and tell them it's time to fight for Tig."

"I'll bring the O'Days their dinner," Gran' said. "You save my boy."

*

Maggie spent the rest of the evening composing a call to arms and e-mailing it to everyone on Tig's list. Responses were quick and supportive. It was midnight when Maggie finally tore herself away from the computer. She took a quick shower and fell into bed, only to be haunted by a nightmare where she and her family were paddling up Bayou Beurre in a pirogue canoe packed with all their belongings, searching for a place to live. Her great-great-great-grandmother, Mag-nolia Marie Doucet Cabot, waved to them from the edge of the bayou, but the Crozats rowed past her.

The morning brought some good news. Maggie made her way into the manor house kitchen and found her father sitting at the kitchen table. "What a relief," she said as she hugged him. "How are you feeling?"

"Depressed."

"I'm sorry, Dad. But you'll get used to taking whatever medication Dr. Jen prescribed, and it'll become routine."

"It's not that." Tug motioned to the stove, where Ninette was making eggs. "Your mother is making me eat healthy."

"That's right," Ninette said. She massaged a handful of kale and tossed it into the pan. "Egg whites with kale, no salt, no cheese." She emptied the eggs onto a dish that she placed in front of her husband. He reached for a bottle of Tabasco sauce, but Ninette pulled it away. "And no hot sauce. Sodium, chère."

Tug reluctantly began eating his eggs, each bite accompanied by a grumble. A timer went off, and Ninette pulled a large baking pan from the oven. The kitchen filled with the scent of butter, brown sugar, and brandy. "Your holiday baked brandy pain perdu?" Tug groaned. "Chère, you're killing me."

"Au contraire, my darlin'. I'm trying to keep you alive."

"We've got to wow our guests, Dad," Maggie said. "And Mom's pain perdu is a wow." She grabbed a biscuit from the bread basket on the kitchen table and headed back to the shotgun cottage, where she finally took a look at the script Tannis had given her the day before. "Oh, dear Lord," she muttered. It was everything she dreaded: stilted, sappy, and downright embarrassing. This was going to be a very long day.

*

"Oh, my, how will I ever go on without my husband, who is still at war?"

Tannis, who was directing a run-through of all the guides, frowned at Maggie. "Where's your accent?"

"I lived in New York for fourteen years before coming back to Pelican. I lost it."

"Well, find it again. Can you cry on cue?"

"I can't and I won't," Maggie said. She'd barely been at work for an hour, but it felt like ten. Her new lime-green ball gown costume was too tight around her ribs and exposed far more cleavage than she was comfortable with. "You know, Tannis, my ancestor, Magnolia Marie, was a smart, strong woman who freed the Doucet slaves before the war even started, ran the entire operation on her own after her husband died, and then outraged the locals by getting remarried to a Union general. That would be a much more interesting character to play."

"I think I need to remind you that your family doesn't own this place anymore, Margaret—"

"Again, it's Magnolia, just like my ancestor."

"Which makes you an *employee*," Tannis said, ignoring Maggie. She pursed her perfectly lipsticked lips. "Who should be listening to her *boss*. Let go of all this family history stuff and stick to the lines as written." Tannis checked the time on her phone. "First tour starts in ten. Places, please." The guides began shuffling out. "Oh, Ione, I almost forgot. I have your costume."

Ione stopped, as did Maggie and Gaynell, who looked miserable in her nineteenth-century pantaloons and suspenders. "It has to be better than mine," Gaynell said under her breath.

Tannis handed Ione what looked like a bundle of rags. Puzzled, Ione unfolded the bundle, which turned out to be a sack of a dress made out of burlap and fabric scraps. Ione turned a cold eye to Tannis. "Tell me this costume isn't what I think it is."

For once, Tannis's omnipresent arrogance faltered. "It's not. You're an indentured servant."

"You mean a slave."

"No, they're different."

"Yeah, one is a word long, and the other is two words long."

"I can trade with her," Maggie piped in, eager to help her friend while at the same time divesting herself of the polyester nightmare she was trapped in.

Tannis shook her head. "Nuh-uh. I need you to play off your connection to Doucet. Visitors eat that up."

"I thought I was supposed to 'let go of the family history stuff,'" Maggie said, relishing the chance to throw Tannis's own words back at her.

Tannis glared at Maggie, and then she turned to Ione. "If you refuse to wear this, I'm afraid I have to terminate your employment. As of right this instant."

"Do that, and I quit," Maggie declared. She was sick of Tannis's mean-girl tactics and contempt for her employees.

"Me too," Gaynell said. She whipped off her newsboy cap, and her blonde curls fell to her shoulders.

"And we're just the beginning, Tannis," Maggie said, furious. "You won't have an employee left at Doucet if you fire Ione."

A sheen of perspiration appeared on Tannis's forehead. There was a murmur of voices. Through the bubbled glass of the room's old window, Maggie could see groups of visitors forming. Tannis snatched the dress from Ione. "Fine, we'll keep you in the gift shop . . . until I find someone who doesn't have your attitude. Now *places*."

Tannis glowered at them and then strode off to browbeat other employees.

"Thank you both. You're good friends," Ione said. "It's bad enough I was demoted to make room for that woman, but to have to wear that horrible costume . . ." Her voice was husky, and Maggie knew her friend was trying to control her emotions. "I think it's time I looked for a new job."

"I think it's time we all did," Maggie said. Her emotional connection to Ninette's ancestral home might be strong, but her loyalty to her friends was far stronger.

*

Maggie managed to slog through a raft of embarrassing tours. She didn't know which was more humiliating: the snickers of some visitors or the faked compliments of others. The one bright spot in her day was a text from Uncle Tig letting her know that the onslaught of positive feedback from PPC employees had had the desired effect on his investors. They were waffling in their support of Harmon's ruthless game plan.

She took comfort in this promising attitude shift as she locked up the manor house. Then she made her way to the overseer's cottage that housed the employee facilities, changed out of the lime monstrosity and back into her street clothes, and headed for her car. Darkness had fallen early due to the short winter days, but Doucet was bathed in the glow of bright holiday decorations. Her mood took a downturn when she saw Steve Harmon leaning against a round Doucet pillar festooned with a swath of red-and-white lights that made it look like a fat candy cane. He had a smug grin on his face as he listened to Tannis Greer, who appeared to be in the middle of an animated monologue. *Now what could bring those two together?* Maggie wondered. Tannis stopped talking, and Harmon responded with a shrug and a quick comment. Maggie's young boss burst into giggles, then flicked her ponytail back and struck a flirtatious pose. Much as Maggie wanted to avoid all contact with the loathsome duo, curiosity won out. She sauntered over to them.

"'Night, Tannis. See you in the morning." She feigned surprise at seeing Steve Harmon. "Hello, Mr. Harmon. I hope you're not here for a tour. We just finished for the day."

"I've already gotten a couple of private ones," he said, leering at Maggie's boss.

Tannis blushed and then put on a more professional face. "Mr. Harmon is discussing a large donation to Doucet. In exchange, we're trying out a few of his suggestions."

"Like living tours?" Maggie said.

"That's just the beginning," Tannis said, gazing at the hedge fund manager with an adoration that trumped professionalism. "There could be restaurants and luxury accommodations and maybe even a little train running around the property."

"Sort of like a plantation Disneyland," Maggie said.

"Exactly," Tannis responded, missing the cutting undertone of Maggie's remark. "But much higher-end. The board of directors is even considering Mr. Harmon's proposal to buy Doucet and privatize it. Ooo, Stevie, we could put in a spa like at Belle Vista and market the place to rich people who need to recuperate after plastic surgery."

Wow, that was a quick trip from "Mr. Harmon" to "Stevie," thought Maggie. She was repulsed by the rapacious couple and made a mental note to start a campaign against the privatization of Doucet as soon as Crozat's future had been secured. "I have to go," Maggie said.

"Keep those great ideas coming, Tannis," Harmon said. "I'll see you later, Miss Magnolia." He had the audacity to follow up the flirtatious comment with another wink.

Maggie strode toward her car as fast as she could without breaking into a run. "Maggie, wait," she heard Tannis call. "I forgot to tell you something." She reluctantly stopped and let Tannis catch up to her. Away from the ambient light of Doucet, the parking lot was pitch dark. Tannis stumbled on the gravel in her spike heels and reached to grab Maggie's arm for balance. Or so Maggie thought. Instead the Doucet manager dug her manicured nails into Maggie's forearm and then leaned in until their faces were only inches apart. "Stay away from Steve or you'll be sorry," she hissed. "He's mine."

Chapter Five

Tannis stormed away. Maggie stood by her car for a moment, so shaken by the strength of the woman's venom that she didn't notice Gaynell and Ione approach.

"What's wrong?" Gaynell asked. "You look kind of freaked out."

Maggie started at the sound of Gaynell's voice. "Sorry. I just had a very weird experience." She shared Tannis's threat with her friends.

"That woman is more than a pain in my posterior; she is pure evil," Ione declared.

"Steve Harmon is the one who's pure evil, and he infects other people with his bile." Maggie sunk back against her vintage convertible.

Gaynell studied her friend. "Do you need to help with dinner at Crozat tonight?"

"No, my parents are handling it."

"Good. I know what'll get your mind off of this whole mess."

"Drinks?"

Gaynell shook her head. "Exercise."

Ione frowned. "I like Maggie's idea better."

"If we go for drinks, all we'll do is talk about all the bad that's happening with Maggie," Gaynell said. "But if we go to DanceBod and do whatever class Sandy is leading, it'll distract us." Then she added, "We can go for drinks after."

"Now I'm on board," Ione said.

Maggie gave Gaynell a grateful smile. "It's a great idea. Thank you. Ladies, let's dance!"

*

DanceBod Fitness Studio was housed in one of the quaint nineteenth-century brick storefronts that encircled Pelican's grassy town square. Sandy Sechrest, the studio's owner and a relative newcomer to town, was a former pole dancer who had saved enough tips to open her own business just months earlier. Pelicaners were generally a soft-hearted lot, not prone to judging a person's present by their past. Sandy was a terrific teacher who made shedding those Cajun and Creole food babies fun, which was enough for the locals.

Maggie and her friends arrived at the studio in time for DiscoBod, fifty minutes of medium and high cardio dance routines set to classic disco tunes. They went into the small locker room and changed into workout gear, then found places on the dance floor. Maggie took a spot next to her cousin, Lia Tienne. Until recently, Lia had managed to stay lithe despite owning Pelican's two popular sweeteries, Fais Dough Dough Patisserie and Bon Bon Sweets. But as Maggie gave her cousin a hug, she noticed that Lia, a Nefertiti-like beauty, seemed to be filling out. Years of creating delectable pastries, pralines, and chocolates had finally caught up to the thirty-six-year-old.

A woman Maggie had never seen before hurried into the studio. She deposited a gym bag on a bench, then searched for a space on the dance floor. Maggie indicated there was room next to her. The woman smiled gratefully and took the space. "Thank you so much," she said. Maggie detected a slight accent that she couldn't place. The woman appeared to be around Maggie's age, but where Maggie was petite and brunette, her new dance-floor neighbor was tall and slim with flaxen hair cut into a bob. *Scandinavian, maybe?* Maggie wondered. *German?* She realized the woman was talking to her and forced herself to focus.

"This is my first class," she said. "I've been wanting to come for months, but I've been too busy. I'm Bea Boxler, the new general manager at Belle Vista."

Maggie felt the usual pinprick of jealousy she got when she heard the name of Crozat's upscale competitor. "I'm Maggie Crozat," she said, forcing a polite smile. "Of Crozat Plantation B and B."

"Really?" The woman seemed delighted. "I *love* your place. It's so beautiful and genuine. Sometimes I fear we've lost that at BV. A little too much resort and too little history."

Maggie was surprised—and a bit gleeful—to hear Bea voice a critique of "BV." "I'd be happy to give you a tour of Crozat sometime," she said, this time with a genuine smile.

"I'd love that, and I'd be happy to reciprocate if you'd like a tour of BV. Let me get my card. And give me yours."

"I—actually, I don't have one," Maggie said, hating that she felt embarrassed by this. "It's more of a helping out my family thing than an actual job."

"No worries. Just call me, and I'll have your number."

Bea dashed over to her gym bag and returned with a business card. She handed it to Maggie, who stuck it in her sports bra. "Thanks," Maggie said, "and welcome to class."

"*Maggie.* Maggie!"

She instantly recognized the voice and turned to see her former coworker Vanessa Fleer in the back row. The zaftig new mother waved to Maggie with one hand and blew her a kiss with the other. Maggie responded with a wan smile. She had helped clear Vanessa of a murder charge only weeks before, which turned the "Loch Nessa Monster" from foe to self-appointed BFF, much to Maggie's consternation. "I gotta work off the baby weight," Vanessa announced to Maggie and the room. She stuck out her derriere and spanked it. "Mama's got way too much junk in the trunk."

Before Maggie could come up with an appropriately fatuous response, Sandy Sechrest, her dancer's body clad in black leggings and a turquoise fitness tank, came bounding into the room. King Cake, Sandy's beloved little rescue mutt, trotted in after her and parked himself in a doggy bed at the front of the studio. "Hey, Pelican!" Sandy yelled into her head mic. "Are you ready to dance?!" Her enthusiasm was infectious, and everyone in the room roared back, "Yes!"

Every session at the studio had a different theme, and tonight's was disco. Maggie and the class Hustled and Bumped their way through Sandy's routines. By the time DiscoBod ended, Maggie was drenched with sweat. But she felt relaxed and happy for the first time in days. Thanks to Gaynell's suggestion, she'd danced off her stress—at least for the moment.

The women retreated to the locker room to change back into their street clothes. Lia sat on a wooden bench and dabbed at her face with a tissue. Maggie noticed that she looked pale. "Lia, are you okay? You don't look well."

"I'm fine. My stomach's a little upset is all."

Lia took a soda cracker out of a small plastic bag in her purse and nibbled on it. Vanessa let out a screech that startled the room and set nearby crows cawing. "You're pregnant!"

"What?!" Maggie said. "That's ridiculous, Nessa. You're just seeing babies everywhere because you've got one."

"Wrong-o, Magnolia. I bet you five dollars Lia's having a baby." Vanessa turned to Lia. "I dare you to tell me I'm wrong."

Lia paused. "You're not." The other women screamed, and Lia disappeared under their hugs. "Careful—I'm having a bad case of morning sickness today." The women instantly pulled back. "I'm so sorry I didn't tell you, Maggie, but Kyle and I wanted to wait until I was into my second trimester. We're still a few weeks away. But I guess I can wear this now."

Lia reached into her purse again. This time she pulled out a thin gold band, which she placed on the ring finger of her left hand, eliciting more shrieks from the women.

Maggie collapsed onto the bench next to her cousin. "Married. A baby. Lia, you are seriously messing with my mind."

Lia looked sheepish. "Kyle and I eloped three weeks after we met. We didn't tell anyone because we thought people would think we were moving too fast. But we knew we weren't. Are you mad at me for keeping secrets?"

Maggie thought about everything Lia and Kyle had endured. Lia's first husband had died of cancer at thirty-six, and Kyle had lost his pregnant wife in a car accident. These two grieving souls found solace in each other, and for that Maggie thanked the universe. "Not one bit. Your life is yours to live any way you want." She hugged her cousin gently, mindful of her condition. "Yay! Gals, let's celebrate."

The group headed out the door for Junie's Oyster Bar and Dance Hall. Waiting outside the studio were Vanessa's ex-fiancé, Rufus Durand, and her soon-to-be husband, defense attorney Quentin MacIlhoney. Despite three previous marriages and an upcoming birthday that would see sixty candles on his cake, Quentin had never sired his own offspring. He'd taken to stepfatherhood with gusto, even commissioning a made-to-order, monogrammed alligator diaper bag for himself.

Rufus pushed a baby carriage toward Vanessa, who sauntered over to it. "There's my little princess," she cooed to the infant inside. "Did you miss your mommy?"

"No, because she was having so much fun with the daddy that made her," Rufus, the baby's birth father, said. He scowled at Quentin, who gave him a jovial slap on the shoulder.

"I'm gonna wipe that frown off your face by telling you I'll be picking up all the costs for little Charli's baptism," Quentin said. He turned his attention to Maggie. "Hey there, Miss Magnolia. Anyone murdered at Crozat lately? My caseload's a little light around the holidays."

"Sorry to disappoint you, but all our guests are alive and well," Maggie said.

"I'm gonna pop into DanceBod and say hi to Sandy." Rufus did his best to sound casual, but it was obvious to Maggie that the police officer, who knew Sandy from her strip club days, had a bit of a crush on the dance instructor.

Good-byes were said, and Maggie's group walked down the street toward Junie's. As they passed Le Blanc's Bistro, Pelican's first high-end restaurant, a limo pulled up to the curb. The limo driver got out and opened the passenger's door. Steve Harmon exited from the vehicle, followed by a beautiful redhead. Maggie was surprised when she recognized the woman. What was Bo's ex-wife, Whitney Durand Evans, doing with the hedge fund manager? "Y'all go ahead," Maggie told her friends, who did so. Harmon appeared to be giving his limo driver instructions, so Maggie approached Whitney.

"Hey, Whitney. What's up? I didn't know you knew our guest."

"I didn't. Well, I do now." Whitney spoke in a jumble of words. "He found me because he saw Xander's painting at Crozat, and he thinks he's a prodigy, so he, me, and his art adviser are having dinner at Le Blanc's, which I've been dying to try, but it's superexpensive, which doesn't matter to Steve at all." Whitney stopped to take a breath. "Zach would be here too," she added, referencing her second husband, who held a middle management position at a nearby oil refinery, "but he had to work late."

"Does Bo know about this?" Maggie asked, keeping her tone measured.

"I texted him and he's on his way. Isn't it exciting?"

Maggie didn't respond. It wasn't her place to share Bo's repulsion at the thought of his young, emotionally challenged son turned into some kind of art world circus act.

Steve Harmon finished conversing with his driver and rapped on the passenger's-side window. "You done? I'm hungry."

Maggie saw the shadow of a figure put a cell phone into a jacket pocket. The limo door opened, and a man got out. "That's the art adviser," Whitney whispered to her. "He's real nice. He explained how we have to bring Xander to New York because he's so talented that if people don't see him in person, they'll think we're lying about his art being done by a kid."

The man stepped onto the sidewalk and into the glow of a streetlight. When she saw who he was, for a moment Maggie couldn't breathe.

"Hi, Maggie," the man said.

Maggie opened her mouth to respond, but no words came out.

"You know each other?" Whitney asked, surprised.

Maggie finally found her voice. "Yes. He's Chris Harper. My ex-boyfriend."

Chapter Six

"Sorry I didn't call to warn you, but this whole trip came together really fast," Chris said.

Still in shock, Maggie nodded. Her ex hadn't changed in the two years since she'd last seen him. A hint of gray in his curly brown hair, maybe. A few more crow's-feet. He was dressed in the uniform of jeans, black thermal Henley shirt, and the utilitarian black eyeglass frames Brooklyn hipsters had appropriated from the 1950s. "How's Samantha?" she asked, aiming for polite small talk. She hoped no one noticed the slight crack in her voice when she said the name of the woman Chris had married instead of her.

"Good. How's your family?"

"Good."

"You look great."

"You too."

Eager to end the forced pleasantries, Maggie was searching for an exit line when Bo pulled up in his SUV and screeched to a halt. He jumped out of the car, slammed the driver's door shut, and strode over to Whitney. "You need to *not* be here," he said, his tone laced with fury.

"Bo, you're being stubborn," Whitney said. "Steve is offering Xander an amazing opportunity. He'd meet professional artists and be introduced to that world at such a young age. Zach and I both think it could draw him out of himself more. And if his paintings sold, they could pay for college someday."

"Zach's a good stepdad, and I appreciate that, but I'm Xander's father, and I will be paying for college. He's finally in a school where he's happy and self-confident, Whitney. He's making friends. After three years, he's *talking* again, for God's sake. You really want to tear him away from all that so some money guy can parade him around to make himself look like a big shot?"

"I want to do what's best for Xander and not deprive him of an opportunity that could change his life."

"In a bad way. We've seen what happens to prodigies when they're not prodigies anymore. They go from being famous to 'used to be famous,' and a lot of them never recover from that."

"May I say something here?" Steve Harmon asked.

"Please do," Whitney said. Bo glowered. Maggie and Chris simply stood there, trapped in the awkward face-off.

"You have no idea if your son will show any kind of a talent when he grows up," Harmon said, "so you might as well milk the moment. This may be as good as it gets for a kid like him."

The rage Bo had tamped down bubbled up. He drew back his fist and was about to send it into Harmon's jaw when the mogul's chauffeur clocked Bo with a punch that knocked him to the ground. Whitney whimpered as Maggie fell to her knees next to Bo.

"Thanks, Dan," Harmon said. He pulled open the restaurant door and addressed Whitney. "I leave in the morning, so it's now or never."

Bo shook off the blow and pulled himself to his feet. "I'm warning you both," he said. "If you even think of taking Xander to New York, I will do whatever it takes to stop you."

Whitney, clearly conflicted, looked from Bo to Harmon. Then she followed the businessman into the restaurant with Chris right behind her. "I'll call you," he told Maggie.

"Please don't," she called after him as he disappeared into Le Blanc's. She turned her attention to Bo, who leaned against his SUV, massaging his jaw. "You should ice that. I'll run into Junie's and get some from the bar."

Bo shook his head. "I've gotta get home and look at my divorce papers. Whitney can't take Xander out of the state without my permission, but I want to make sure there aren't any loopholes I'm missing. I'll get in touch with my lawyer first thing in the morning to lock everything down." Bo pulled open the driver's door, jumped in, and started the engine. "I'll call you."

"Please do."

Bo began backing out and then hit the brakes. "Wait a minute—who was the other guy who said he'd call you? The one with Harmon?"

Maggie paused. "That was Chris."

"*The* Chris? Ex-boyfriend Chris? From New York?"

"Yes. But please, so not important right now. I'll explain after you've made sure Xander's not turned into some kind of art gallery sideshow."

Bo frowned, muttered a string of expletives, and then roared out of his parking space. Maggie was alone, which she welcomed after the ugly confrontation that had just taken place. She took a few deep breaths to center herself and then headed down the block to Junie's. "Maggie . . . Maggie . . ." the air whispered. At least she thought it was the air until she heard the yappy bark of a small dog. Sandy Sechrest, with King Cake on a lead, materialized out of the shadows, startling her. "I swear," Maggie coughed out, clutching her heart, "if I survive tonight, it'll be a tribute to some hardy Crozat genes."

"I'm so sorry," Sandy said. Maggie noticed the young woman was trembling, despite her fleece hoodie. "I need to know . . . was one of those men Steve Harmon?"

"Yes, he's staying at our B and B."

Sandy's trembling increased. "F—f—for how long?"

"He's leaving tomorrow."

"Oh, thank God." Then Sandy burst into tears and began running back to her studio. King Cake, thinking it was a game, barked happily and nipped at her heels.

Strangest night ever, Maggie thought to herself as she made her way toward Junie's. She found Gaynell and Ione parked at the hangout's turn-of-the-century bar. Junie's was the kind of place that was pitch dark on summer's sunniest day. It smelled like a century of beer, jambalaya, and mildew, and the locals couldn't have loved it more. The ashes of Junie, the bar and grill's late owner, sat in a bedazzled urn atop the bar, next to the stuffed body of her deceased pet alligator. Junie's son, JJ, had inherited her business and her wardrobe, and he treated them both with tender, loving care.

Like his mother, JJ believed more was more, so he and the restaurant were resplendent with holiday decorations. Large ornaments hung from the tin-tiled ceiling, and small Christmas trees decorated each table. JJ wore a festive sequined red tunic and had clipped a sprig of holly to his hair.

Maggie pulled up a barstool next to Gaynell. "Lia had some first trimester fatigue, so she went home," Ione said. "What took you so long?"

Before she could respond, Old Shari, the nonagenarian bartender, eyed Maggie and then placed a shot of bourbon in front of her. "You need this," she declared. Maggie marveled at the ancient woman's instincts and knocked back the shot.

"It's been a night," she told her friends and filled them in on everything that had happened, from her ex-boyfriend's sudden appearance to Bo getting decked by Harmon's goon. She finished by recounting her strange rendezvous with Sandy.

"It sure sounds like she has some kind of history with this Harmon man," Gaynell said.

"I know," Maggie said. "She seemed almost terrified to see him."

"It must have been a shock for you, seeing Chris again after all this time," Ione said. "And here of all places."

"Yes," Maggie said. "It was." Old Shari refilled Maggie's shot glass and gave her a sympathetic wink. *Helene Brevelle may be our town voodoo priestess, but Old Shari is definitely the Pelican cocktail psychic,* a grateful Maggie thought to herself. She wasn't ready to elaborate on her feelings about Chris's unexpected reappearance in her life, and her friends were sensitive enough not to press for details. She assumed he would leave the next day with his boss, and she could file the experience under Life's Little Surprises. Maggie suddenly felt a chill that countered the bar and grill's clammy warmth. It was accompanied by a foreboding message: *Never assume anything.*

The three women finished their drinks and said their good-nights. Maggie wrote off her anxiety as an aftereffect of the day's disturbing events. But her ominous premonition was borne out when she returned home and found her mother hauling Steve Harmon's suitcase onto Crozat's veranda. The mogul watched as she refused his driver's offer of help. "I want the satisfaction of throwing Mr. Harmon out myself," Ninette said. She let go of the suitcase and gave it a shove with her small, sneakered foot. The pricey-looking bag tumbled down Crozat's front steps.

"You found out what Harmon's up to, didn't you?" Maggie asked her mother. "Uncle Tig and I have been trying to fight off his scheme to take over Preferred Properties. We didn't want to tell you because we were afraid it would affect Dad's health."

"Your father saw Uncle Tig's address on an e-mail and thought it was for him, so he opened and read it. We know everything." She marched down the stairs and faced off with Harmon. "I have never expelled a guest from our property, but doing so tonight has given me a great deal of satisfaction. Count your blessings that I made my husband take a sleeping pill or you'd be leaving here in an ambulance."

"I only stayed at Crozat to get a sense of how to monetize this place," the multimillionaire replied. "I'll be sending you a bill for any damage you caused to my suitcase when you drop-kicked it, and you can send the check for repairs to me at Belle Vista Plantation Resort and Spa. Come on, Dan."

Harmon grabbed his suitcase and got in the limo, which kicked up clouds of dust as it drove away. "If I had a gun, I'd shoot out their tires," Ninette said.

Maggie had never heard such a venomous tone from her kind and gracious mother.

It scared her.

*

In the morning, Maggie readied herself for a day of bad acting at Doucet by applying a heavy coat of concealer to hide the bags lurking under her hazel eyes. She then pulled her thick brown hair into a ponytail that she could tuck under her Southern belle wig. As she got into her car, Marco pulled up beside her in his rental van. He hopped out and helped one of his Japanese charges from the van. Both looked exhausted. "Your mama's cooking is so good that Akira tried to ignore the fact that he's hypoglycemic and had a little too much dessert," Marco told Maggie. "We spent the night at the hospital."

"Oh, no, I'm so sorry. Akira, I sympathize with how hard it is to resist my mother's treats. If you need anything, let us know." Both men nodded and yawned. They trudged toward the house, and Maggie took off for work.

She arrived at Doucet with only a few minutes to spare. She threw on her wig and wriggled into the despised lime ball gown. "Well, hello, y'all." Maggie greeted her first tour group with an accent thick as two-day-old gumbo and then launched into the tour's new scripted patter. "I'm the mistress of Doucet Plantation. Welcome to my home. Did y'all bring me a gift of a pineapple? You may wonder why I ask. Well, I'll tell you. A pineapple is a rare and exotic fruit here in the 1860s, so if you've brought me one, I know you are a family of wealth and pedigree. But even if you haven't brought me one, as honored guests to my home, you'll still be the 'pine-*apple*' of my eye." Maggie sympathized with her visitors as they cringed at the terrible dialogue forced on her by Tannis. "Follow me, if you will."

Maggie spent the next twenty minutes leading her group from room to room, spewing Tannis's clumsy mix of fact and fiction as she showed off the home's antique doo-dads and ornate Victorian furnishings. The final stop on the ground floor was the men's parlor. She noticed a long streak of water and dirt on the floor, which struck her as strange. It hadn't been there the night before when she locked up the manor house.

The last thing Maggie needed was a visitor slipping and getting injured, so she steered her group around the mysterious stain. Then she forced her attention back to the tour. "This is where the menfolk retire after a meal," Maggie said as she pulled open the room's pocket doors. "It's where they do manly things like smoke cigars and play cards and drink whiskey. I miss my dear husband so very, very much." Maggie laid on her accent even more and, following Tannis's directions, added a shaky timbre to her voice to maximize the dramatic effect. "Oh, how I wish he'd return from the war."

A gawky teen visiting with his family chortled. "The dummy's awesome," he said, pointing into the room. "I like how the first thing your 'husband' did when he got back from the war was get wasted."

Puzzled, Maggie leaned into the room to see what he was talking about. A man sat slumped in a red velvet wingback chair. At first glance, she thought he was one of Tannis's guest actors brought in to play a role in her ludicrous new format. She stepped closer and stifled a gasp.

The man was Steve Harmon. And Maggie could tell from his waxy complexion that the ruthless businessman had done his last deal.

Chapter Seven

Maggie stood frozen.

"I don't think that's a dummy," an elderly woman on the tour said.

A concerned murmur went through the group. Maggie collected herself. "Oh, boy, it looks like one of our cast members might have been the one to hit the whiskey. Which kinda makes him a dummy, doesn't it?" She broke character and spoke in her regular voice, earning the first genuine chuckle of the tour. As she spoke, she pulled the pocket doors shut. "We'll let him sleep it off. Anyhoo, now that we've completed exploring the ground floor of Doucet, why don't we step outside for a breath of fresh air?"

Maggie steered her group onto the veranda. She saw Gaynell, in her boy's attire, leading a few guests up toward the house. With her was Little Earlie Waddell, editor in chief of the *Penny Clipper*, Pelican's free community periodical. Ad sales were slow during the holidays, so the twenty-something was picking up extra cash by joining Doucet's cast of characters on a part-time basis. "Why, there's my son and his tutor," Maggie riffed to her tour. "Excuse me for one minute." Not wishing to alarm them, she walked rather than ran over to Gaynell and Little Earlie. "You need to take my group," she told them in a whisper. "Something's happened. I can't explain right now, but make sure everybody stays out of the men's parlor."

"Okay," Gaynell said as she and Little Earlie exchanged confused glances. They hustled the guests up the plantation home's wide front stairs. Maggie waved to her group. "I must attend to some important plantation details," she called to them, reverting to Southern belle mode. "Buh-bye, y'all! Enjoy the rest of your tour."

Maggie sauntered away. As soon as she was sure that she was out of the group's eyeline, she dashed back to the house. She threw open the men's parlor pocket doors and entered the room, closing the doors behind her. Maggie approached Steve Harmon's body, careful not to disturb anything in the room, and put two fingers on his wrist dangling over the arm of the chair. She found no pulse and noticed the stain of a sticky red-brown liquid on his shirt pocket that she feared was congealed blood. She pulled her cell phone out of her décolletage and dialed 9-1-1. A dispatcher answered, and Maggie blurted out, "I need to report a male who appears to be deceased."

"Maggie Crozat, is that you *again*?" Delphine Arnaud responded. Delphine always seemed to be the dispatcher on duty when Maggie stumbled across a dead body.

"I'm not at Crozat, Delphine," Maggie said. "I'm at Doucet."

"Well, that's different."

"But," Maggie had to acknowledge, "the man in question was one of our guests."

"Of course he was." Delphine sighed. "Pelican PD is on its way, as are the EMTs."

Maggie ended the call and left the parlor. She pulled the pocket doors shut and dragged a carved black walnut bench in front of them, blocking access to the room. Then she hiked up her hoop skirt and ran to the gift shop. Ione was restocking a Christmas tree with ornaments for sale as Tannis retrieved credit card receipts from the cash register. Maggie checked to make sure there were no customers around and then told the women, "I need to talk to you. In private." Ione and Tannis followed her into the gift shop office. "There's a dead man in the manor house."

Both women gasped. Ione crossed herself. "Who? How? What exactly—"

Maggie held up her hand. "No time for questions. The police are on their way. They may want to talk to people . . ."

Maggie paused. Intuition and the red stain on his shirt told her Harmon didn't die of natural causes, but it would be irresponsible to bring that up until it was confirmed by medical professionals. ". . . because what happened is so unusual," she continued. "Anyway, we need to round up all the visitors and staff in a way that doesn't create some kind of panic."

"Oh, no," wailed Tannis, who seemed on the verge of panic herself. "What do we do?"

Before Maggie could respond, Ione jumped in. "We're going to tell them a man passed away on the property and the police may want to speak to them, just pro forma. We'll gather everyone here in the gift shop and put out the chairs we use for rental events. We'll refund the visitors' money and give them free tickets for another visit. And little gift bags." She called up a list of inventory on the gift shop computer. "Let's see . . . bookmarks, postcards, Mardi Gras beads. The car decals aren't selling, so we can throw those in too. And something real special. I know, the Christmas ornaments shaped like bonfires. Tannis, can you think of anything else?" The manager shook her head. "I'll put in a 'Visit Plantation Country' brochure. Those are wonderful. And I'll call Burnside Plantation, explain we have a situation here, and see if they'll honor our tickets for today. It'll funnel people into their restaurants and gift shop, so I don't foresee a problem."

Maggie marveled at her friend's efficiency. Ione's demotion to Tannis's lackey was unfathomable. "I'll message the other guides and tell them to herd everyone this way," she said, then headed out of the office.

"Maggie, wait," Ione said. Her tone was somber. "Was the man anyone we know?"

"It was someone *I* know. A Crozat guest." Maggie stopped, remembering Tannis's relationship with the late financier. Then she said, "Steve Harmon."

Tannis let out a shriek and started to sway. Ione grabbed her, put a hand over the manager's mouth, and guided her to a chair. "Control yourself. You'll scare our visitors."

Tannis nodded and then burst into tears. Maggie heard the whine of a police siren grow louder as a patrol car approached. "You take care of Tannis," she told Ione. "I'll take care of everyone else."

*

Once the other guides received Maggie's text alert, they maneuvered their groups into the gift shop, where she explained the situation. The staff was more concerned than the guests, who seemed to view a dead man and police interview as a unique vacation story to bring home along with souvenirs and laundry. They were disappointed to hear the plantation would have to close for the day due to the emergency, but any ill will dissipated when Maggie handed them each a goody bag and announced that their tickets would be honored at Burnside Plantation. As insurance, she placed a call to Lia and ordered a buffet of pastries, which thrilled the staff even more than the guests.

As she walked back to the manor house, Maggie's cell phone rang. She looked down and read, "Private Caller." "Hello?" she said, a little wary.

"Hey, it's me. I see you didn't change your cell number."

Maggie's heart sank as she recognized the voice. "Hi, Chris. I'm kind of in the middle of something."

"Sorry, but I have a problem. I'm at St. Pierre Parish Airfield, and Steve hasn't shown up. I know he checked out of Crozat last night, but I thought he might have gone back for some reason."

"I know where he is," Maggie said, choosing her words carefully. "You need to meet me at Doucet Plantation."

"Your mom's old place? Maggie, what's going on?"

"Just get here. I'll give you directions."

"Don't need them. I remember how to get there."

Maggie ended the call and rushed over to the Pelican EMTs, Cody Pugh and Regine Armitage. "This way," she said as she led them and their gurney to the men's parlor. Regine picked up Steve's wrist to take his pulse, then let go of it. She looked at Cody and shook her head, confirming Maggie's diagnosis.

"Nothing for us to do now except turn this over to Pelican PD," she said.

"He was murdered, wasn't he?" Maggie asked.

Regine pointed to the darkening red splotch on the late mogul's chest. "Unless a red pen burst in his shirt pocket, I'd say there's a pretty good chance someone stuck a knife in him."

Maggie and the EMTs were distracted by the sound of heavy footsteps and men's voices. Bo and acting Pelican police chief Hank Perske appeared in the room's doorway. Bo gave Maggie a slight nod; they had learned to underplay their relationship when around the rigid, taciturn Perske. "We'll take it from here," Perske announced to the room.

"He's all yours," Cody said as he and Regine packed up their gear.

"Officer Belloise will take your statement," Perske said to Maggie. "The coroner needs to determine the cause of death, which may or may not be from natural causes. Either way, it's important to tap your memory while it's fresh."

"Of course."

Maggie stepped outside the room, ducking under the police tape that Artie Belloise was threading across the parlor doorway. His Pelican PD partner, Cal Vichet, waved to Maggie. "Hey there, Maggie. We meet again."

"We meet all the time, Cal. My boyfriend works with you, plus you're a regular at Junie's."

"Well, if you know that, then you're a regular too."

"True," Maggie acknowledged.

Artie finished blocking off the parlor and cut the tape. "All righty," he said to Maggie. "Let's find somewhere to talk."

"We can go to the employee lounge."

"They got any snacks there?" asked Artie, who was the chubby baseball to Cal's lean bat.

"Afraid not."

"Dang," the officer grumped. "I like these murders better when they happen at Crozat. Your mama's one terrific cook."

"We don't know it's a murder," Maggie said. Both officers gave her skeptical looks. "Fine. Let's go."

"I'll start interviewing the other folk soon as I finish up here," Cal said. "Come over when you're done, Artie."

"I ordered a bunch of pastries from Fais Dough Dough for the visitors," Maggie told Cal. "They should be there soon."

"And so will I," Artie assured his partner. "Let's get steppin', Maggie. I see a Fais Dough Dough-nut in my future."

Maggie and Artie retreated to the employee lounge, where she recounted her discovery of Steve Harmon's body. "Thinking about it, one important thing is that I didn't see any evidence of forced entry," she said. "I've opened all the doors to this place so many times, I'd notice if anything was different. And nothing was."

"Interesting," Artie said. "Our techs will check, but it sure don't sound like it was forced entry."

"No. Whoever did this had a key. Or made a copy of a key."

Maggie heard a sound coming from the bathroom. "Someone else is here," she said and knocked on the bathroom door. No one responded. "We know you're in there; we heard you."

Artie got up and pounded on the door. "Pelican PD, open up *now*," he ordered.

The bathroom door flew open, revealing Little Earlie. "I would have come out, but I didn't want to disturb you," he said.

"Yeah, right," Maggie scoffed. Little Earlie's dream was to turn the *Penny Clipper* into a real newspaper, and there wasn't a small story that he didn't try to blow up into a big one. And if Harmon had been murdered, the story was already big.

Artie extended his hand. "Give me your notebook."

"Don't have one."

"I'm light on collars this month. An arrest for obstruction of justice would put me right with my boss."

"Fine," Little Earlie said. He reluctantly pulled a reporter's notebook out of the pocket of his ersatz nineteenth-century jacket. "Doesn't matter anyway. I got it all up here." Little Earlie tapped his head.

"Lord knows what you got up there, but it better not be anything you heard in this room," Artie said.

Artie opened the door, and Little Earlie started out, almost colliding with Chris. He and Maggie exchanged quick greetings. "Artie," she said, "this is . . . an old friend of mine from New York, Chris Harper. He worked for Steve Harmon."

"Really?" Artie eyed him. "You got any contact information? We might need to have a conversation."

"Um, sure. Here's my card." Chris, perplexed, pulled a card out of his wallet and handed it to Artie, who placed it in his wallet.

"Thanks. Maggie, I'll be in touch if I need to ask you any more questions. I might have to go over a few things. Might be best to do it at Crozat next time."

"Around dinnertime?"

"Or breakfast. Maybe lunch. Any meal's good with me. I better get over to Cal before all of Lia's treats are gone."

"And to interview guests and staff."

"Right. That too."

Chris watched Artie go and then turned to Maggie. "Okay, what's going on?"

She debated how to break the bad news to Chris and decided blunt was the way to go. "Chris, I'm so sorry, but Steve Harmon is dead."

He stared at her. "*What?*"

"I found him this morning in the men's parlor. And there's a good chance—well, not good, poor choice of words, sorry about that—there's a strong chance he was murdered."

"Oh, my God." Chris collapsed onto one of the lounge's beat-up plastic folding chairs. "This is unreal. It can't be happening."

He ran his fingers through his hair over and over again, and Maggie got a catch in her throat. She remembered the anxious gesture so well from their years together. "Let me get you some water," she said, pulling herself together.

"No." Chris jumped up. "Thanks, but I need to make some calls. I have to let his wife, Emme, know. And Dan. And—"

"Whoa. Wife? He was married?"

"Yes, for years."

Maggie sighed. "Oh, boy. I have more bad news. I'm pretty sure he was having an affair with my boss."

To Maggie's surprise, Chris shrugged and said, "Yeah, well, that's Steve." He paced for a minute and then said, "Before I call anyone, I should talk to the police. Who's the head guy?"

"Hank Perske. You can't miss him. He's about six foot six and built like a five-hundred-year-old oak tree."

"Thanks. I'll be back. Wait for me."

Chris hurried out the door. For the first time all day, Maggie was alone. Exhausted, she yanked off her wig, folded her arms on the lounge's old card table, and rested her head on them. The image of Steve Harmon's lifeless body haunted her. His death may not have occurred at Crozat, but he had been the family's guest. *Our B and B is starting to feel like a roach motel*, Maggie thought glumly as she recalled an old commercial Tug once dug up on the Internet and showed her. *Guests check in, but they don't check out.*

"Maggie?"

She lifted up her head as the lounge door opened partway. "There you are," Bo said. He came into the room and pulled a folding chair next to her.

"Do they know how he died?" she asked.

"Ferdie Chauvin took a look at him," Bo responded, referencing the Pelican coroner. "He won't commit to anything until he does an autopsy, but he's fairly certain Harmon was stabbed in the chest, most likely with a long, thin blade."

Maggie shuddered. "That's so gruesome."

"Even though the cause of death hasn't been confirmed, Perske asked me to start compiling a list of possible suspects."

Bo pulled out a piece of paper and placed it in front of Maggie. When she read it, she suddenly felt sick to her stomach. "No. I refuse to believe it."

"I started with the most likely one."

There was a single name on the page: Bo Durand.

Chapter Eight

Maggie pushed the paper across the card table back to Bo. "That's ridiculous. You're being dramatic."

Bo shook his head. "Harmon was taking advantage of my son. I went after him on the street. I threatened him. Any decent detective would consider me a 'person of interest,' and I happen to be better than decent at my job. So . . ." He pointed at his name on the paper.

"Fine, if you're going to be stubborn about it. But there are plenty of other names you can add to that list, like my boss, Tannis, who had a thing for him, and probably *with* him. And there's—" Maggie stopped.

"What?"

Maggie sighed and then said, "There's my entire family. Harmon wanted to put us out of business. I know why my father almost had a stroke." She filled Bo in on Steve Harmon's campaign against her uncle. "If he managed to push Tig out, we'd be collateral damage. Harmon would control

Crozat and get rid of us faster than green grass through a goose."

Maggie noticed a pen on the lounge's old wooden floor. She picked it up, took Bo's piece of paper, wrote on it, and then handed it back to him. "Maggie Crozat, Ninette Crozat, Tug Crozat, and Charlotte Crozat," Bo read. He looked up at her with skepticism. "You put your grand-mère on this list?"

Maggie nodded. "I'm trying to do like you did and be honest about how we all hated him. And we're people who've only known him a few days. Considering the range of his business activities, that list could go international."

This brought a rueful smile to Bo's handsome face. "Good point." He waved the sheet of paper. "I think we're going to have a lot of company here." He pushed back his chair and stood up. "I better check in with Perske. I'll see you in a bit." Bo gently kissed the top of Maggie's head, which sent a charge surging down to her toes. "By the way, as long as we're all about honesty here, that dress is butt-effin'-ugly."

*

Maggie spent the next several hours helping Ione and Gaynell entertain Doucet's visitors as they waited to be interviewed and released by Pelican PD. She drummed up stories about Doucet's past from the family vault of anecdotes. When she finally ran dry, Gaynell pulled out her guitar and did an acoustic set of original tunes to the toe-tapping delight of the guests. A few even danced to the Cajun-inspired ditties and bought CDs from the tour guide-musician. The atmosphere was more like a party than a death investigation, and Maggie heard a few disappointed groans when Chief Perske sent the message that guests and staff were free to go.

Maggie, Gaynell, and Ione retreated to the employee lounge to change into their street clothes and grab a late lunch. Ione noticed Maggie was toying with her food rather than eating it. "What's wrong? I've had your mother's oyster stew, and it's as good on day two as day one."

"I'm not very hungry."

Gaynell, whose guileless looks belied a sharp intellect, eyed her. "How exactly did this man die?"

"We won't know for sure until the coroner does an autopsy." This was true but skirted the question that Maggie knew her friend was really asking.

Gaynell, however, had no intention of letting Maggie off the hook. "You think he was killed, don't you?"

Instead of responding, Maggie speared an oyster and lifted it to her mouth. Then her mind flashed back to Bo's list of suspects, and she let the oyster fall back into her lunch container. "It's looking that way," she said. She fastened the container's lid and then stood up. "I can't eat right now. I want to see what's going on out there."

"Okay, hon," Ione said. "We're here if you need us."

Gaynell nodded. "What she said."

Maggie managed a smile for her friends, and then she headed outside. While the coroner's van was long gone, the number of law enforcement vehicles seemed to have grown, and Maggie noted the all-too-familiar Pelican PD mobile evidence van had made an appearance. She scanned the scene for Bo but didn't see him. She did, however, see Chris and turned away, not in the mood to negotiate their weird dynamic. But it was too late. Chris waved and jogged over. "Hey," he said, panting slightly. He'd never been a particular fan of exercise in any form. "How crazy is this whole thing?"

"Pretty crazy," Maggie acknowledged.

"Steve's people are on their way up from New Orleans."

"Aren't you his people too?"

"I was. I don't know now." Chris once again ran his hands through his hair. "Man, I wasn't prepared for this. I mean, it's such a freaky situation."

"A very freaky situation," Maggie said, sticking to an inane mimicking of Chris's comments.

"The police won't tell me squat. If you hear anything, being a local and all, can you let me know? Please?"

Chris's plea was tinged with vulnerability. His boyish take-care-of-me vibe had seduced Maggie in the past, but now it only annoyed her. "I'm sure Pelican PD will share the details they feel are relevant when the time is right," she said, not caring how stiff she sounded. The last thing Maggie wanted was to be a conduit of information for her ex, and she hoped that a side benefit of Steve Harmon's unexpected demise would be Chris's quick return to New York.

"I know you have to say that, but if you do hear something, I'm staying at Belle Vista." Chris made a rote move to kiss Maggie on the cheek and then stopped himself. Instead he took off for the Doucet parking lot.

Maggie heard weeping and looked across Doucet's wide verdant lawn to where Cal Vichet was escorting Tannis from the manor house. The young woman had fallen apart since learning of her lover's death. Her usually slick blonde pony-tail was in disarray, and tears turned her mascara into black rivulets that dribbled down her cheeks onto her navy suit. "I swear, I didn't care that he was married," she sobbed to the officer. "He was going to leave his wife for me." Cal snorted. "Stop that, it's true," Tannis yelled at him. "And I'm not the only one around here who had a key to the manor house. She did too."

Maggie assumed Tannis was pointing at her. Then she realized her boss was pointing behind her and turned to see Ione leaving the overseer's cottage, followed by Gaynell. "Ione has a key," Tannis said as she continued to point an accusing finger at Maggie's friend. "And she hates me. I took over her job, and she was ticked off about all the changes I was making to improve Doucet. She was giving me a terrible time. I wouldn't be surprised if she killed Steve and tried to frame me because I fired her."

"What?!" Maggie yelped. "That's slander."

"Yeah!" Gaynell chimed in.

"She's only here because y'all forced me to keep her on. Curse my kindness; it led to murder," Tannis exclaimed, her voice a screech by the time she hit the word "murder."

Gaynell, Maggie, and Ione let loose a chorus of protests. Cal held his hand up in the air. "Ms. Greer, you're free to go," he said to Tannis, adding, "for now. We'll be in touch."

The officer crooked his finger and beckoned to Ione. "We need to talk."

"We already talked, Cal," she responded.

"We need to talk *more*," he said. Cal started toward the gift shop and motioned for Ione to follow him. As Maggie watched her friend take dejected steps after the officer, she feared someone else she cared about would soon be added to Bo's suspect list.

*

With Tannis a hot mess and both she and Ione targets of suspicion, it fell on Maggie to inform the Doucet staff that the plantation would be closed for at least the next day and possibly longer. She asked them not to speak to reporters about what had happened and assured them they would be compensated for any length of closure, knowing full well that Tannis would flip her associate-business-degree lid when she heard about it. *Too late*, Maggie thought, smug with satisfaction. It was her holiday present to Doucet's hardworking employees. Gaynell then helped her rebook scheduled tours to Burnside Plantation, which was starting to view Doucet's woes as *their* holiday present.

By the time the two women were done, the early night of winter had fallen. Gaynell threaded her fingers together and stretched her arms above her head. "I could use something to wash down the day," she said. "Junie's?"

Maggie shook her head. "I should go home and check in with my folks."

"Well, if you change your mind, text me. And if you need anything, anything at all . . ."

Maggie smiled at her friend. "Thanks, Gay."

Gaynell took off. Maggie turned off the computer and locked up the gift shop. She stepped outside and slipped on her hoodie as she walked to her car. With the sun down, the air was chilly. She would have felt alone and a bit spooked had it not been for the bright lights and murmur of conversation emanating from the evidence van.

As Maggie drove down the road that snaked along the west bank of the Mississippi, it occurred to her that there was another possible murder suspect in Pelican, someone who was hiding a painful secret. She crossed the river, noting the shadows of partially built bonfires that lined both the west and east levees. A few miles after crossing, instead of heading home to Crozat, she made a left onto Main Street and followed it into town. The Pelican Chamber of Commerce had okayed additional holiday decorations, and now giant snowflakes lit by white LED lights hung over every intersection. They reminded Maggie of the festive, giant snowflake-slash-star that hung over the Manhattan intersection of Fifty-Seventh Street and Fifth Avenue every Christmas, and she got a brief pang of nostalgia.

Maggie parked near the village green's bandstand, which served as Papa Noel's Cajun home prior to Christmas. The role of Papa Noel was usually played by Father Prit, the resident priest of Saint Theresa, Pelican's Roman Catholic Church. His Indian accent betrayed him to even the youngest child, but they adored his enthusiastic embrace of the local custom. However, this holiday season, Father Prit was in Rome to participate in the Vatican's Christmas Eve Mass, led by his idol, Pope Francis. Local men who took turns filling in for the priest had to endure the complaints of children who missed "Papa Prit."

She strode across the green to DanceBod. The studio space was dark, but Maggie could see a light shining from Sandy's office. She gave the door a hard knock and waited. Sandy peeked through the studio's window and then opened the door. King Cake yipped a greeting. "Hey," Sandy said. "I finished my last class about twenty minutes ago."

"I actually didn't come by to dance. I wanted to talk to you."

"Oh," Sandy said. "All right. Come on in. I'll get us some coffee."

Maggie followed Sandy and King Cake through the studio into the DanceBod owner's office. Sandy had brought a homey look to the old room. Staple-gunned Indian fabric covered its worn walls, and teal ottomans served as seating. A small carved desk hosted a laptop computer and coffeemaker. On the opposite wall was a door that led to Sandy's living quarters. DanceBod was both business and home to her.

Sandy poured coffee into two paper cups and offered one to Maggie, then took a seat next to her on an ottoman. "So," she said, "what's up?"

It had been a long, difficult day, and Maggie didn't have the energy to tiptoe around the topic. "Why were you so alarmed to see Steve Harmon?" she asked Sandy.

Maggie noticed Sandy's body tense up under her purple leggings and exercise tank top that read, "BeLIeVE." King Cake jumped into her lap and snuggled protectively. "Has he left Crozat?" she asked, a tremor to her voice. "Is he gone?"

"Yes," Maggie said, adding to herself, *in a manner of speaking.*

Sandy closed her eyes, sucked in air through a long inhale, and then slowly blew it out. She didn't open her eyes. "When I was dancing at the Cajun Classy Lady," she said, referring to the strip club outside Baton Rouge that was her former workplace, "Steve Harmon was a regular whenever he was in town. And there was an incident." The dancer paused. "One night about a year ago, he was waiting by my car when I got done with work. At first he was all flirty, and I tried to fend him off in a polite way. But then it got physical. He tried to kiss me, and when I wouldn't let him, he grabbed me. I tried fighting him off but ended up falling and banging my head so hard on the ground that I passed out, which probably saved me from something worse happening."

Sandy opened her eyes. Maggie sensed she was relieved to have shared her story. "In a way, I owe him. I'd saved enough by then to get this place started, so after my run-in with him, I quit the Lady and came here. Sometimes when I'm low on cash, I think maybe I should go back and pick up a few shifts to bring in some tip money. But then I look at this." Sandy pulled the hair back from her right temple to reveal a jagged scar. "It's where my head hit when I fell. I needed almost twenty stitches. It reminds me that I can never go back. Instead, I make myself work double hard here."

Maggie took Sandy's hand and held it between hers. "I am so sorry. And so glad you chose Pelican as your new home. I think this town's collective cholesterol level is going to drop a lot thanks to DanceBod."

The dance instructor managed a small smile. "Thanks, Maggie."

"You need to know something," Maggie said. "Steve Harmon is dead."

Sandy's eyes widened in shock. "Oh, my God."

"And there's a chance that he may not have died of natural causes."

"Oh, my *God*," Sandy said again, shock turning to fear.

"The police will be talking to a lot of people, including my own family. There's a good chance they'll want to talk to you too."

Sandy picked up King Cake and held him to her chest. The pup rested his head on her shoulder. Maggie noticed the dance instructor was shaking. "Do I need a lawyer?" Sandy asked.

"No. Well . . . not yet. Someone will. Hopefully it won't be you or me."

"If he was killed, it wasn't me. I swear."

Sandy's teeth were chattering. Maggie felt for the woman. "I can't imagine you killing anyone," she said. It was the semitruth. She had learned over the last few months that pretty much anyone was capable of murder. Yet watching the vulnerable woman in front of her, she genuinely doubted Sandy could stick a knife in Steve Harmon and then sashay back to DanceBod to teach locals how to salsa. "I thought you should know."

"Yes. Thank you."

Maggie drained her coffee cup and disposed of it in a wicker trash bin. Sandy and King Cake walked her to the studio's front door. "Could you do me a favor and not tell my story to anyone unless you have to?" Sandy asked as Maggie hovered in the open doorway.

"I promise." Maggie appreciated that Sandy had tacked on the "unless you have to." If pressed by Pelican PD, she would have to reveal Sandy's traumatic confrontation with Harmon. But until then, she would safeguard the story.

Maggie stepped outside and heard Sandy lock the door and throw a dead bolt behind her. She had a feeling a lot of Pelicaners would be throwing their dead bolts that evening. She crossed the village green to her car and then stopped short. Leaning against the car was Chris. He was engrossed in checking his phone and didn't see her. Maggie debated her next move. Should she walk home? A brisk several-mile evening stroll would be good for her. She could pick up her car in the morning. *Coward*, she scolded herself and made her way to the convertible.

"Hello," she greeted Chris coolly.

"Oh, hey," he said, looking up from his cell.

"How did you know where to find me?"

He held up his phone. "The Find Me app. I never deleted you, and apparently you never deleted me either."

Maggie fumed. She'd meant to delete the entire app, but once she'd settled into Pelican, she had forgotten about it.

With everyone in the small village about an arm's length away, finding each other generally proved easy.

"The app's wonky, so I didn't know exactly where you were," Chris continued. "I figured I was safe waiting by your car. It's not like you were gonna walk home, right?"

"Right," Maggie said, wishing she had. Something about Chris, in addition to his general presence, was bothering her, but she couldn't land on what it was.

"I wanted to tell you I'll be sticking around the area for a while. I'm helping Steve's wife, Emme, handle the details of his death. I'll be appraising the artwork in their New Orleans place as well as Belle Vista."

"Thank you for letting me know." Maggie made a move toward her car door, hoping Chris would get the hint, but he didn't move.

"Look," he said, "I know you're angry at me. I did a crappy thing, and there aren't enough ways to say I'm sorry. But I think I've become a better person since then. I hope someday you'll stop hating me and maybe even let me be your friend."

Chris repeated his nervous habit of running his hands through his hair, and Maggie suddenly realized what was bothering her. "Your wedding ring," she said. "You're not wearing it."

"No." Chris looked down at his bare finger. "That's the first thing to go when your wife files for divorce."

Stunned, Maggie didn't know what to say, so she said nothing.

"The second thing to go is your business, if your wife comes from money and can afford a way better lawyer than you can. Samantha got the gallery. And I scrounged around, broke and unemployed, until I got a job as Steve Harmon's art adviser."

"Oh. I thought maybe you were freelancing with him on top of running the gallery. I'm sorry. About everything."

"Yeah, I'm guessing you're probably not. And that's okay. I get it. But I hope you'll think about being my friend. I could use one."

Chris turned and walked across the green, head down and shoulders slumped—a man defeated. Maggie got into her car but didn't start the engine. She processed what Chris had shared with her. He was wrong. She did feel sorry for him. But it was mixed with sorrow for her own loss. She had loved their life together in New York, every high and low of it. When Maggie thought Chris had thrown her over for the love of his life, it was brutally painful, but she forced herself to accept it. But to learn that everything they had built together—their relationship, the art gallery, a home—had been cast aside for an impulsive failed marriage? Maggie's mood swung from sad to angry.

A gentle rap on the car window snapped Maggie back to the present. She looked up to see Bo and rolled down the window. "Hope I didn't scare you," he said. "I was going to send a text, but then I saw you in your car and had make sure you were all right. I don't want you hanging around in the dark with a murderer out there."

"So it's confirmed," Maggie said. "Someone killed Steve Harmon."

Bo nodded. "There's other news too," he said, his tone grim. "As predicted, Perske took me off the case."

"No." Maggie opened the Falcon's door and got out. She put her arms around Bo and held him tight. "I'm so sorry. Cal and Artie are great officers, but they can't do the job that you do."

"They're not replacing me."

"Then who is?"

Bo didn't respond, and she knew he was about to utter the one name she dreaded hearing. "Rufus," he finally said. "Perske's bringing him back as lead detective on the case."

Maggie's stomach churned. In a case where every member of her family was a potential suspect, the lead investigator was a man whose own family had hated hers for one hundred and fifty years. Rufus Durand's holiday gift was a chance to live his dream of making the Crozats' lives miserable.

"Oh, no," she said. "I think we'd better get a lawyer."

Chapter Nine

Bo did his best to allay Maggie's fears. "Give Rufus a chance, chère. Please. The mayor won't reinstate him as police chief yet, so this is his chance to prove himself. And I don't think he's blowing smoke when he says he's changed because of Charli. If he starts to mess with any of you, I swear on the Durand family Bible that I'll take care of him myself."

Spurred by her affection for Bo, she finally agreed to his plea. And she respected his loyalty to his cousin. As her late Grand-père Crozat used to say, "The ties that bind family are tied tightest of all." This was as true of Bo, Rufus, and the rest of the Durands as it was of the Crozats. So she would honor Bo by trusting him when he said Rufus was no longer a conniving, lowlife bully.

Rain started to send a rat-a-tat-tat on the canvas roof of her old convertible as she drove home, so Maggie parked her car inside the family garage at the far end of the Crozat property. She pulled her jacket over her head and dashed from the garage into the manor house kitchen, where Ninette was arranging an appetizer of shrimp remoulade on top of avo-cado halves. "Sorry I'm late," Maggie said as she replaced the jacket with an apron. "I had to talk to Bo about some things."

"Involving Mr. Harmon's death, I'm assuming." Ninette pulled a foil-wrapped loaf of French bread out of the kitchen's industrial oven. Maggie unwrapped the loaf and sliced it into thick hunks. She plated the shrimp remoulade and garnished each dish with a slice of bread. She then dampened paper towels and placed one on each plate to keep the bread moist. "Cal and Artie stopped by," Ninette said, as if the officers had paid a casual social call. "They searched Mr. Harmon's room and chatted with us."

"You mean interviewed you, Mom."

"Yes." Ninette turned on the rice cooker and then stirred a cast-iron pot filled with shrimp étouffée. With crawfish out of season, shrimp was her crustacean of choice for the evening meal. "They spoke to our guests first, and at least one of them mentioned overhearing me banish Mr. Harmon from the premises."

"I wonder who ratted you out."

Ninette managed a wan smile. "This isn't a 1930s gang-ster movie. I was pretty vocal when I evicted him. By law, people have to share what they see or hear or know regarding a questionable death."

"Unfortunately, it's not questionable anymore."

"Oh."

"I should have warned you that we were possible sus-pects. I didn't want to stress Dad. Or you. Because of the

Hodgkin's." Ninette was a non-Hodgkin's lymphoma survivor, and as much as she pooh-poohed any possible return of her cancer, Maggie always feared a recurrence.

"Oh, chère." Ninette put down the wooden spoon she was using to stir the étouffée and went to her daughter. She stroked Maggie's hair. "I've been cancer-free for years. You need to stop worrying about that."

"I don't know how to do that. I love you too much. Anyway, we need to let Uncle Tig know about Harmon."

"He already knows that he passed away."

"Dad called him?"

"No," Ninette said. She washed her hands and took a buche de Noel out of the refrigerator. "Marco did."

Maggie was surprised to hear the tour guide's name. "I thought that he and Tig broke up again."

"They did. But apparently they're still good friends."

This was less of a surprise. Her uncle's infectious charm lured many a suitor, but he was upfront with them about his priorities. Some people rescued animals; Tig rescued decrepit buildings. He was devoted to rehabilitating these strays of the architectural world and giving them a second chance. Even the most besotted boyfriends eventually wearied of playing second fiddle to old edifices and moved on.

Except for Marco.

Marco and Tig had been off and on for years, but Maggie knew the relationship was always on in Marco's heart. He was too civil to stalk her uncle, but Maggie guessed it was a bit of a battle for Marco not to give in to the urge.

"It's getting late," Ninette said. She placed some leaves and berries made of colored marzipan on top of the buche de Noel, adding a festive touch to the sponge cake faux Yule log. "You need to put out the appetizer."

"Right. Will do." Maggie noted the dark shadows under her mother's eyes. While monitoring her father's stress level was critical, she reminded herself to also keep an eye on her mother. She gave her a gentle kiss on the cheek, then loaded a tray with the plates of shrimp remoulade and pushed through a swinging door into the manor house dining room. She laid an appetizer at each table setting and walked into the front parlor. Gran' was conversing with the O'Day family while Marco's Japanese tour group huddled together, taking turns showing each other photos on their phones. As soon as the tour guide saw Maggie, he hurried over to her.

"Can you believe it about that Harmon guy?" he said after a quick air kiss. "Everyone knows he was a first-class you-know-what, but still, to get murdered like that . . ."

"How did you know he was murdered?"

"Mags, it's *Pelican*. Everyone knows everything. But I'll be honest, I am *glad* that guy is dead. He was a depraved mofo who didn't deserve to share the same earth as our boy Tig." Marco spat out the words with hatred but then quickly reverted to his usual sunny self. "Thank goodness Tig is in Italy, or he'd be suspect numero uno. He found a tiny, almost abandoned village he thinks can be rehabbed as a destination hotel and spa. Look, he sent pictures."

As Marco swiped through the pictures on his phone, pride etched on his face, Maggie suddenly wondered if unrequited love might drive someone to prove themselves by committing a desperate act like murder. Then she recalled with relief that the night of Steve Harmon's murder, Marco was at the hospital caring for a sick tourist. He had an alibi and so did Tig, as Marco had just reminded her.

Her attention drifted from the photo stream to the O'Days. While their daughters futzed with their cell phones, Lindy O'Day and her husband, Tom, a man in his early forties of average height and weight with nondescript features, were engaged in a conversation with Gran'. But Maggie noticed that Lindy seemed preoccupied. Her gaze wandered, and her lips pursed in a frown. Maggie tried to shake off her distraction and focus on Tom and Gran', but her artist's eye, attuned to the slightest change in features, could tell Lindy was struggling.

Maggie made a decision. "Dinner's ready, y'all," she announced. She walked to the dining room door and held it open for the guests. When they were all through, Maggie made sure to grab a seat next to Lindy. Gran' looked at her, surprised. The Crozats held to a rotating schedule that ensured one family member dined with the guests while the others served and helped in the kitchen. It was Gran's turn to socialize, but when Maggie telegraphed a warning glance, Gran' took the hint and retreated to the kitchen. Maggie focused on Lindy. "It's so terrible about Mr. Harmon, isn't it? I hope it hasn't distressed you too much."

Lindy dropped her fork on her plate and didn't bother to pick it up. She looked down at the table. "No," she said, her voice barely audible. "He was just another guest."

Maggie's intuitive sense set off alarm bells. *She's lying*, she thought. *Big time.* "Are you sure you're not upset?" she pressed.

Lindy O'Day raised her head, and her eyes met Maggie's. She was about to speak when her husband touched her arm. "Honey, the girls have downloaded some fashion game app that I can't make sense of. Maggie, do you mind if Lindy and I switch seats so she can take a look at it?"

"No problem," Maggie said politely.

Lindy turned away from Maggie and rose to change places with Tom. "Sorry about that," he said to Maggie with a sheepish grin. "But we'd risk a major meltdown if I messed up a game on my girls' phones."

"I hear you," Maggie said, flashing her sunny cruise-director smile. "Now tell me all about your day."

She pretended to listen as Tom shared the details of the O'Days' day. But she was sure his fear wasn't of risking diva drama from his daughters, who seemed perfectly happy playing on their phones and ignoring their mother. He didn't want to risk his wife opening up to Maggie. Maggie had the unnerving feeling that Tom O'Day wasn't the milquetoast he appeared to be. And that the secret the O'Days were harboring might be dangerous.

Perhaps even deadly.

Chapter Ten

In the morning, Maggie helped her mother serve Marco and his tour group breakfast. The O'Days had texted that they were skipping breakfast to get an early start, and Maggie was convinced Tom had manufactured this excuse to keep Lindy away from her. She assumed the family would be checking out ahead of schedule and was surprised they hadn't bolted already.

After breakfast, Maggie filled two carafes with coffee and packed a basket full of baked treats to sell by the bonfires. Ninette had made a variety of pralines in addition to traditional brownies and blondies. She'd also baked a large pan of her popular coconut pecan bars. Maggie pulled a windbreaker over her black hoodie. The rain had passed, but the sky was heavy with clouds. She put on rubber boots to protect her feet from the soggy grass, then placed the coffee carafes into a cooler and added some water bottles. She used a bungee cord to strap the basket of baked goods to the top of the cooler and hauled her load across the road to the Crozat roadside stand by the levee. Gopher, the family basset hound, tagged along, hoping for errant crumbs dropped by customers.

Maggie set out the coffee, water, and treats and then glanced up to the top of the levee. Plantation handyman Bud Shexnayder and Lee Bertrand's great-nephew, Chret, were stacking logs on the Crozat pyramid. Tug was with them. She saw her father reach for a log, but Bud stopped him, and Tug backed off. He was still not operating at full capacity and was being forced to take it easy until the doctors landed on the right blend of medications to stabilize his blood pressure and stress level.

"Good morning, Miss Magnolia."

Maggie recognized Rufus's voice and turned to find herself face-to-face with the officer. A doughy man in his late thirties with thinning blond hair, he was easy to write off as a good ol' boy. But Maggie had learned he was more like an alligator. Rufus might appear to be hibernating when he was actually calculating the perfect time to launch an attack. "Morning," she said. She gestured to the spread in front of her. "Help yourself to whatever you want. My treat."

"Well, that could be classified as bribing an officer, but given how tasty your mama's baked goods are, I will look the other way." Rufus scanned the array and settled on a rum praline. He took a seat at the card table and folding chairs that Maggie had set up for customers and motioned for Maggie to join him. "So," he said, "tell me the tale of how you found Mr. Harmon."

Maggie once again detailed the circumstances leading up to her discovery of the late financier. When she was done, Rufus nodded. "That lines up with what you told Artie."

"Of course it does, because it's the truth."

"Whoa, watch the attitude. I'm just doing my job, which is to interview suspects. Which right now appears to be a boatload of Crozats."

Maggie seethed. As she expected, Rufus was milking an opportunity to stick it to her family. "If you're serious about talking to suspects, I recommend taking a hard look at Tannis Greer. She had a thing for Harmon and got vicious when she saw the dirtbag, may he rest in peace, flirt with me."

"Yeah, well, Ferdie Chauvin established a time of death, and Miss Greer has an alibi. She was with Little Earlie. He corroborated her statement."

"What? What were those two doing together? And what time frame are we talking about? I may also have an alibi."

"Ferdie says Harmon went to his heavenly maker somewhere between two and five AM. Where were you during those hours?"

"Sleeping," Maggie muttered.

"Alone?"

Maggie opened her mouth to protest his insinuation and then realized it was a good question, one that could establish her own alibi. Unfortunately, the answer was, "Yes. Alone."

Rufus nodded and then looked up at the top of the levee. "I think your dad's trying to get your attention."

Maggie followed his glance and saw Tug waving to her. "Did we get some logs delivered?" he called.

Maggie glanced behind to the right of the stand and saw a large bundle of them. "Yes," she called back.

"Hey, Rufus, any chance you can bring them up here?" Tug yelled.

Rufus got up and walked over to the logs. "My back's been acting up," he told Maggie. He rubbed a spot on his spine. "I gotta pass."

Maggie shot him a skeptical look. "Seriously?"

"Sorry, Tug," Rufus called out. "No can do."

Tug started down the levee, but Maggie held up her hand. "No, Dad, I'll do it." She faced Rufus, furious. "My father is in no shape to haul logs anywhere, and I think you're a fakin' lazy-butt."

Maggie bent down and channeled her anger into dragging the bundle of logs. She couldn't move them more than an inch. She tried again with less success. She let loose a stream of cuss words and kicked the bundle. Rufus put a hand on her arm.

"Calm down, Magnolia Marie. And congratulations. You just dodged a murder rap."

"I *what?*"

"Harmon wasn't killed in the house. We found evidence proving he was killed elsewhere and dragged into the room."

Maggie flashed on the moment she'd arrived at the murder scene with her tour group. "There was water in the hallway," she said. "And dirt. A streak of it. Like something had been dragged across the floor."

"Exactly. Now you just showed me that you couldn't move a bundle of logs, so I don't believe there's any way you could drag a hundred-and-fifty-pound body up a flight of steps into Doucet. You also let me know that your father isn't up to it, and I can't image your Gran' or tiny mama having the strength either."

Maggie dropped the bundle's mesh handle. "Oh. Wow. Rufus . . . that was kind of brilliant."

"No 'kind of' about it."

"You're right." Once again, Maggie had misjudged Rufus. But this time, he'd done the one thing she never expected him to do—stand up for the Crozats. "Ru, I'm sorry. And I'm especially sorry I called you a lazy-butt."

"You can make it up to me by nosing around Sandy Sechrest and letting me know if she's seeing anyone."

"Will do," Maggie promised. "To be honest, I didn't believe Bo when he said you've changed. But I truly believe you have."

"Yeah, well . . ." Rufus looked down at the ground and scuffed pebbles back and forth with his shoe. "When you have a kid, you want to be the best person you can be for them. And that person isn't someone who's petty and bullies people and carries stupid grudges years old. If there's anyone who should be throwing 'sorrys' around here, it's me. So . . . I'm sorry."

"Apology accepted," Maggie said, marveling at the positive new direction of their relationship. Rufus looked up and acknowledged Maggie's response with a small smile. She furrowed her brow. "Well, now that we've cleared the air and you very generously got my family and me off the hook, I need to point out that there's no way Ione would have the strength to drag Harmon's body either. Right?"

"Probably not."

"Good," Maggie said. "Feel free to mention that to Mr. Acting Chief Perske. But I have to tell you, I really think there's something suspicious about that whole Tannis-Little Earlie meet up."

"I had exactly the same feeling. Earlie said they're writing a script together, trying to take advantage of all the film production that's come our state's way these last few years. Then again, 'writing a script' could be code for going at it. Earlie says they both fell asleep, which could have given either of them the chance to sneak out and do in Harmon, but I don't see her having the heft to drag a body. Or Little Earlie either, for that matter. If I blew on him, he'd flutter off like a dandelion. Still, it could have been a team effort, so I'm keeping an eye on both of them."

"Of course, it could have been a team effort with any of us too," Maggie felt compelled to point out.

"Yeah, I thought of that, but my big old gut doesn't buy it. If you offed the guy, I could see you marching into Pelican PD headquarters and announcing to anyone who would listen, 'I killed the SOB, and I'm not sorry—now lock me up.' I couldn't see you *or* your kin sneaking around. Y'all would own your bad ways."

"That would be classified as a backhanded compliment, but I'll take it. I'm sure you're breaking some rule telling me all this. I truly appreciate it."

"Chère, it's Louisiana. We only follow the rules we like."

Maggie laughed. "True. You're really good at your job, Rufus."

"Thanks." Rufus flashed an impish grin. "And you're pretty good at my job too."

Then he picked up the bundle of logs with ease, placed it on his shoulder, and marched up the levee to Tug.

*

For the next two hours, Maggie focused on providing customers with their morning sustenance. Eventually everything was gone except for a few water bottles, which Maggie brought up to the men—and one woman—working on the bonfire. Gaynell had joined Chret, her boyfriend, in the effort. "With Doucet closed today, I needed something to do with myself," she told Maggie as she stacked a log on the pyramid.

"I need to bring the sales supplies back to Crozat, but that can wait a bit," Maggie said and joined her friends and family in building the bonfire. She fell into a rhythm of hauling and placing logs, and the mindless task provided her with a welcome break from the stress of the last few days. The ring of her cell phone disrupted the calm, especially when Maggie saw that the caller was Tannis.

"Maggie, this is Tannis Greer," her boss said, apparently including her last name so Maggie could differentiate her from the other Tannises in her life—of which there were none. "I'm calling to provide you with updates on Doucet. We'll be closed for at least another two days, per the request of Pelican PD. I also want you to know that Ione Savreau has been placed on unpaid leave."

"What?! Why?"

"She's a suspect in a murder investigation, and I think her presence creates an uncomfortable and possibly dangerous situation for the staff."

Maggie felt a surge of pleasure at the news she was about to deliver. "It just so happens that I have a little inside information on this issue. While I can't reveal my source, I can share that the police do not view Ione as a suspect."

"Sorry, but I don't consider pillow talk between you and your detective boyfriend a reliable source."

"I didn't hear it from—"

"Until whoever murdered Steve—Mr. Harmon—is caught, Ms. Savreau is out. I'd recommend you put aside your personal relationship with her and acknowledge that this is a business decision for the benefit of Doucet Plantation. Have a good day."

Tannis quickly ended the call before Maggie could protest. Ione's plight made building a bonfire feel superfluous, so Maggie lugged the cash box and empty cooler back to Crozat. She needed to think, and for that she needed privacy. She was on her way to the shotgun cottage when she heard frustrated exclamations coming from the B and B office. Maggie stepped into the room and saw Gran' typing furiously on the computer keyboard. "More bad reviews posted on Trippee.com," she said. "They were dated from yesterday, which means Trippee had time to receive my warning that trolls are targeting us, but apparently the website's fraud alert and review approval department operate at cross-purposes. Oh, fudge."

"What's wrong?"

"Every time I send an e-mail, I get some form response thanking me for contacting Trippee and warning me that not every e-mail can be answered individually. What does that even mean?! Oh, shi—ver me timbers, I got another one. Mo—mmy funny, there's another. Ahhh!"

Maggie had to laugh at her grand-mère's creative take on cussing. "Here," she said, motioning to Gran' to get up. The older woman did so, and Maggie replaced her at the computer. "I'm forwarding all your e-mails to Tig's people. They've been trying to track down our troll from their end but haven't had any luck yet. Preferred Property places ads on Trippee, so I'm sure the website will 'trip' over themselves to help them out . . ."

Gran' shook her well-coiffed head.

"Sorry, couldn't resist," Maggie said.

"Well, I guess the misery of the last few days has earned you a terrible pun or two. It won't be two, will it?"

Maggie stood up and gave her grand-mère a hug. "I'm done."

"On a positive note, Lindy O'Day wrote a lovely review and even countered the negative ones with positive comments. So that's something."

Ninette appeared at the door. She held Jasmine, Xander's favorite foster puppy, in her arm. "I was feeding our furbabies when I heard a car coming down the drive. I looked out, and I think it might be Mr. Harmon's limo."

Maggie and Gran' exchanged a look. "That's odd," Gran' said.

"Very," Maggie agreed. "I'll take care of this, Mama."

She left the women and walked down Crozat's wide hall to the front door, opening it as the limo came to a stop. Dan, Steve Harmon's driver, got out and walked around the car to open the passenger's door. An attractive brunette in her late forties got out, giving Dan a warm smile as she did so. Maggie found it curious that the woman had chosen to sit next to Harmon's driver rather than be chauffeured by him. They exchanged a few words, then Dan looked down at the ground and shook his head. The woman placed a hand on his arm in a comforting gesture and walked up the stairs to where Maggie stood.

"Hello," she said. "I'm looking for a Maggie Crozat."

"You found her." Not quite sure how to proceed, Maggie went with extending her hand, which the woman gave a limp shake. "I'm Maggie."

"I'm Emme Charbonnet Harmon," the woman said. "Steve Harmon's widow."

"Oh," Maggie said, affecting more surprise than she felt. Maggie's instincts had beat Emme to her introduction. "I'm so sorry for your loss."

Emme gave a slight nod of acknowledgment. "Thank you. I was told you're the person who found my husband. I'm on my way to the morgue to make arrangements for Steve's transportation and wanted to stop by for a quick chat."

She sounds more like a travel agent than a widow, Maggie thought. "Come in. I'll get us some coffee. Does Mr. Harmon's driver want to join us?"

"No, Dan prefers to wait by the car. He's devastated by Steve's death."

Well, at least one person is. "Why don't we go to the front parlor?"

Maggie gestured for Emme to follow her. As they walked, Maggie sent a quick text to Ninette and Gran', alerting them to this odd development. By the time she and Harmon's widow entered the parlor, Gran' was there waiting. Ninette showed up a minute later with coffee and pastries. Maggie introduced her mother and grand-mère to Emme, who responded to their expressions of sympathy with the same miniscule nod that she'd given Maggie. The four women sat down on the room's ornately carved nineteenth-century settee and chairs. When Emme crossed her legs, Maggie noticed that her black pumps boasted the trademark red soles of an expensive shoe brand. Her black-and-white print wrap dress and black pashmina shawl seemed equally high-end.

Ninette poured coffee as Gran' passed the plate of pastries. Emme chose a croissant. "Delicious," she said as she nibbled on it.

"Thank you," Maggie responded politely. "They're from my cousin's shop in town, Fais Dough Dough."

"As in d-o-u-g-h? Clever." Emme finished her croissant. "So tell me how you found Steve."

The abrupt change of conversation caused Ninette to swallow the wrong way, and she coughed until tears came to her eyes. Gran' gave her several sharp pats on the back, and she finally stopped. Emme didn't seem to notice. "I was leading the first tour of the morning," Maggie said. She chose her words carefully, not wanting to upset Harmon's widow. Although judging from Emme's behavior thus far, that didn't seem cause for concern. "One of my guests saw your husband first. He thought he was a dumm . . . a prop . . . not real. But since Mr. Harmon was a guest here, I immediately recognized him. I transferred my tour group to two other guides and checked to see if he was still breathing."

"But he wasn't."

"No."

"You're sure."

"Yes," Maggie said. *This conversation is getting stranger by the minute.* "As were the paramedics when they arrived. Anyway, once it was determined he was . . . deceased . . . I stepped back so I wasn't in the way of the medical professionals and law enforcement."

"Because you thought he might have been murdered."

"Yes. There was a stain on his shirt. Where his heart was. A red stain."

"A blood stain."

"That's what I assumed."

"Well," Emme said, "all right, then."

There was silence as Emme sipped her coffee. Maggie exchanged subtle, perplexed glances with her mother and grand-mère. Then Gran' finally spoke. "So . . . you're a Charbonnet."

"Yes," Emme said.

"Are you by any chance related to Adelaide Charbonnet?"

"She's my mother. Do you know her?"

"We were at Newcomb together. And we were debutantes the same season."

"Really? What a small world."

"Oh, yes, a small world, a very small world." If Maggie had any doubt this was a bizarre conversation, her grand-mère's reaction dispelled it. When Gran' was uncomfortable, she had a tendency to lay on her accent and repeat words until she sounded like a Southern parrot.

Emme finished her coffee and placed the cup on its saucer. "Well, thank you for your time and hospitality. Dan and I need to go now."

All four women stood up. "I'll walk you out," Maggie said. Emme followed her out of the room and down the hall until they reached Crozat's old oak front door. Ninette and Gran' tagged along behind them. "If you have any other questions, please feel free to call me," Maggie said. "I'll help in any way I can."

"Thank you," Emme said, "but I'm satisfied."

She walked outside to the waiting limo. Dan opened the passenger's door for her, and Emme rewarded him with a warm smile. Maggie was again struck by her familiarity with the man. Dan got into the driver's seat, and the limo slowly made its way down the earthen drive out onto the road, where it disappeared toward Pelican.

"What on God's green earth was *that*?" Ninette said.

"She was either the most self-contained widow on the planet," Maggie said. "Or . . ."

"Someone who wasn't too sorry to see her mate slip the surly bonds of earth," Gran' said. She thought for a moment and then turned to her granddaughter. "You know, this means that Adelaide Charbonnet lost her son-in-law. I assume she's still living in New Orleans, where the family's had a Garden District home for generations. Given our shared history, I feel that good form dictates I pay her a condolence call, don't you?"

Maggie nodded. "Absolutely. And I'd be happy to join you in that call."

She and her grand-mère shared a knowing look, which Ninette caught. "Oh, dear," she said. "You two are going to nose around the Charbonnets, aren't you?" She frowned. "Be careful. As if Mr. Harmon's murder wasn't enough, his widow's visit gave me the shudders."

"Me too," Maggie said.

"Well, chère," Gran' said, "if you find Emme Charbonnet Harmon unsettling, just *wait* until you meet her ogress of a mother."

Chapter Eleven

Gran' and Maggie planned their visit to the Charbonnet clan in New Orleans over a lunch of leftover shrimp étouffée. "You two should stay overnight," Ninette said. She saw the amused look Maggie and Gran' shared. "That's right, I'm on board now. Give yourself plenty of time to find out everything you can about these people."

"Good idea, Mama," Maggie said.

"And here's another one. Remember your high school classmate Lulu Colombe? She went into hospitality and works as the general manager at the Reveille Orleans Hotel, which is part of a larger boutique hotel chain, the Orleans Group. Your dad and I have run into her at some travel trade shows, and she's lovely. I'm sure she'd give you a fair hotel rate. Plus, she may have some suggestions about how we should deal with our negative reviews."

"Mom, you are on a roll. I'll shoot her an e-mail through the hotel website."

Maggie sopped up the last of her étouffée sauce with a hunk of French bread and left for the B and B office. An Internet search yielded the Reveille Orleans website, and Maggie dashed off an e-mail to her old friend Lulu. She then sent a text to Bo and Rufus alerting them to the widow Charbonnet's odd visit. By the time she finished feeding the family's rescue puppies and kittens and helping her parents prep for the B and B's cocktail hour, it was early evening. Her phone pinged a text: "Junie's in 30?"

Tug, who was opening a bottle of red wine, glanced at Maggie's phone. "Bo?" She nodded. "Go. We can handle tonight. Maybe he's got some new intel on what all's going on with Mr. Harmon's passing."

"Thanks, Dad."

Maggie gave her father a kiss on his weathered cheek and left the manor house for the shotgun cottage, where she changed into slim black jeans, black boots, and a snug, long-sleeved, purple V-neck T-shirt. She pulled her hair into a high ponytail and wrapped a purple ombré knit scarf around her neck, then threw on a black leather jacket. After a quick check of her makeup, she left the cottage for her convertible.

It was a clear night, and the sky was crowded with stars, a sight Maggie had missed while living in New York. The bonfires loomed like large dark shadows on the levee and spooked her a bit as she drove by them. But Pelican was bright and full of holiday cheer, enabling Maggie to shake off the vaguely ominous feeling she'd had as she drove by the bonfires.

She parked and walked into Junie's. Bo waved to her. But he wasn't alone. Rufus was with him, alternating between drinking a beer and tossing fried crawfish in his mouth. Maggie brushed aside her disappointment at not having Bo all to herself and took a seat between the two men. Rufus pushed the bowl of crunchy crustaceans toward her. Maggie hesitated. "Come on," he said. "No better Cajun popcorn anywhere around. You know you want some."

Maggie caved and popped one in her mouth, where it released its juicy, slightly spicy flavor as soon as she bit into it. "That is so good. Thank you."

Bo reached into the bowl and helped himself to a handful of the popcorn. "I asked Ru to join us because he just spent some quality time with Emme Harmon."

"Ah," Maggie said. "And . . . ?"

"Well, I wouldn't exactly call her a Merry Widow, but she sure ain't a grieving one. I half-expected her to hold a mirror under Harmon's mouth to make sure he wasn't breathing." Rufus took a big swig of beer. "Now the chauffeur guy on the other hand seemed real sad. I'd say it's cuz he's out of a job, but the way Harmon's widder woman was clinging to him, looks like he's got a new job, if you know what I mean."

"I know what you mean, Ru, no need to raise your eyebrows up and down like an old-timey comedian," Maggie said, trying to suppress an amused smile. "I picked up on that too. I'm not sure how he feels about her, but she's definitely into him."

"I'm gonna take a hard look at where both of them were during the time of the murder," Rufus said. "Especially her. Mrs. H better have herself a good, strong alibi."

Bo frowned. "I hate that I'm sidelined here. I'd like to poke around the Charbonnet-Harmon dynamic."

"Gran' and I are already on it," Maggie said. She shared the plan to ferret out more information on the family under the guise of a condolence call.

"Nice," Bo said with a sly smile. "You know, I haven't been to the Big Easy in a while. I think I'll take a couple of vacation days and meet up with you there. Get your reactions to the family fresh from meeting them. And if there is anything suspicious going on, well . . . not a bad idea for me to be there and keep an eye on you and your Gran'."

Maggie's phone pinged an alert. "Oh, this is perfect! An old friend of mine manages Reveille Orleans, and she got back to me that she's comping us a room. I'll see if she can comp two and tell her I'll return the favor with a free stay at Crozat."

"So one room for Gran' and one room for . . ." Rufus winked and raised his eyebrows up and down again.

"Knock it off, Rufus," Bo said, giving his cousin a dirty look.

"Yes, enough with the eyebrows," Maggie added, glad that thanks to Junie's barely there lighting, neither man could see her blushing. She and Bo, both skittish from prior failed relationships, had yet to consummate their romance. Bo's ex-wife, Whitney, moving to Pelican had complicated things for Maggie. Although Whitney and her second husband, Zach, seemed to have worked through a rough patch in their marriage, Maggie still felt insecure compared to the statuesque beauty that was the former Mrs. Bo Durand. And now with her ex, Chris, wandering around town, she had a feeling Bo was experiencing his own trepidations.

"Hey, Maggie, my friend, speaking of favors . . ." Rufus nudged her and pointed toward Junie's front door, which Sandy Sechrest was closing behind her.

Maggie rose and walked over to the dance instructor. The two exchanged hellos, and then Maggie, mindful of the promise she'd made Rufus to check out Sandy's relationship status, asked, "So . . . are you meeting someone here tonight?"

"No," Sandy responded. "Just getting takeout."

"Dinner for one, huh?"

"For two, actually," Sandy said. "Me and King Cake. JJ always gives me some bones for the little guy."

"Well, why don't you join me, Bo, and Ru? We've got space at the table."

Sandy smiled. "Thank you, I'd love that. Let me just put in my order with JJ."

Sandy headed to the bar, and Maggie returned to her table. "Good news, Ru. Seems your only competition is her pup."

Rufus nodded. "I can work with that."

Bo shook his head. "I don't know, Ru. I've seen that dog. He's a hotty."

He gave his cousin a wicked grin, and Rufus elbowed him. "Shut up, you. Hey, she's coming."

Rufus jumped up and pulled out a chair for Sandy. "If you did stuff like that for Vanessa, you might still be together," Maggie teased sotto voce.

"Ignoring you," he whispered back.

The foursome made small talk while waiting for JJ to bring over Sandy's food, and Maggie was happy to see that Sandy seemed to enjoy Rufus's company. The pungent aroma of JJ's jambalaya preceded its arrival at the table. "Here you go, darlin'," JJ said as he placed it in front of Sandy. "Stop by the bar when you're leaving for King Cake's bones."

"Thanks so much." Sandy inhaled the dish's scent. "This smells unbelievable. I've been waiting for it all day."

Sandy began to eat. Bo's phone alerted him to a text, and he checked it. "We're set for tomorrow," he told Maggie. "Perske approved my vacation days. He's only too happy to off-load me for a bit."

"Where are you going?" Sandy asked.

Maggie jumped in before Bo could answer. "New Orleans. Just overnight. My grand-mère wants to visit an old friend." Bo gave Maggie a puzzled look but said nothing.

"Yeah," Rufus said. "An old friend who happens to be the mother-in-law of our recent murder victim."

Sandy, who was about to take another bite, put her fork down. "Mr. Harmon, right?" She was trying to keep her voice normal, but Maggie noticed the dancer's hand was shaking.

"Yeah, and what a tool he was," Rufus said. "I don't think his widow was too sorry to see him lying on a morgue table."

Sandy stood up. "I totally forgot, I'm supposed to walk King Cake twice tonight. Thanks so much for letting me join you. I better go or who knows what surprises I'll find in the studio later." Sandy gave a small laugh at her attempt at a joke.

"Oh," Rufus said, disappointed. "I'll get JJ to pack up your dinner."

"No, that's okay. I'll see y'all again soon."

Sandy hurried out the door, and Rufus slapped himself on the forehead. "Stupid, stupid, stupid. She's eating dinner, and I'm talking about murder. Wait, she forgot the bones for King Cake. I'll grab them for her."

Rufus pulled out his wallet, threw down money for his meal, and then took off. Maggie watched him get the bones from JJ and leave. She turned back to the table and found Bo staring at her. "What?" she asked, keeping her tone as innocent as possible.

"You know something," Bo said. "About Sandy. And Harmon."

Maggie searched for an excuse and then gave up. "Ugh, sometimes I hate dating a detective. Yes, Sandy told me about an ugly run-in she once had with him. But it was in confidence, and I promised I wouldn't share it unless I had to."

"Maggie, chère, this is a murder investigation, not a gal-pal sleepover. The sooner we solve it, the sooner everyone who's under suspicion isn't anymore. Don't you want that?"

"Yes." Maggie sighed. "When Sandy was working as an exotic dancer at the Cajun Classy Lady, Harmon developed a thing for her. He assaulted her in the parking lot, but she managed to get away from him." Maggie felt terrible for betraying her friend. "But it happened a year ago, and I'm sure it's not related to his death. She seems so fragile. I can't imagine her resorting to murder." Maggie paused. "What are you going to do?"

"What I have to do. Tell the lead investigator on the case: Rufus."

It dawned on Maggie what Bo was saying. "Who will do absolutely nothing with the information unless he's forced to because he's sweet on Sandy."

Bo smiled. "Exactly." He leaned over and kissed Maggie. "I'll get us another round. I think we could both use it."

Bo made his way to the bar, and Maggie felt a sense of relief. But she knew they were merely stalling the inevitable. The assault on Sandy would have to come out, making her a prime suspect. Maggie hoped that for the dance instructor's sake, the question of who killed Steve Harmon would be answered in New Orleans.

Chapter Twelve

Maggie got up early to prepare for her overnight stay. The Charbonnets were conservative old money, and Gran' had instructed her to dress accordingly. Maggie only owned one suit, a black skirt and jacket set bought ten years earlier to wear at Grand-père Crozat's funeral. She put it on, pulled her hair back with an old headband left over from a brief preppy phase in high school, and applied a subtle shading of makeup. She then rolled her overnight suitcase into the living room of the cottage. Gran', who was already there, gave her an approving once-over. "Well done," she said.

"I look like someone on trial whose lawyer made her dress to impress the jury."

"Well, then it should impress Adelaide. Wait—" Gran' scrutinized Maggie's legs. "No pantyhose?"

"Ugh, I hate them," Maggie whined. "Don't make me."

"I'm sorry, but this is a pantyhose crowd," Gran' said. "If you go bare-legged, Adelaide will immediately dismiss you as some kind of hippie." She pointed toward Maggie's room. "Back you go."

Maggie dragged herself to her room, kicked off her black pumps, and forced on a pair of pantyhose. She returned to the living room. "There," she told her grand-mère. "Happy?"

"It's not about being happy, chère. If it were, we wouldn't be going at all. The cloistered world of New Orleans privilege is not my favorite."

Gran' pulled on a navy jacket over her pale-blue silk blouse. "You're wearing your sorority colors," Maggie said. "Was Adelaide a Kappa with you?"

"Oh, no." Gran' flashed a devilish smile. "Adelaide was a Chi O."

"I have to wear pantyhose, but you get to stick it to her with rival sorority colors?" Maggie crossed her arms and faked a pout. "That is so not fair."

"One of the few benefits of aging is you pretty much get to do whatever the h-e-double-hockey-sticks you want." A car horn toot came from outside. "Our carriage awaits."

Gran' left the shotgun cottage, and Maggie followed, pulling both her and Gran's suitcases. Bo, who had parked in front of the house, retrieved the luggage from Maggie and put it in the back of his SUV. "Xander wanted to see Jasmine, so he's in the house with your parents."

"And he's okay just being with Mom and Dad? That's wonderful." Maggie knew this marked more socialization progress for Xander.

"I know. Whitney will pick him up in half an hour, but that's half an hour more than he would have spent on his own with anyone a few months ago. And I have to show you this. He's doing a portrait of Jasmine with the paints you gave him. I took a picture of it."

Bo took out his phone and showed Maggie a photo of a painting in progress. A rudimentary sketch covered most of the canvas. But Xander had painted Jasmine's tiny face. The artwork went beyond mere rendering, somehow managing to convey the pup's happy energy. "Wow," Maggie said. "I think I've run out of words to say how talented he is. The student may soon surpass his teacher."

"No way," Bo scoffed. He closed the app and stuck his phone in the back pocket of his jeans. "I know squat about art but enough to know how good you are. Xander may be exceptional for his age, but who knows what it'll be in ten or twenty or even thirty years? That's why I fought so hard to keep Harmon away from him. Maybe hard enough to murder, according to Perske." Before Maggie could respond, Bo jumped into the driver's seat. "We better get going."

*

The drive to New Orleans was uneventful, and they got to the city in under an hour. Bo transitioned from the interstate to US 90 and got off at the Carondelet exit. He navigated his way to St. Charles Avenue, where he made a right onto the famed street. After Jackson Avenue, he waited for a streetcar to pass and then made a left across the tracks, followed by a right onto Prytania Street into the heart of the Garden District. They drove by block after block of beautifully restored historical homes, each one more impressive than the next. All of them glowed with holiday decorations. From one balcony hung a purple fleur-de-lis with the words "Joyeux Noel" illuminated by tracer lights. A large display suspended from another balcony announced, "Merry Christmas, Y'all."

Bo finally stopped the car in front of a mansion so elegant it shamed all the others. Three stories high on a wide green lot, the house was painted a sedate taupe. Forest-green shutters adorned its many windows, and a lacey wrought-iron balcony wrapped around the second story, supported by filigreed iron columns. Tiny white lights were threaded through meticulously pruned topiaries that stood sentinel on both sides of the black front door, which sported an elegant wreath. The property was enclosed by an elaborate wrought-iron fence, and each fence post was topped by a sturdy iron fruit. "Pineapples," Maggie said.

"Yes," Gran' replied. "The archetypal symbol of welcome. But also a symbol of wealth. For those who recognize it as such."

"Yowza," was all Bo could come up with. He got out of the SUV, opened the back passenger's door, and helped Gran' out. "Rufus asked me to see what I can find out about this clan while I'm down here, so I'm gonna do that while you two are paying your social call. Maggie, text me when you're done, and I'll come get y'all."

Maggie nodded. She hopped out of the car, and her heels immediately sunk into the mossy grass between the car and the sidewalk. She extricated herself and knocked the sides of her shoes against the sidewalk curb to get rid of the mud and grass clinging to her shoes. "I am so not cut out for this world."

"You're visiting, not moving in, so I trust you can pull it off," Gran' said. "Come, dear. And be sure to put a smile on. A small one, with a mild hint of superiority. Like this." Gran' formed a smile that managed to convey both warmth and high status, and Maggie tried to mirror her. "Oh, dear. Well, do your best."

Bo jumped back in his SUV, waved, and roared off as if he couldn't get away from the fancy neighborhood fast enough. Maggie pressed a discreet button next to the front gate, and it silently swung back as if by magic. The front door opened as they approached it, and an African American woman dressed in a starched maid's uniform appeared. "I think we entered a time tunnel and emerged in the 1950s," Maggie muttered to Gran', who gave her a warning poke in the ribs.

"Hello," the maid greeted them. Maggie noted her voice was deep and mellifluous. "You must be Mrs. and Miss Crozat. Mrs. Charbonnet is expecting you."

Maggie and Gran' followed the woman into a two-story entrance hall that featured an ornate staircase laced with holiday pine garlands and Palladian windows dressed with gold velvet curtains. A large crystal chandelier shot small rainbows onto the hallway's wallpaper, which carried the pineapple theme into the home's interior. They were led through a small parlor into a larger one. Ornate crown molding encircled the room, which was anchored by a carved marble fireplace. A tall, impeccably decorated Christmas tree dominated one corner of the room. Something was missing from the holiday decor, and it took Maggie a moment to realize what it was. The air was devoid of the pine scent that infused Crozat during the holiday season. The Charbonnet decorations were in perfect taste but artificial.

The maid motioned for them to take a seat on a centuries-old settee upholstered in gold and green brocade. A woman who had been sitting in a wingback chair upholstered in the same fabric stood up to greet them. She was Gran's contemporary and dressed with equal elegance in a pale-yellow silk shantung skirt and a patterned red-and-pale-yellow silk top. The room's crystal chandelier, much larger than the one in the hallway, occasionally flashed a rainbow onto the woman's white hair. She held out her arms to Gran'. "Charlotte," she said with a smile that had the high status of Gran's but lacked its warmth.

"Adelaide," Gran' responded. The two women shared an air kiss. "This is my granddaughter, Magnolia Marie." Maggie was surprised for a moment by her grandmother using her full name.

"Such a pleasure to meet you, my dear," Adelaide said. Maggie responded in kind, resisting a sudden urge to curtsy.

Adelaide motioned for Gran' and Maggie to take a seat. "Mahalia, you can bring the coffee," she instructed her servant, who nodded and disappeared. Maggie sat with her legs crossed at the ankles like the Catholic schoolgirl she once was while the octogenarians shared a few minutes of small talk. Then Gran' deftly segued to the subject of the late Steve Harmon.

"Adelaide, we are so sorry for your loss," Gran' said.

"Yes, well . . ." Adelaide left the sentence unfinished.

"Since we were close to the tragedy, I wanted to express my condolences in person and answer any questions you might have. Especially since Magnolia discovered the bod . . . your son-in-law."

Adelaide's face creased in horror. "Oh, dear, no thank you."

"Well, if you change your mind, feel free let me know," Maggie said, jumping into the conversation, which she regretted when Adelaide looked at her as if she'd expelled gas. Desperate for a change of subject, Maggie glanced around the room and landed on a photo of Adelaide's daughter and Steve Harmon's widow, Emme Charbonnet Harmon. Emme appeared to be in her early twenties in the picture and was clad in a heavily beaded white gown with a matching cape whose train was arranged around her feet. She wore a crown and held a scepter, looking straight into the camera with a grim, defiant expression. "What a nice picture of Emme," Maggie lied.

Adelaide immediately took the bait. "Oh, thank you. That's from her debutante season. She was queen of Rex." Adelaide couldn't have sounded more proud if her daughter had discovered the Ark of the Covenant.

"Rex?" Gran' responded. "How outstanding."

"Yes," Adelaide said, warming to her subject. "She was also a maid in Proteus and had so many parties offered up in her honor, I wouldn't be surprised if she broke a record." Adelaide gave a sad sigh. "I always expected she would marry one of the established families in the city. A Poche or a

LaPeyre. Instead . . ." She left another sentence dangling and then turned to Maggie. "When did you come out, dear?"

"Huh? Oh. I didn't."

Adelaide gaped at her. "A Doucet *and* a Crozat who didn't come out?! My goodness." To Maggie's discerning eye, the woman looked both amazed and a bit repulsed. "I assume you were at least baptized." Adelaide chuckled at what she considered a joke.

"Oh, my goodness, yes," Gran' said. "At St. Louis Cathedral. You were there, dear. Remember? The marvelous reception afterward at Commander's Palace?"

Adelaide seemed flustered. "Yes, of course. How silly of me. I blame A-G-E syndrome."

Both older women faked laughter. Mahalia brought in a silver coffee service, gave a tiny bow, and disappeared. Just then, a woman called, "We're home," from the hallway. A minute later, Emme appeared, followed by Dan and a middle-aged man who had the jowly look of a frat boy gone south. If Emme was surprised to find Gran' and Maggie there, she didn't let it show, instead sharing polite greetings.

"You know Emme and Daniel," Adelaide said. "And this is my son, Philip Charbonnet."

Philip gave a slight nod, not bothering to hide his lack of interest. "We made arrangements for him," he said. It took Maggie a moment to register that he was referring to Steve Harmon, and she was taken aback by the man's blatant disdain for his late brother-in-law. "I told Emme that Charles Petite called to express his condolences and we should all meet for a drink—"

"But I'm not interested," Emme interrupted, glaring at her brother.

Wow, they're already trying to line her up with another husband, Maggie thought. It was obvious Emme's attraction to the family chauffeur was not going to fly with her mother or arrogant brother.

"Philip, Magnolia is a Doucet *and* a Crozat," Adelaide said.

This roused Philip from his bored stupor. "Really?" he said, gracing her with a smile that was more of a leer. "That's quite a pedigree."

Oh, dear Lord, no, no! "Well, all we have to show for it is a beat-up old plantation that barely squeaks by as a bed-and-breakfast," Maggie said, hoping this would serve as a turn-off.

"At least you still have your plantation," Philip grumbled.

"Yes, ours perished in a fire," Adelaide said. She gestured to a heavy antique sideboard. "Sadly, this piece is the only thing that survived. Philip, Emmaline, join us for coffee and cake."

"If you'll excuse me, I have to make a few more calls about Steve's funeral," Dan said, taking his lack of inclusion as the dismissal it was.

"I'll go with you," Emme said quickly. "Thank you both for stopping by. I do appreciate it." She followed Dan out of the parlor, and both Philip and Adelaide shot the couple a look of disgust as they left the room.

*

As Gran' and Adelaide reminisced about their days at New-comb College, Maggie endured an hour of Philip's ham-fisted flirtations. His sandy hair was thinning, a muffin top spilled over the leather belt holding up his chino pants, and the rosacea blooming on his face and nose warned of a drinking problem. None of this dimmed his arrogance. Philip Charbonnet was a catch, according to himself, and no one was more surprised than he that three wives had already fled his company.

"Oh, my goodness, it's almost dinnertime," Gran' said, finally picking up on one of the desperate glances Maggie threw her way.

"You must stay for dinner," Adelaide said.

"Great idea, Mama," her son echoed. Philip leaned in toward Maggie, who sat as far back in her seat as she could without tipping it over.

Nooooo! "That's very nice of you," she said, "but I have plans with my boyfriend." *Take the hint; please take the hint*, she thought, knowing in her heart that Philip wouldn't.

"Charlotte, I insist you dine with us and spend the night here as well," Adelaide said. "You can't stay in the *Quarter*." She shuddered as if the very word might transmit a disease.

"Adelaide, dear, you've twisted my arm," Gran' said. "I would love to stay with you. Bo can bring in my suitcase when he comes to pick up Maggie."

"I texted him, and he's on his way, so why don't we wait outside?" Maggie said. She practically yanked her grandmother up from her chair and through the front hall. "Thank you so much for your generosity, and again, our condolences," she called back to her hosts as she hurried out the front door. Once outside, she collapsed against the closed door with a groan. "Those people are horrible. And thanks for delivering me to that wolf. I can't stand people who think just because a family's parked itself in Louisiana for a couple of hundred years, their last name gives them some kind of special status."

"I'm sorry, chère, but it had to be done. If I'm going to be accepted as one of them, I need to act like one of them. Which means pretending I'd be thrilled if my darling grand-daughter became the bride of an odious dipsomaniac."

"Are you sure you want to stay here tonight, Gran'? The whole atmosphere is more than unpleasant. It's kind of creepy."

"It will give me the chance for one-on-one time with Adelaide. I may be able to ferret some useful information out of her."

"Okay," Maggie said with reluctance. "By the way, I had no idea I was baptized at the Cathedral. I thought I was baptized at Saint Tee's."

"You were, but that old bat doesn't remember," Gran' said, gesturing toward the house. "I must say, tripping her up was a delightful moment. And their plantation did not 'perish in a fire.' They let it run down until it was uninhabitable and then sold it to a chemical company because they needed the cash. The sideboard Adelaide pointed out is probably the only piece they couldn't unload on a secondhand furniture dealer."

Maggie gazed at the Charbonnets' elegant, pristine mansion. "It's all a facade."

"Yes, and as much as they despised Mr. Harmon, I'm sure his millions were the only thing propping it up."

"I wonder how the family went off the rails like that."

Gran' sighed and shook her head. "The son is not the father. Philip Senior was lovely and very intelligent. Philip Junior is neither."

"How did Senior end up married to that gorgon?"

"You know, your generation assumes no one had premarital sex in previous generations," Gran' said, "but there was a reason certain 'premature' babies came out a surprisingly healthy weight and size. Like Philip Charbonnet Junior."

"Ohhh," Maggie said, catching on to Gran's implication.

"Yes, 'ohhhh.'"

A light rain began to fall, and Gran' shivered. "Go back inside," Maggie said. "We'll bring in your suitcase. By the way, just wondering . . . are red and yellow the colors of Adelaide's sorority?"

"They are indeed. And as you can see, much less flattering than mine." Gran' winked and kissed Maggie on the cheek. "*Je t'aime*, chère."

"*Je t'aime.*"

Gran' scurried up to the front door, knocked, and was let in by Mahalia. Maggie pulled her jacket over her head, choosing the rain over spending another minute with Phil Junior. She saw Dan emerge from a side entrance to the Charbonnet house carrying an umbrella. He took quick strides toward her. "I thought you could use this," he said, offering her the umbrella.

"Thanks, but that's okay. My ride should be here any minute."

"Well, until then . . ." Dan held the umbrella over both their heads. Maggie noted the man looked exhausted. His lids were rimmed red as if he'd been crying.

"I'm sorry about Mr. Harmon's death. I can see how hard it's been on you." The driver gave a slight nod. "You and your boss seemed to have had a very close relationship."

Dan stared at her. "My boss? They didn't tell you, did they?" Dan gave a mirthless chortle. "Of course they didn't."

Maggie was growing uncomfortable and desperately wished Bo would arrive. "I'm sorry, Dan, but I don't understand. What didn't they tell me?"

To Maggie's surprise, Dan's eyes filled with tears. "I didn't work for Steve—I worked *with* him. Steve was my stepbrother."

Chapter Thirteen

Rather than continue what promised to be a very interesting conversation standing outside in the rain, Maggie convinced Dan to join her and Bo for a drink. She texted Bo that they would meet him at Aggie and Johnny's, a comfortable dive bar on the lower reaches of St. Charles Avenue. Soon the three were sharing a pitcher of A and J's cheap domestic beer. But Dan barely touched his stein. Instead, as he told his story, he passed it from hand to hand in what was almost a nervous tic. "My mom married Steve's dad," he said. "Our childhood sucked. We were technically middle class—nice house, good neighborhood. But Steve's dad was abusive, and my mother was an alcoholic. Steve and I bonded, though. Kind of an 'enemy of my enemy is my friend' thing. His mom died of breast cancer when Steve was only a few years old, and I never knew who my dad was, so we basically had each other."

"God, how sad." Maggie was starting to see where some of Steve Harmon's miserable behavior stemmed from.

"I was a couple of years younger than him, and he looked out for me. Sheltered me when one of our parents was on a tear. Made sure I had food and got to school. He was brilliant and ambitious and earned a college scholarship. When he started his own business, he brought me into it. I have no idea what I would have become without him. I owe Steve my life." Dan finally picked up his beer and downed it without a pause.

"Which," Bo said, "I'm guessing is why you went to jail for him in the insider trading scandal."

Maggie was confused. "What scandal?"

"I used my free time to stop in at NOPD headquarters and run background checks on the family," Bo explained, "and learned a few interesting things."

Dan picked up the pitcher and refilled his glass. "The SEC went after Steve's company for insider trading. A couple of us got nailed and went to jail for a few years. That's why I'm not in finance anymore. Banned for life."

"But not Steve Harmon," Bo pointed out.

Angry, Dan leaned in to Bo. "Hey, they never proved Steve knew about it."

"But you're not saying he didn't."

Dan slumped back in his chair. "What does it matter, anyway? He's gone." He took a napkin and wiped his forehead. It didn't escape Maggie that he took a surreptitious wipe of his eyes as well. "Look," he said to Bo, "I'm sorry I clocked you outside the restaurant the other night. Try not to hold it against me. I'd appreciate anything you can do to find Steve's killer."

"We're all over it," Bo said. He cast a glance at Maggie that Dan picked up on.

"We?" Dan asked. "Not to insult you, Maggie, but aren't you an artist?"

"She is," Bo said. "And it gives her a skill that a lot of people don't have. She picks up visual details that other people, even trained law enforcement officials, might miss."

"But I'm in no way a professional," Maggie hastened to add. "I just help out if I can." Dan nodded, and Maggie decided to take a chance on bringing up a delicate subject in a light manner. "Speaking of my artist's 'eagle eye,' I noticed Emme seems very fond of you."

"She's a good person," Dan said, his tone evasive. "To be honest, marrying Steve was more an act of rebellion than love for her."

"I can see that," Maggie said. "The easiest way to rebel in the Charbonnet world would be to marry outside of their race or religion."

It was Bo's turn to look confused. "How so?"

Maggie pointed to a small charm hanging around Dan's neck on a thin gold chain. "I noticed your chai."

"You do have an eye for details," Dan said. He turned to Bo. "'Chai' is a Hebrew symbol for 'life.' We're Jewish."

Bo's look of confusion disappeared. "Ah. Not a popular choice of spouse for some of the old money crowd."

"Our generation and the ones after us couldn't care less," Dan said. "But Mother Charbonnet is still ticked off about it. And Emme's brother, Philip, was no fan of Steve's. The irony is that Steve couldn't care less about his faith. I'd even say he was embarrassed by it. Not me. I'm proud of my heritage *and* my religion."

"Dan," Maggie said, "it's obvious Emme and Steve's marriage wasn't a happy one. Is there any chance she—"

Dan didn't even let her finish the sentence. "No, no effing way. Emme would never harm anyone. I told you; she's a good person, a fantastic person. Don't even think about her as a suspect."

Bo and Maggie exchanged a look. Whether or not Emme could be dismissed as a suspect was debatable, but Dan's reaction confirmed that the woman's affection for her brother-in-law was reciprocated. "If you're going to look at anyone in the family for Steve's murder," he continued, "I'd give Philip Charbonnet a good, hard look. The guy's a leech and a scumbag, and I wouldn't put anything past him, including murder if he thought he'd benefit from it."

Bo paid for the beer, and he and Maggie left Dan with Gran's suitcase and a promise that they'd let him know about any developments in the investigation of his step-brother's death. Bo begged off dinner with Maggie's friend Lulu Colombe. "I never get down to New Orleans, and I feel like taking a wander in the Quarter," he said. "Gives me time to think."

"I could use some thinking time too," Maggie said. "I'll pass on a ride and take the streetcar there."

Bo took off. Maggie texted her friend to say she was on her way and then crossed St. Charles Avenue to a transit stop. After a moment, she saw lights up ahead and heard the comforting rattle of a streetcar. It rumbled up to where Maggie stood, and she climbed aboard. She found a seat on a worn wooden bench and stared out the window as the old, olive-green streetcar creaked and lurched toward the Quarter. Every day seemed to bring a new suspect in Dan Harmon's murder. Tannis, Sandy, Emme, Philip, even Adelaide Charbonnet. Maggie wouldn't have been surprised to learn the octogenarian had driven a knife through the heart of the son-in-law she despised. But Maggie's intuition told her that these were only a few names on a long list of people who might have murdered the financier.

The streetcar conductor announced the final stop, and Maggie exited the car with the other passengers. She crossed busy Canal Street, where the streetlamps were wrapped with festive white lights, and walked past the antique shops of Royal Street into the heart of the French Quarter. Maggie made a left onto Bienville and saw the US and Louisiana flags flying over the arched doorways of the Reveille New Orleans Hotel. She approached the entrance and smiled when she saw Lulu bouncing up and down as she waved to her. Lulu still possessed the bubbly energy of the pep squad captain she once was. A career in hospitality was the ideal choice for her. "Maggie, hey!" Lulu called out as she bounced and waved. *"Laissez les bon temps rouler!"*

Maggie strode up to Lulu, who enveloped her in a bear hug. Lulu might have been tiny, barely clearing five feet, but she had the strength of a martial artist, and Maggie flinched from her tight squeeze. Lulu didn't notice. "I am so glad you're back in town," she said as she took Maggie by the hand and led her through a sumptuous lobby decorated with velvet couches in silvery tones and a thick Aubusson rug in pastel shades. A Christmas tree decorated in the same color scheme as the couch and rug stood next to an antique table covered with brochures for the local tourist sites. "We'll go talk in my office, then move this party over to Antoine's for dinner."

The two women walked through a stunning courtyard with a large, burbling fountain encircled by lush potted poinsettias. Lulu unlocked a door, and Maggie followed her into a small office crammed with files and brochures for local tourist attractions. Lulu stepped over a box of flyers for bus tours of New Orleans and took a seat at her desk. Maggie pulled more flyers off the only other chair in the room and sat down. "We'll save catching up for dinner," Lulu said. "Now tell me what's going on with your bad reviews." She listened as Maggie explained the vitriolic reviews and then read a few on her computer. "Well, the good news is they're so nasty they reek of trolls, and legitimate travelers would be skeptical about them. But newbies, people who don't travel a lot, might believe them."

"We haven't had any new bad reviews, but we can't get rid of the old ones, and they're dragging down our overall rating. What do we do?"

"Keep trying to get Trippee to help you out. And while you're waiting, write a pleasant reply to each slam. When readers see you respect the respondent and are trying to address their 'problem,' it makes you seem like a caring, engaged proprietor and buys you goodwill. Also, see if you can get guests to counter the comments with positive replies. And celebrity endorsements help a lot. We've had a few that really upped our profile." Lulu rattled off the names of an Oscar-winning actor, a legendary rock star, and a former president. "Have you had any celebs stay with you?"

"Um . . . all I can come up with is one of the WGNO sportscasters. And I can't even tell you which one."

Lulu crinkled her nose. "That's not going to get you any traction. It's interesting y'all made it through those other murders without seeing a big drop in business, and then these reviews suddenly come out of nowhere."

"I don't think it's out of nowhere. There's a—well, there was a hedge fund financier who developed a thing for hotels. He's been trying to oust my uncle Tig from Preferred Properties. I'm sure the bad reviews are somehow tied to him."

"You said 'was.'"

"He's dead. Murdered. Not at our place," Maggie added hastily. "They found him at Doucet."

"Wait. Steve Harmon?"

"Yes. You know him?"

"He's infamous around here. He pulled the same stunt with the Tonrie Hotel Group that he was trying with Preferred Properties. Only the Tonrie Group didn't survive his machinations." Lulu did a search on her computer. "Ah, here. He started a negative campaign against the company's management, and it got brutal. He pushed them out and wound up buying a bunch of the company's properties at bargain prices, including Belle Vista up by y'all."

Lulu began explaining Harmon's maneuverings in detail, and after fifteen minutes of corporate backstabbing, lawsuits, firings, and hirings, Maggie's head ached. "These Wall Street guys are ruthless," she said. "It's amazing they're not bumped off on a daily basis." But she had acquired a new piece of information. "I had no idea the Tonrie Group was gone. That's why Harmon went to Belle Vista after we booted him out. He owns it."

"He shuffled properties from one company to another," Lulu explained. "Belle Vista's now part of the Gerner Group. Here's an article about it. I'll print it out for you."

Lulu did so and handed the paper to Maggie. The article was a puff piece, probably written by Harmon's own personal publicist. Maggie gave it a desultory scan. Then she saw a quote attributed to a familiar name, and she sat straight up in her chair.

"Unbelievable," she muttered.

"What is it?"

Maggie held up the sheet of paper. "I owe you, Lulu. Thanks to this article, I now know who's responsible for our bad reviews."

Chapter
Fourteen

Lulu understood when Maggie canceled their evening plans. "I want to share all this new information with my law enforcement friend," she explained, opting to keep her relationship with Bo vague. She remembered Lulu as the kind of girl who would screech at the word "boyfriend" and insist on "all the deets."

"No problem," Lulu said as they walked toward the hotel lobby. "We'll have so many reasons to get together now that we're in the same business."

This comment threw Maggie. "I'm really not in the hospitality business. I'm still an artist. I'm just helping my family out."

"Okay," was Lulu's skeptical response. She handed Maggie two key cards. "You and your friend have the best rooms in the hotel, side by side on the fifth floor. If you need anything, let the staff know. I'll see you the next time you're in town."

Lulu gave Maggie another rib-crushing hug and then headed back to her office. Maggie texted Bo to meet her at Gumbo Ya Ya, a casual eatery near Jackson Square. She stepped outside, where the air was heavy with humidity and full of chatter and music. People spilled off the crowded sidewalks onto the street, dodging cabs and delivery drivers. Even though the French Quarter felt more like Disneyland than a metropolis, Maggie was buoyed by its infectious energy. She'd been so wrapped up in Crozat's affairs that she hadn't realized how much she missed city life. When she'd returned to Pelican many months earlier, it was supposed to be a visit, not a relocation. The powerful pull of her tiny hometown still surprised her.

She stopped to glance inside a gallery filled with oil paintings depicting the wrought-iron balconies that graced the Quarter's historic homes and thought of her art studio back home at Crozat. She vowed to take a break from tourism and sleuthing to resume her art career. That was one point in New York's favor: she never had to deal with distractions like murders that threatened her family's personal and professional security.

Her cell phone vibrated. She checked it and saw a text from Bo: "Last-minute shopping. Give me an hour." The message reminded her that she still had some shopping of her own to do. While she already had a stack of presents at home, it would be fun to fill it out with a few unique gifts from the Big Easy.

She headed over to Chartres Street to a shop selling culinary antiques. After browsing its historic treasures, she settled on a nineteenth-century copper saucepan for her mother. At a nearby bookstore selling new and used volumes, she bought a 1940s *History of Gumbo* for her father, a Walter Moseley first edition for Ione, and a Cajun songbook for Gaynell. For Gran', who enjoyed "snooping on people's lives," Maggie purchased several new and vintage biographies. Next stop was a children's clothing store, where she picked up adorable onesies sporting Mardi Gras images that would be perfect for Lia's babies. She had one last present to buy. But it was the one that stumped her. While Maggie had a few utilitarian presents for Bo, she still lacked one truly special gift, which bothered her. Shopping for Chris had never been a problem. Anything hip, arty, or artisanal made him happy. But Bo's interests were harder to pin down. His passions were his son, his job, and—she hoped—her. Maggie debated sticking a bow on top of her head and offering herself to him, then instantly dismissed the cheesy idea.

She stood on the corner of Royal and Iberville, brooding. A jazz band, followed by a second line of drunk tourists, danced through the street. Growing impatient, she crossed Royal to avoid them and found herself in front of a menswear shop. Draped over the shoulders of the mannequin in the window was a handsome black leather bomber jacket. She stepped into the shop and walked out ten minutes later with the perfect present for Bo.

*

Maggie made a quick stop at the hotel to drop off her purchases and then headed to Gumbo Ya Ya. She found Bo sitting at a wrought-iron café table for two in the restaurant's courtyard. Large bowls steamed at both place settings. "I ordered us each seafood gumbo," he said. "So what did you and your friend Lulu discover?"

"Guess who provided a quote about how fantastic his boss was for a press release?"

"Your guest from the Midwest, Tom O'Day."

"What?! How did you know?"

Bo held up his phone. "A text from Rufus, who may make a better detective than police chief."

"Oh, once he gets the chief position back, he'll never give it up again. He likes the power too much. Did he find out anything else about him? Was he able to connect him to our negative reviews?"

"Not yet. And even if he does, I don't think there's anything you can do about it legally. O'Day can always say those were his opinions and he's protected by free speech laws."

Maggie dumped the cup of rice that accompanied her gumbo into the bowl and gave it a hard stir. "I can't wait to get home and talk to the O'Days. Although Lindy wrote a very positive review and then posted comments that countered her husband's negative reviews. Ugh, I'm so confused."

"At least one mystery is sort of solved. Let's relax and enjoy that."

Maggie nodded and dipped her spoon into the thick gumbo. She was hungrier than she realized, and for a few minutes, she and Bo ate in companionable silence. They finished their gumbo and ordered coffee.

"So how was your time in the Quarter?" Maggie asked as she sipped her chicory-enhanced brew.

"Good. Wandered a little, got a few more Christmas presents. Look what I bought Xander." Bo held up what looked like a voodoo doll. "It's actually a doggy chew toy for when he gets to take home Jasmine."

"I love it. And so will he."

"Aside from investigating Harmon, how was your get-together with your friend Lulu?"

"Okay." Maggie paused. "She thinks of me as a fellow hotelier. Not an artist."

"I'm sorry. But who cares what she thinks? The important thing is how you think of yourself. Right?"

"I guess. But sometimes, especially these days, I forget."

A loud crack of thunder startled both of them. A flash of lightning instantly followed, and then rain poured down on the stone courtyard as if a spigot in the sky had been turned to full blast. Maggie and Bo jumped up from their seats, both dripping wet.

"I'm totally soaked," Maggie said.

"Me too." Bo grabbed her hand. "Let's get out of here."

They paid the bill and ran back to the hotel, getting more drenched with each step. They finally reached Reveille Orleans and collapsed with laughter under the overhang. "I've taken baths where I didn't get this wet," Maggie said. She gave herself a shake and sprayed Bo with water.

"Hey! Right back at ya."

Bo gave his head a fierce shake, and Maggie giggled as she recoiled from the dowsing. "You win," she said. "We'd better get upstairs and dry off. The last thing either of us needs is to catch cold."

Bo pulled open the hotel door, and they dashed inside. A quick elevator ride took them to the fifth floor, and they walked down the covered outdoor hallway to their adjacent rooms. Maggie stopped at her door. "Do you want to come in?" she asked, her voice soft and hesitant.

Bo looked down at her from his six-foot-plus height. "Yes," he said. "But I won't."

"Oh." Maggie was glad the hallway was dimly lit. Bo couldn't see her flush of humiliation. "I'm sorry, that was so . . . I don't know what it was, but I shouldn't have opened my stupid big mouth."

"You had the guts to say what we were both thinking." Bo took her hands in his. "I want us to be together. And we will. But when it does happen, I don't want it to be because circumstances threw us together, and you suddenly had an empty hotel room. And God knows, not in the middle of a murder investigation. Call me repressed, but I don't find them sexy."

Maggie had to smile at his last comment. "Okay. Well . . . good night."

"Good night." Bo kissed her and then disappeared into his hotel room. Maggie leaned against a rail post and watched as the rain fell into the hotel's courtyard below. She waited for her heart to stop racing, then took a few deep breaths and disappeared into her own hotel room.

*

The next morning, Maggie awoke to a text from Gran': "Ready when u r, if not sooner!!" She managed to pull Bo away from the sumptuous hotel breakfast buffet and his third helping of muffaletta frittata, and they drove uptown to the Charbonnet's home. Gran' was waiting for them at the front gate with her overnight bag and started to climb into the car before Bo came to a complete stop. "Thank you for rescuing me," she said, heaving her suitcase into the back of the SUV. "That place smells of mildew and a decaying lifestyle."

"Did you pick up any useful gossip?" Maggie asked.

"Aside from Adelaide being a rabid racist and anti-Semite, which I'm sure comes as no surprise, not much else from her but a whole lot from my new 'bestie,' Mahalia—their 'girl,' as Adelaide so-two-centuries-ago calls her. Philip Charbonnet is the proverbial prodigal son who's been forced by business failures and a foreclosure to move back to the family homestead. Emme and Steve Harmon were only staying with Adelaide while the Uptown home that they recently bought was being renovated. And if you think the Charbonnet home is grand, Mahalia says the Harmons' place makes it look like an outhouse. Adelaide and Philip are assuming that with Steve gone, Emme will be much looser with the Harmon multimillions. *But* Emme despises her mother and brother, is madly in love with Dan Levy, and has no intention of turning over one pretty penny to her miscreant relatives."

Gran' stopped for a breath. "And Mahalia offered up one particularly vital piece of information. Adelaide doesn't drive and hasn't for years. So as much as I'd like to finger her as the perp—ooh, what fun to talk like a television detective—unless she was chauffeured to the murder site, I regret that she has an ironclad alibi."

"Well, much thanks to Mahalia for all that dirt," Maggie said. "She's our source at Chez Charbonnet."

"I'm afraid not for much longer," Gran' said with a wicked grin.

Maggie gave her grand-mère an admonishing look. "What did you do?"

"My dear friend and fellow Newcomb alum Cissy Bennett lost her husband a few years ago. She adores traveling but misses sharing her adventures with someone. She was in need of a companion, so I connected her with Mahalia, whom she hired over the phone. My only regret is that I won't be there to see Adelaide's face when Mahalia gives notice."

"I'm assuming Cissy was another competitive Kappa."

"Oh, no, dear. Cissy was in Pi Beta Phi. You might call Adelaide an equal opportunity offender. Bo, chère, are you still with us, or have we lost your attention with all the family and sorority machinations?"

"I have to say, I feel a little out of my element listening to these one percenter problems. So I've been thinking. Do you know what the main motivation for murder is?"

"Money? Jealousy? Revenge?" Maggie guessed.

"Anger? Passion? A thirst for justice?" offered Gran'.

Bo shook his head. "Humiliation. Which is the thread connecting pretty much all the reasons you listed. And Philip Charbonnet sounds like a man who's suffered a lot of humiliation in his life—not to mention he was in the shadow of a phenomenally successful albeit despised brother-in-law. Ru and I need to take a hard look at his personal and professional history."

"While you're doing that, I'm going to pay a visit to Belle Vista," Maggie said. "That place has been dogging me lately. I met the general manager at dance class, and she seemed nice. I'll take her up on the tour she offered and see if I can find out any new info on Harmon. But first, I need to have a chat with the O'Days. They're behind the bad reviews, Gran'. At least he is."

"*What?*" Gran' exclaimed. "Son of a gumdrop, that ticks me off. We need to start screening our guests for basic decency. If there isn't an app for that, there should be. Maybe I'll create one."

Maggie laughed. "Well, if anyone can, it's you."

*

Bo dropped Maggie and Gran' at the shotgun cottage and took off. Maggie set down her suitcase and then strode over to the garçonnière, where the O'Day family was staying. She rapped on the door, and Lindy O'Day opened it. The expression on her face told Maggie that this was not a welcome visit.

"We're checking out early, and I'm pretty busy," Lindy said. She remained planted in the doorway. "We can drop off our keys on the way out."

"I wanted to thank you for the positive review on Trippee."

"Oh." Lindy relaxed slightly. "You're welcome. We've enjoyed our stay."

"That surprises me, considering all the slams your husband posted under a pseudonym. I saw his name attached to a brownnosing quote about Steve Harmon in a newspaper article. It was also attached to the title of vice president, marketing. So it wasn't too much of a leap to figure out he was our troll."

Lindy's shoulders sagged, and she dropped her face into her hands. When she lifted her head, Maggie saw tears streaking her face. Lindy moved out of the doorway. "Come in," she said. "Please."

Maggie followed Lindy into the garçonnière. The bottom floor of the hexagonal two-story edifice was a living room; a staircase led to two small bedrooms upstairs. Lindy pulled a half-packed suitcase off the room's loveseat, and she and Maggie sat down. "Tom took the girls to Bon Bon to pick up a few final treats and some souvenirs," Lindy said. Maggie didn't respond. She had learned silence often served as a prompt for people to share, which proved true for Lindy. "I am so, so sorry about those horrible reviews. Tom used to work for an investment company that Harmon's hedge fund absorbed. There were layoffs when that happened, and Tom lost his job. I work as a librarian, but my salary is pitiful. Steve Harmon had been using some of his own fortune to cherry-pick distressed companies. He bought a small boutique hotel chain in Ohio and offered Tom a job at the new addition to the Harmon real estate portfolio, but on one condition."

"He'd help bring down my uncle Tig so Harmon could gain control of his company, Preferred Properties."

Lindy nodded. "He had us book a stay here because you can only post on Trippee.com if you've utilized a travel business's services."

"I'm well aware of Trippee's policy."

"You have to understand—Tom hated doing it, but he was desperate. You do—did—not want to get on Steve Harmon's bad side."

"Yes, I'm getting that impression big time."

"Since Steve was staying here to check out the place, he could have posted the reviews himself. But he was a master at getting other people to do his dirty work." Lindy's tone was bitter. "What are you going to do?"

"Well, legally I can't really do anything. Of course, I could report Tom to whoever replaces Harmon as his boss and threaten to take the story to the media. This would probably get him fired, even though he was basically acting as Harmon's surrogate."

"Yes. Like I said, Steve had a way of staying clean while throwing people under the bus. He even did it to his own stepbrother, Dan, during that insider trading scandal."

Maggie pondered her options. It was hard not to sympathize with anyone who found themselves in Steve Harmon's crosshairs. Was there a way of turning the situation into a positive? "Let's start with this. Tom owns up to what he did and apologizes to my uncle, my parents, and anyone else he slammed. He deletes all his negative reviews and, wherever he can honestly do it, replaces them with glowing recommendations."

For the first time in days, Lindy brightened. "Yes. Yes, he can absolutely do that."

"And instead of leaving, why don't you finish out your stay here, then both of you hit every travel blog you can find and write rave reviews about Crozat. But not because you have to. It will be because you enjoyed a fantastic vacation at a wonderful B and B. Like most of our guests do."

"Thank you, thank you so much." Lindy was weepy with gratitude. "I'll talk to Tom as soon as he gets back with the girls. They'll be thrilled. They were so disappointed that we were going to leave before the bonfires."

As Maggie made her way out of the garçonnière, she was showered with more thanks from a relieved Lindy O'Day. "It's just a way of making things right," she told Lindy. *It's also a way of keeping two more potential suspects around*, Maggie thought but didn't say. *Because if there's anyone who'd be happy to see Steve Harmon dead, it's you for the way he used your husband.*

Chapter Fifteen

Ninette and Tug were relieved by Maggie's news that she had solved the mystery of the bad reviews and supported the deal she had cut with Lindy O'Day. "Great work, chère," Tug said as he helped his wife put away the breakfast dishes in the manor house kitchen. "I think Tig will be on board with turning the O'Day family from foes to fans."

"I'll call him. But I don't think they were ever really foes. They were more like hostages of Harmon's brutal style of doing business." Maggie took a last swig of her coffee. "Oh, I almost forgot. We had a delicious dish this morning at the hotel that would be a great addition to our brunch menu, Mom."

"Really? What?"

Maggie was amused by the edge in her sweet mother's voice. Cooking always sparked a competitive streak in Ninette. "Muffaletta frittata. I'll see if I can get the recipe from Lulu."

"No need," Ninette said. "I can figure out my own take on the dish. Tug, I'll be putting together a shopping list for you."

"Yes, ma'am," her husband responded with a smile and a wink at his daughter.

Maggie left the kitchen, happy to see her parents engaged in something besides worrying about Crozat's future. She went into the office and placed a Skype call to her uncle. His face soon filled the screen. "Buongiorno, cara mia," Tig greeted his niece.

"I'm assuming you're still in Italy."

"Si. I found un bello villagio tucked away in the Abruzzo region. It's pretty much abandoned, but with some TLC, it'll make a great destination hotel."

"Bene. Anyway, I have something positive to report for a change." Maggie filled him in on the situation with the O'Days.

"Bravissima," Tig responded with a dimpled smile. "I'm impressed by your crafty thinking."

"Just trying to help save the family biz, mio zio."

Tig laughed. "Hey, Marco's still there, right? Tell him I say hi."

"I'll do better than that. I'll tell him you send your love."

"Maggie—"

She disconnected the call before her uncle could protest. "Crafty me," she murmured with a sly grin. Then she pulled out her cell phone and texted Bea Boxler, the Belle Vista general manager she'd met at DanceBod. Bea immediately texted back an invitation to stop by the plantation cum resort. Maggie returned to the shotgun cottage, showered, and picked out an outfit that was professional without being dowdy. She paired the black skirt she'd worn to the

Charbonnets with a teal-green blouse, black pumps, and *no* stockings. She ringed her hazel eyes with teal liner and added black mascara. A swipe of coral lipstick, and she was done. She grabbed her leather jacket from the small front closet and headed for Belle Vista's stately digs.

*

"And last but not least, this is the White Ballroom, where all six of the Tucker daughters enjoyed lavish weddings prior to the Civil War."

Bea Boxler led Maggie into a spectacular room, white from floor to ceiling with white velvet drapes and ottomans upholstered in a matching white silk. Maggie's appreciation of the view was dimmed by it coming at the end of a two-hour tour of Belle Vista's rooms, gardens, and outbuildings. Her feet were killing her, and much as she hated stockings, she wished she had worn them since they might have prevented the nascent blisters on her feet. She prayed the final stop on the tour would be the Belle Vista Café, where she could finally sit down and subtly steer Bea into a conversation about her late boss. She'd also worked up an appetite traipsing around Belle Vista's hallowed grounds, and the food at the upscale planation resort was rumored to be five-star.

"This ballroom is like walking into a cloud, isn't it?" Bea said, her undefinable accent giving the sentence a sing-songy lilt.

"Yes," Maggie said, forcing herself back into the moment. "I wonder if any of the grooms had trouble finding their brides in here. With their white wedding dresses, they would have blended right in."

Bea gave a thoughtful nod, and Maggie got the impression she'd taken the wisecrack seriously. It occurred to her the general manager might have been raised in another country and didn't quite get Maggie's style of humor.

"You don't have a ballroom at Crozat, do you?"

"I'm afraid not. But we have a party tent." Maggie cringed as she thought to herself, *Could that sound any tackier?*

"Yes, we have one as well. They do come in handy." Bea might as well have been talking about a pocket wrench. "Our business increased by a good thirty percent after we added the spa facilities. Do you have a building on the property you could renovate?"

"Well, there is the garage," Maggie said. "It's from the 1920s, so it's not architecturally distinct." She began warming to the idea. "But it's got good bones and lots of space."

"It sounds perfect. Let's talk more about this over lunch. I can give you lots of tips. It will be so much fun to have another friend here in the hotel business."

Maggie appreciated Bea's enthusiasm and was happy to make a new friend, but having the second person in two days assume she was in the hotel business pushed a button. While it was a logical assumption to make, it highlighted how much Maggie's world had changed since she'd moved back to Pelican. The life she knew as an artist seemed to be fading away. She was starting to miss who she was and wasn't sure who she was becoming. Maggie wondered if thirty-two was too young for a midlife crisis. *Stop it,* she then admonished herself. *These are high-class problems.*

"Let's go to the café," Bea said. "I had the chef prepare a salad of our homegrown lettuce and fresh crab. You'll have to accept my apologies. The lobster that was supposed to be flown in from Maine this morning was delayed by weather."

Now that, Maggie thought to herself, *is* really *a high-class problem.*

Maggie followed Bea out of the mansion, resisting the urge to remove the shoes from her sore feet and walk barefoot. Belle Vista Café was lodged in the plantation's former conservatory, a glass confection resembling a large music box. Tables had replaced plants, but the chintz linens bloomed with fat magnolia and gardenia blossoms. The maître d' greeted Bea with subservience and sat the two women at a table impeccably set with silver, fine china, and crystal. Bowls brimming with salad and large chunks of crab were placed in front of them, and steam rose from a basket of fresh bread. Maggie was particularly happy to see a full champagne glass next to each place. She picked hers up. "To new friends," she said.

Bea smiled. "How lovely." She picked up her own glass. "To new friends. Cheers."

The women toasted and then began eating. The rumors about the café's cuisine were true. In fact, if restaurant ratings offered a sixth star, Maggie would have awarded it to the crab currently melting in her mouth. She showered compliments on the food and atmosphere and then steered the conversation toward Steve Harmon. "What happened to your boss was awful," Maggie said. "What a traumatic event for everyone here."

"Yes, it's been difficult. But we've managed to keep up the high standard people expect from BV."

Wow, right to business. "Do you know what's going to happen to the resort without Mr. Harmon?"

"As opposed to many of his other properties, Mr. Harmon owns—owned—BV outright. His wife inherited it, and she's been very receptive to my ideas and generous with the staff. It's sad, of course, but I think we'll be fine. Perhaps even better."

File that under motive. For Emme and *Bea. As well as anyone else who might be in Harmon's will.*

Maggie decided it was time to kick into gossip mode. It wasn't an approach she was fond of, but it got results. "I heard from a friend that Mr. Harmon had a bad reputation with women." Maggie lowered her voice. "Like, sexual harassment bad."

Bea looked perturbed. "Really? I know nothing about that." She pursed her lips. "I think it's terrible when people feel the need to say scurrilous things about a person who has departed, especially under such tragic circumstances. Mr. Harmon was always a gentleman with me."

"Well, I'm glad to hear that." But Maggie didn't believe it. Bea was a stunning woman with a model's body. Given Steve Harmon's predatory nature, it was hard to imagine him passing up a chance to hit on his lovely underling. Maggie had also noticed Bea's eyelid flicker slightly when she defended her boss. She was either lying or there was more to the story than she was willing to share.

Sensing a slight chill coming from Bea, Maggie decided to broach a new topic. "I hope I'm not being rude, but I noticed you have a slight accent."

"Oh. Yes." Bea smiled and the chill evaporated. "I was raised in Europe and attended boarding school in Switzerland. Then I worked in London for a number of years until I came here, so my accent is what you might call a mishmash. But we must stop talking about me. I want to hear about Crozat Plantation. How have you managed to keep it in your family for all these years?"

Maggie recognized the question for what it was: an attempt to change the subject. She responded with a rote history of her family's home that Bea seemed to find fascinating. Or perhaps she was faking interest. Maggie couldn't tell. One thing Maggie found interesting was the fact that Bea never asked her about finding Steve Harmon's body. The death of Bea's boss seemed the equivalent of a clogged toilet in a guest room: unpleasant but easily handled.

A young man in a business suit approached the table. He looked familiar to Maggie, but she couldn't place him. "Hey, Bea, we lost our Santa for the Christmas Eve brunch. He decided to spend the holidays with his daughter's family in Alexandria."

"Then you need to find another Santa." Bea's tone was polite but annoyed.

"I know," he responded defensively. "But I thought I should tell you."

"Thank you, Harrison. But next time, let the conversation be, 'We lost our Santa but I replaced him.'"

Harrison. "Sweet potato pralines," Maggie blurted.

The others looked at Maggie as if she'd lost her mind, but then Harrison gave a nod of recognition. "Right. The Crozat food stand by the bonfires. Those pralines are awesome. Nice to see you."

"You too."

There was an awkward silence. "Okay then," Harrison finally said. "Guess I better find a new Santa."

Harrison plodded off, and Bea sighed. "He's rather hopeless. But then again, he *was* deeply affected by Mr. Harmon's death. He seemed to see him as some sort of mentor." The concept of the financier mentoring the awkward twenty-something seemed as ludicrous to Bea as an elephant tap-dancing. But at least there was someone besides Dan Levy who grieved the loss of Harmon.

The lunch finished with a delectable vanilla mousse topped with a spun sugar garnish in the shape of the plantation's initials. After cups of French press coffee, Bea led Maggie back to the plantation's manor house, where they walked through Belle Vista's hallway, which doubled as an art gallery, on their way to the exit. Maggie noticed Emme at the far end of the gallery, listening to a man as he pointed to one of the many paintings lining the walls. The man pointed out another painting, and Maggie saw that it was Chris. "Maggie?" he said, as startled to see her as she was to see him.

"Hi," she said. "I'm here touring Belle Vista. Bea was nice enough to show me around."

"Ah," he said, nodding. "Emme's asked me to appraise Belle Vista's artwork and see if there are any hidden masterpieces in the collection. But so far it seems the Tuckers were more interested in their own portraits than any artists of note."

"Typical of new money, which is what they were in their day," Emme said. Maggie noted the statement would have been laced with derision had Emme's snob of a mother spouted it. But coming from Emme, it simply sounded like a historical fact.

"But you do have an Audubon print." Maggie pointed to an exquisitely detailed rendering of a pelican. "That's certainly valuable."

"It's a copy," Chris said. "Worth fifty dollars at most."

"Oh. I just thought because of its unique size and the fact that the print looks hand-colored . . . I guess my art history is a little rusty."

"No worries; it happens all the time with Audubon prints and knock-offs, especially good ones like this," Chris assured her. Maggie knew he was trying to make her feel better, but she still felt mortified by her mistake.

"Oh, this reminds me of something I wanted to ask you," Bea said to Maggie. "I've noticed some souvenirs at other plantations feature unique renderings of their buildings. Have you seen those? Do you know where I can get them?"

"From me," Maggie said. "They're my paintings. I reproduce them on souvenirs to sell at local historical sites."

"What a nice hobby," Bea said.

Maggie felt a flush of humiliation. To Bea, and probably to many others, that's what her passion had devolved to—a hobby. She was formulating a response when Chris jumped to her defense. "It's not a hobby. Maggie's an artist, and a terrific one." Maggie flashed him a grateful smile.

"Really?" Emme sounded impressed. "I'd like to see your work sometime. I wouldn't mind replacing some of these dead white people with more contemporary paintings."

She gestured toward the gallery's artwork and then suddenly tensed up. Maggie saw Harrison heading in their direction. "Hey, Bea, wanted to let you know I think I scared up another Santa," he called to his boss. He froze when he saw Emme. "What are you doing here?"

"I own Belle Vista now, Harrison," Emme said, her tone measured. "You know that."

"Is *he* here?" Harrison demanded. Maggie saw a vein pulsing on his forehead. "What am I saying? Where else would he be except following you around?"

"Harrison, don't," Dan said, startling Maggie, who hadn't seen him come in.

"Get out of here," Harrison yelled at Dan. "*Now.*"

"Son, please . . ."

"Wait, what?" Maggie was confused by this unexpected twist. "Son?"

The others ignored her. Emme took a step toward the young man. "Don't you *dare* talk to your father that way."

"Can you please take this somewhere less public?" Bea said, exasperated with the family drama.

"Dan is Harrison's father?" Again, the others ignored Maggie. She caught Chris's eye, and he gave a helpless shrug. Maggie hovered between feeling trapped by and absorbed in the family's dysfunction.

"Shut up, shut up!" Harrison choked out the words as he fought off tears. "The murderer got the wrong person," he shouted at the man Maggie now knew as his father. "He should never have killed Uncle Steve. He should have killed *you*."

Chapter Sixteen

Even the reserved Bea Boxler gasped at Harrison's outburst. Emme pulled her hand back as if she was going to slap the young man but restrained herself. "Your father is a thousand times the man your uncle was," she said through clenched teeth. "And if you continue to abuse him and hold him in less regard than the vicious SOB that was my late husband, you can forget about family loyalty and find a job somewhere else."

"Emme, it's okay," Dan said. "Let him be. He's grieving. He was very close to Steve." He turned to his son, who looked away, refusing to give his father the satisfaction of eye contact. Maggie felt for Dan. He looked drained and near tears himself. "We're leaving, Harry. But please . . . if you need me, I'll always be there for you."

Dan laid a hand on Emme's shoulder and guided her down the hallway. "I'll text you later," Chris muttered to Maggie, and then he followed his patron out the door.

"Hey, Bea, is it okay if I take a break for a few hours?" Harrison said, his eyes cast down at the floor.

"Take as much time as you need."

Maggie felt a need to speak. She was uncomfortable being a mute observer. "Harrison, I'm so sorry about your uncle."

Harrison stared at her. She'd finally gotten somebody's attention. "You're the one who found him, weren't you?"

"Yes. Do you want to talk about it?"

The young hotelier shook his head. "No. Not now. I'm not ready. But someday."

"Well, when you are, I'm there for you. And know that the police are doing everything possible to identify Mr. Harmon's killer."

"You're good at solving murders, aren't you? I read about what happened at Crozat and how you worked with the police to nail the killers."

"I don't know if I've got any special gift for it. But since your uncle was our guest, I'm very invested in the case, and I promise I'll do everything I can to help the police find who killed him."

"Thank you. I appreciate that." Harrison gave Maggie the faintest glimmer of a grateful smile, then took off in the opposite direction from his father.

Bea sighed. "Well, that was unpleasant. I don't know about you, but I could use another glass of champagne."

Maggie released the breath she hadn't realized she'd been holding. "I could use a whole dang bottle."

*

A bride-to-be calling about the possibility of renting the White Ballroom for her wedding forced Bea to pass on a second round of champagne. She and Maggie agreed to find a time to meet at Junie's, and Maggie took off. She called Rufus as soon as she got in her car. "I'm curious. Did y'all get a copy of Steve Harmon's will?"

"Yeah, after a few threats to go all Louisiana law enforcement on his team o' New York lawyers' backsides. I had to plow through a lotta legalese and some small bequests to household staff and business employees, but basically the bulk of his estate was split between his wife and some foundation he probably set up for tax reasons. He also left a nice chunk of change to his stepbrother, Dan Levy, whose alibi checked out. One of the Charbonnet-Harmon's live-in housekeepers . . . yeah, I said 'one of.' Like they say, it's good to be the king. Bottom line, the housekeeper verified in seriously unpleasant detail that Levy was laid up with a stomach virus the night of Harmon's murder. Anyway, I gotta go. I'm taking Charli to a Mommy and Me class."

"Rufus, that is so adorable."

"A daddy's gotta do what a daddy's gotta do. Which sometimes means going to a class called Mommy and Me."

Rufus signed off, having revealed nothing that Maggie didn't already assume. As she drove toward Pelican, she mulled over what she'd witnessed at Belle Vista. The

Harmon-Levy-Charbonnet dynamic felt straight out of a telenovela. She found it exhausting and a little depressing. But Maggie knew what would lift her spirits: sugar.

She made a left into town, pulled into the parking lot behind Fais Dough Dough, hopped out of the car, and headed into her cousin's shop. The tantalizing scent of cinnamon and vanilla instantly soothed Maggie. She was surprised and happy to see Ione behind the counter. "Welcome to Fais Dough Dough-licious," Ione said.

Maggie smiled at her friend's play on words and gave her a hug. "I'm so glad you're working here."

"When Lia heard Tannis laid me off, she hired me to help out for the holidays, bless her heart. What can I get you?"

"I'll take a cinnamon raisin croissant. And then I'm going next door for a big old dose of chocolate."

"Doubling down on the sweets, huh? Rough morning?"

"*So* rough."

Ione went behind the counter and retrieved a croissant for Maggie. It managed the croissant hat trick of having a perfectly crispy crust, moist center, and buttery layers. Ione refused Maggie's attempts to pay for the pastry, ignoring her protestations as she gently pushed her through the open doorway connecting Lia's two shops. "This girl needs more sugar, stat," Ione told Kyle, Lia's husband, who was manning Bon Bon's counter.

"I'm on it," he said with a grin, and Ione returned to Fais Dough Dough. "What can I get you, Maggie?"

"Surprise me. Is Lia in the back? I'm going to say hi."

Kyle got to work assembling a small box of candy, and Maggie went into the store's workroom, where she found Vanessa Fleer-soon-to-be-MacIlhoney piling baby clothes onto Lia's lap.

"I'm giving her every little thing my Charli's outgrown," Vanessa explained after the women exchanged hellos and hugs.

"You found out you're having a girl?" Maggie asked her cousin.

"She's having twins," Vanessa announced before Lia could respond.

"*Twins?!*"

"Yep," Vanessa said, adding with pride, "I figured it out before the doctors."

"She did," Lia said with a sheepish look. "We were trying to keep it a secret, but it's hard with Vanessa around."

"That is so true," Vanessa agreed with a nod.

Maggie and Lia exchanged an amused look. Maggie bent down and wrapped her arms around her cousin. "This is such amazing news, Leelee. I couldn't be happier for you and Kyle."

Vanessa clapped her hands together excitedly. "And, Lia, I saved the best for last. A present for you, not the babies." Vanessa reached into her large canvas bag and pulled out an oversized T-shirt decorated with a jokey graphic of a sexy woman's torso in a bikini. "You wear this over your big old belly and it looks like *you're* the one who's wearing the bikini. It's hilarious. Try it on."

"Why not?" Lia took the shirt, then stood up and pulled it over her head. The café au lait coloring of her mixed-race heritage ended at the neck, where the cartoon white woman's bodacious body began. All three women burst out laughing.

"You're right, Nessa," Maggie said. "It is hilarious."

"Sorry I couldn't get one in your skin color, Lia."

"That's okay," Lia said. "It's the thought that counts."

The women dissolved into more laughter. Quentin MacIlhoney appeared in the back doorway and observed the scene. "I'm here for my future missus, but if she's having this much fun, maybe I should come back later."

"I'm good to go, honey bunny," Vanessa said with a wave to her fiancé.

"Quentin, how do I look?" Lia struck a silly model's pose.

"Like a client I'd be bailing out of jail after she beaned her husband with a longneck beer bottle."

"I have to show this to Kyle."

Lia started for the door and then stopped suddenly. She clutched her stomach. Maggie ran to Lia and helped support her as the pregnant woman doubled over. "Lia, what's wrong?"

"I don't know. I've got a real bad cramp." Lia cried out in pain. Fear etched her face. "Oh, God, Maggie. I think something's wrong."

Chapter Seventeen

Vanessa convinced Lia and Kyle not to waste time waiting for an ambulance. "Trust me, Quentie will get you there way, way faster," she declared. "Don't worry about anything here. I'll look after Bon Bon."

Quentin rushed the others to his purple Bentley. Kyle helped Lia into the back of the car while Maggie jumped into the front seat. The defense attorney pulled out a police siren and placed it on the roof of the sedan. "Buckle up, folks. Kyle, hold on tight to your lady."

Maggie barely got her door closed before Quentin activated the police siren, tore out of the parking lot, and raced toward the hospital at the speed of a Formula One driver. The shriek of the siren hurt Maggie's ears. "Is that thing even legal?"

"Nope, but there's not an officer in the parish who's gonna stop me."

"Why not?"

"It's Louisiana, chère. For every cop in the family, there's also a scofflaw who's gonna need a good lawyer."

Vanessa was right about Quentin's driving. They got to the hospital in the time it would have taken an ambulance to reach Bon Bon. The defense attorney pulled into a handicapped spot in front of the ER entrance and slung a handicapped placard onto his rearview mirror. "What?" he said off of Maggie's look. "I've got a golf handicap."

Kyle flagged down an orderly, who rushed toward them with a wheelchair. "It's going to be okay, sweetie," Kyle told his wife, holding her hand as they headed into the ER. Maggie and Quentin followed close behind.

"No worries, sir, we'll get her in right away," the orderly said. "Your friends can wait here."

The orderly disappeared down a hallway with Kyle and Lia. The automatic doors to the ER whooshed open, and paramedics wheeled in a gurney accompanied by a police officer. The man on the gurney alternated between writhing in pain and screaming a stream of profanity. Quentin sniffed the air. "I smell gunshot residue." Maggie wouldn't say the lawyer's eyes lit up, but they came close to it. "Which means I smell the possible need for a lawyer. If you'll excuse me . . ."

Quentin dashed down the hall after the gurney, leaving Maggie alone in the waiting room. She collapsed into a hard plastic chair, which hadn't grown more comfortable in the days since her father's recent health scare. That visit had a happy outcome. She prayed it would be the same for Lia.

A cluster of doctors walked by, and Maggie noticed Dr. Jen was among them. The doctor saw Maggie and split off from her colleagues. "Hi," she said to Maggie. "Is something wrong with Tug? I thought he was doing well on the last medication I prescribed."

"He is. I'm here because of Lia. She's pregnant with twins and experienced some painful cramping."

"Hopefully it's just that—a cramp. Dr. Fran Vella's the obstetrician on duty this afternoon, and she's fantastic. By the way, I was going to call you. I have some really good news." Jen took a seat next to Maggie. "I'm moving to New York. I took a position with Columbia Presbyterian."

"Oh. Wow. That's great, Jen. Congratulations." Maggie feigned happiness, but she was disappointed. She liked Jen and had hoped to rekindle their friendship.

"Thanks. When you move back, we'll get to hang out together. You can show me your favorite places in the city. I'd love some tips from an insider." Maggie smiled but said nothing. "My parents are freaking out," Jen continued, rolling her eyes. "I keep telling them I can't imagine spending the rest of my life in the town where I grew up, and they think I'm nuts. You're the only person around here who gets it." The doctor's beeper buzzed, and Jen stood up. "I have to get back to work. But text me how Lia is, and your dad too. I'll be here until mid-January, and before I go, I'll make sure I transfer his case to Dr. Marchand. He's wonderful. I'm so excited about New York. We'll have a blast."

Jen gave Maggie a hug and strode off. *Coward*, Maggie scolded herself. Why hadn't she told Jen that she was ambivalent about returning to New York? She was pondering this when Quentin hastened over. "Seems like I landed myself a client. Easy peasy self-defense case. A little holiday present from Laborde's Bar and Grill, home of the drunken bar fight. Anyhoo, I've called a car service to take you back to Bon Bon when you're ready. Tell Vanessa I love her and we're having the good champagne when I get home tonight."

"Will do."

Quentin took off, and Maggie remained in the cold plastic chair, absorbed in her own thoughts. She tabled the dilemma about her future and focused on something that felt less taxing: analyzing the suspects in Steve Harmon's murder. Bea Boxler was the most interesting new addition to the long list. Some might simply find her reserved, but Maggie sensed the cool professional exterior was a front. It was time to play Internet detective and see what the web might reveal about the mysterious woman.

Maggie was so absorbed in her own thoughts that she didn't hear Kyle approach. "You've been here this whole time?" he asked.

"What do you mean?"

"It's five o'clock. We came in almost two hours ago." Kyle took a seat next to Maggie and rubbed his temples.

"How's Lia?"

"She's going to be okay. And so are all three babies."

"Three?!" Maggie sat up straight. "Are you telling me—"

"She's pregnant with triplets."

"Triplets? Oh, Kyle. Congratulations, that's beyond wonderful."

"The doctor wants Lia on bed rest for at least the next week, but my guess is it's going to last for longer than that. I'm going to stay with her tonight and take her home in the morning. Ione can handle Fais Dough Dough, but we may have to close Bon Bon for a while."

"Don't worry," Maggie said, squeezing her cousin-in-law's hand. "We'll make sure that doesn't happen. I'm heading back there now. If you need anything, call me."

"Will do." Kyle smiled and squeezed Maggie's hand back. "I swear, where would we be without our Magnolia Marie?"

"That sounds like the lyrics to a really bad country song."

*

As soon as Maggie left the hospital, she called Crozat to share Kyle and Lia's news with her family. "Triplets? Oh, my goodness." Gran' laughed. "Well, as the mother of twins, I'll be offering our dear Lia a few tips on how to parent multiples while maintaining your sanity."

"I'm going to make Kyle and Lia a week's worth of meals," Ninette said. "I'll have your dad drop them by."

"I'll tell Kyle. I know they'll appreciate it."

"Triplets!" Gran' and Ninette repeated in unison.

Maggie ended the call and moved on to her next task. When she walked into Bon Bon a half hour later, she found Vanessa completing a transaction with a group of tourists. "Well, what do you know?" Vanessa said. She pointed to Maggie. "This is Magnolia Marie Crozat, the artist responsible for the mugs and mouse pads you bought. Maybe she'll auto-graph them for you." Vanessa held up a permanent marker. "What do you think, Maggie?"

"Uh, sure," Maggie responded. She was taken aback by Vanessa's sales savvy, considering her former Doucet coworker was infamous for being a lazy employee who could barely operate a cash register. Maggie took the marker from Vanessa and autographed souvenirs as the tourists handed them to her. They showered her with thanks and left for their mini–tour bus. "Wow, Vanessa, nicely done. Thank you."

Vanessa blushed and waved her hand dismissively. "Weren't nothing. How's Lia and her babies?"

"She's going to be fine, but get this. She's expecting trip-lets, not twins. She'll be on bed rest for a while, though."

To Maggie's surprise, tears rolled down Vanessa's cheeks. "Nessa, what's wrong?"

"It's my fault. I gave her that stupid T-shirt. I almost made her laugh out one of her babies."

"Oh, no, no." Maggie felt for Nessa, who often over-reached in her eagerness to make friends. She went around the Bon Bon counter and gave the weeping woman a hug. "Lia loves the shirt. It was a hilarious present." Vanessa shook her head, not willing to be let off the hook. "I'll tell you what. Lia's going to be on bed rest for at least a week or two. If you want to help the Bruners, they could use someone to mind the store. You could even have Charli here with you."

Vanessa immediately cheered up. "I'd love that. I felt like I did important stuff working here today, Maggie. I think it was the Lord's way of showing me how to make myself useful."

Maggie's cell pinged, notifying her of a text from Tannis: "Doucet open tomorrow. Be there eight sharp." She groaned. "Or you could replace me at Doucet."

Vanessa shook her head vigorously. "No, thank you. That Tannis girl is a real you-know-what."

"Oh, yes. I know exactly what."

Maggie's phone sounded another text alert, and she muttered an epithet. "What do you want now, Tannis?" But the text wasn't from Tannis. It was from Chris: "Can you talk? Meet me at Le Blanc's." Maggie ignored the unpleasant feeling in her stomach and texted back, "Okay. Give me five."

She went over a few shopkeeping details with Vanessa, popped over to Fais Dough Dough to update Ione on Lia's condition, and then walked down the street to Le Blanc's. Chris was waiting for her at the bar. He motioned to a glass of wine in front of the place next to him. "I ordered you a Chardonnay. I haven't forgotten your favorite wine."

"Thanks," Maggie said, although she had a feeling the rendezvous would require a stronger drink.

"After the crazy dose of family drama at Belle Vista today, I figured it was time I told you the real reason I signed on for this trip."

"Okay. I'm listening."

Chris took a swig of his drink, which Maggie assumed was his usual Scotch on the rocks. "I've been Steve's art adviser off and on for about a year. I know he can be a nightmare, but it's been an awesome experience. We became friends. He even taught me how to fly his plane, this sweet Piper Aerostar. Like they say, rich is better. Anyway, when I heard he was flying down to Louisiana—and owned a place near you—I convinced him he needed me to come with him so I could evaluate all of his art down here. But that was an excuse. I wanted to talk to you. Face-to-face." Maggie found the last statement ironic since Chris seemed unable to make eye contact with her. "The stupidest thing I've ever done in my life is dump you, Maggie. It was a panic move. I never should have walked out on you. I never should have married Samantha. I totally own my mistake. And I want to make it up to you. I'd like another shot at our relationship. Because one thing really became clear to me over the last two years." Chris finally turned to face Maggie. "I still love you."

A battery of responses collided in Maggie's brain, all of which were variations on the same theme. "No," she finally said. "I went through months of emotional torture, but I can finally say that I've moved on. And honestly, Chris, I don't think you're still in love with me. I think you're in love with what we had together. Which is over. I'm sorry. But no."

Chris nodded. "I thought that would be your first reaction."

"It's my only reaction."

"But if you're not ready to come back to New York for me—"

"It's not a question of ready. It's actually not a question at all."

Chris ignored her. "Come back for yourself. I feel bad that my crappy behavior chased you out of the city. Don't lie to me and say you don't miss it, because I know you do. You belong there, Mags. I worry about you, out here a hundred miles from nowhere. You're a terrific artist, and you've gotten even better in the last couple of years. I'll give Smalltownville credit for that. But don't you want to share the power of your art with the world? You can't do that from Pelican, Louisiana."

"To reiterate, we are over, and now so is this conversation." Maggie hopped off her barstool. She was angry, exhausted, and close to tears but refused to give Chris the satisfaction of seeing he had affected her. "You've forgotten the 'Smalltownville' you have such disdain for is where I was born and raised, so to put it down is to put *me* down. No matter what choice I make about my future, I can promise you it will never be a comment on Pelican, because I love this town and pretty much everyone in it."

"'No matter what choice I make'? So you haven't made up your mind."

Maggie gave a small, frustrated scream and mimed pulling out her hair. "Good-bye, Chris. I don't know how much longer you'll be in the area, but feel free not to contact me again. Ever."

With that, she stormed out of the upscale restaurant, slamming the door behind her.

*

Maggie lay awake staring at the shotgun cottage's pickled cypress ceiling for most of the night. At dawn, she gave up trying to sleep and took a cold shower, hoping it would shock the exhaustion out of her. Between that and a cup of black coffee, she felt close to functional but restless. She tiptoed into her grand-mère's room. "Gran'?" she whispered. Gran' opened one eye. "If anyone's looking for me, I'm going to my studio to paint for an hour or two. I need to think about something besides murder or my future."

"Paint flowers or butterflies," Gran' murmured. "You can't go wrong with those." She closed her eye and went back to sleep.

Maggie made her way through a thick early morning fog to her studio. She inhaled the scent of oil paints hanging in the air and felt better. Then she dabbed a rainbow of colors onto a palette, placed a canvas on her easel, and studied it thoughtfully.

A half hour later, she was still staring at a blank canvas.

For the first time in her life, Maggie felt blocked. She threw down her paintbrush in frustration and began closing up the studio. The sound of rustling leaves drew her attention to one of the studio's two large windows.

Suddenly, an explosion blew out the glass from one of the windows, followed by a burst of flames. Maggie ran to the front door and tried pulling it open, but it was jammed. She fled to the back door and found it stuck as well. There was another explosion, and flames shot up outside the studio's other window, cutting off Maggie's last possible escape route.

Someone was trying to burn down Maggie's art studio—and take her down with it.

Chapter Eighteen

"Help!" Maggie cried out as she struggled in vain to open the door.

She could feel heat radiating through the windows. Suddenly the glass blew out of the second window, and Maggie ducked as shards and splinters shot all over the room. Flames outside the studio licked at the window ledge. Maggie grabbed the fire extinguisher that she had on hand for emergencies and doused them before they could find their way inside and ignite any of the studio's many highly flammable contents. She continued to yell for help as she sprayed. She heard a cacophony of voices outside. With a bang, someone kicked the front door open. Marco stumbled inside. "Wow," he gasped. "I had no idea I could do that." He grabbed Maggie's hand and pulled her out of the studio. Tug had a hose trained on one window while the O'Days and the

Japanese tourists threw buckets of water on the other. Within minutes, both fires were reduced to smoldering ashes.

Maggie leaned over, placing her hands on her knees as she gulped in fresh air. Ninette and Gran' rushed to her side, each woman taking a turn to hug her. "Here, drink this," her mother said, offering a bottle of water that Maggie gratefully chugged down.

"Y'all saved me," Maggie said to the group, coughing between words. "Thank you, thank you. Arigato."

"Arigato is right," Tug said, spraying water on the fires' embers. "Lucky for us Marco's group was out for a morning power walk. I now know the Japanese word for 'fire!'"

"I told everyone you were in there, and you've never seen people move so fast," Gran' said. She placed her hands on her heart. "Mercy, what a scare. It's going to take a morning gin fizz to snap my nerves back in place."

"You and me both," Marco said.

"I'll make a pitcher," Gran's said. "Guests, *venez avec moi*." She started back to the manor house with the O'Days, Marco, and his tour group close behind her. Maggie heard the whine of fire engines. A tanker truck from the Pelican Volunteer Fire Department mowed down foliage as it carved a path through the brush to the studio. Behind it was a police car. Chret Bertrand and Little Earlie Waddell, both dressed in firefighting gear, jumped off the fire truck as Cal Vichet and Bo leapt out of the squad car. All four men ran toward Maggie's studio. Chret, Earlie, and Cal slowed down when they saw the fire was out, but Bo continued on to Maggie.

"Are you okay?" he asked. She nodded. He wrapped her in a hug and then released her. "What the hell happened?"

"No idea. I was getting ready to paint, and then the fire broke out. I couldn't open either door. I couldn't get out."

"That's because someone didn't want you to," Cal, who had joined them, said. He motioned to Bo and Maggie to follow him, which they did. Cal stopped at the studio's front door and pointed at the bent door handle. "This was messed with until it was broken. Same with the back door."

"Someone tried to kill me," Maggie said. She spoke slowly, unable to believe what she was saying.

"This is a crime scene now." Bo's tone was terse.

Cal gave a grim nod and then headed to the patrol car to fetch police tape.

Bo took Maggie's hand and led her to where Chret and Earlie were training water on the fire's embers. "Lucky we had fog this morning," Chret said. "There was enough dampness in the air to prevent this from turning into an inferno."

Little Earlie's attention was focused on Cal, who was wrapping yellow police tape around the studio. "What's going on?" the *Penny Clipper* editor asked.

"Nothing that you're gonna be writing about," Bo said.

"So it wasn't an accident." Little Earlie pondered this thought. "Well . . . maybe I should write about it. Not the details, but say that due to suspicious activity, Maggie is being guarded twenty-four-seven. Whether it's true or not, at least it might make whoever's trying to take her out think twice about it."

"It's not a bad idea, Bo," Maggie said.

Bo hesitated. "All right. But you better stick to that 'no details' promise, or the next thing on fire will be your printing plant. Meanwhile, you and Chret gather some ash and dirt samples. I want to test them and see if an accelerant was used."

"Yes, sir. I'll see you later at Doucet, Maggie."

"Not today. I think I've earned the right to call in sick."

"Ha," Earlie said. "Are you breathing? Are you walking? Then good luck with Tannis."

*

Earlie's skepticism was well founded. "Sorry, but no can do," was Tannis's instant response to Maggie's request. "It's too difficult to replace you on short notice."

"I'm sorry for inconveniencing you, but being the victim of an attempted murder can be a bit traumatizing."

Maggie's sarcasm was wasted on her boss. "Are you injured?" Tannis asked.

"No, but—"

"If you can get to the phone, you can get to work."

Maggie gave up. "Fine," she said with a sigh. "I'll be there."

"There's that can-Doucet spirit! Your first tour is at ten. I'll see you at nine thirty."

On the drive to work, Maggie brooded about which of the many suspects in the case of Steve Harmon's murder might be ruthless enough to incinerate her. She had no trouble fingering anyone in the Harmon-Charbonnet clan, as well as nonfamily member Bea Boxler. But now that she'd gotten to know the O'Days and Sandy Sechrest better, it was harder for Maggie to picture them as would-be assassins, especially since the O'Days had helped save her life. Tannis, however, was another story. Maggie could see the obnoxious general manager doing whatever it took to rid herself of an amateur sleuth with a pretty decent track record of catching killers. *Or maybe I want it to be Tannis so I can be rid of* her, Maggie had to admit to herself.

Fortunately for the Doucet guides, local officials, fearing the site of Harmon's death would become a ghoulish tourist attraction, deemed the parlor off limits. Since Tannis had no time to adjust her scripts to this new development, the guides happily returned to their original tour spiels. Between curiosity seekers, vacationers, and families enjoying the holiday break, Maggie's tours were packed, and the day flew by. She bid her last group good-bye at five o'clock. As soon as they were out of sight, she made a furtive beeline to the parlor.

Maggie glanced around the room. She hadn't been inside since Harmon was killed, and while his grisly death lent it a creepy vibe, nothing else seemed amiss. Her gaze landed on a portrait above the room's pink marble fireplace. Her great-great-great-grandmother, Magnolia Marie Doucet, stood next to her second husband, Jeremiah, a Union general that she had married after the Civil War amid great scandal. Two adolescent boys stood in front of the couple. The older of the two, Denis Doucet Junior—known as "TiDenis"—radiated the intelligence of his late father, who died weeks after the war broke out after a bad fall from a horse. TiDenis's young brother, Georges, who was rumored to be slow, had a dull look in his eyes, which stared past the portrait art-ist. Jeremiah's hands rested protectively on his challenged stepson's shoulders, which never failed to move Maggie. She considered the parlor a shrine to her ancestors and hated that it would forever be marred by Harmon's murder.

"I'm so sorry," she said out loud to the portrait. It occurred to her that Magnolia Marie and her family were the only witnesses to his death. "If only you could talk," Maggie murmured, focusing on Magnolia Marie's eyes, which were hazel like her own.

Suddenly, for a split second, her ancestor's eyes seemed to come to life. Maggie froze. And then, just as quickly, the sensation was gone.

Maggie shuddered. *I'm starting to lose it*, she thought.

She took one last look around the room and exited, mak-ing sure to lock the door before heading to her car. As she drove home, she began to relax. Still, Maggie couldn't shake the feeling that the parlor—and possibly even the Doucet family portrait—held an important clue that might pinpoint a killer.

Chapter Nineteen

As soon as Maggie got home, she was set upon by her basset, Gopher, and Jolie, the mother of the pups the Crozats were fostering. The pooches jostled each other in their efforts to lick and nuzzle her. "You really know when a human needs some love, don't you?" she said, taking turns massaging the pups' ears. "How about a walk?" At the sound of their favorite word, both dogs barked and leaped into the air.

Maggie retrieved their leashes from the shotgun cottage and led them down the dirt path to her studio. The trio reached the old schoolhouse-turned-art studio, and Maggie circled it, evaluating the damage. The windows, broken and charred, would have to be replaced, as well as the burnt wood frames surrounding them. The one-room interior bore the scars of the fire that Maggie had managed to put out before it turned into a conflagration. The acrid smell of smoke still clung to the air and stung her nostrils.

Maggie's eyes watered, as much from the realization that her refuge was temporarily gone as from the fire residue. She mourned the works-in-progress that had been damaged beyond repair by smoke and water and wondered how she'd come up with the money to replace ruined supplies. Tug had contacted local contractors, searching for someone who could rebuild the studio as soon as possible, but all were either taking the holidays off or building a bonfire. "I promise we'll fix it up better than new," he'd told Maggie when he called with a progress report, "but I won't even be able to get an estimate until the New Year."

She heard leaves crunch under footsteps and tensed. Gopher and Jolie assumed alert positions. When Bo emerged from the brush, the basset hound and mutt barked joyous greetings. "I saw your car, but you weren't at either house, so I thought you might be here," he said. She bit her lip and nodded. Bo came to Maggie and held her in his arms while she allowed herself a good cry. "Thanks," she said after a few minutes. "I needed that."

Bo used his thumb to wipe away the tear stains under her eyes. "Let's go back to the shotgun cottage. It stinks here."

Maggie scrunched up her nose. "I know, right?"

The two strolled back toward the plantation's main grounds, stopping to let the dogs sniff and out-pee each other. "I need to tell you something," Bo said. He paused and watched Jolie tussle with a pinecone as if it were an enemy rodent and then continued. "I saw you at the bar with Chris."

Maggie stopped walking and put her hand on Bo's arm. "Bo, that was nothing. Chris was pushing me to meet, so I forced myself to see him and shoot down any fantasy he had about us getting back together."

"Good. But, Maggie . . . if you need to go back to New York, I would never stop you. I'd miss you like crazy. But I wouldn't hold you back. Frankly, you might be safer there."

"Spoken by someone who's never ridden the subway at four in the morning."

"I'm serious."

"I know. You're the kindest and the most generous boyfriend ever. And you don't have to worry. I'm not going anywhere right now."

"You said 'right now.' Not 'never.'"

"I did, didn't I?" Maggie pondered her slip. "I feel zero pull back to Chris. Less than zero. But his being here reminds me of my life in the city. And sometimes I do feel a pull back to that. A small one. I'd be lying if I didn't admit that."

"I get it. Thank you for being honest." Bo leaned down and kissed Maggie, his lips lingering on hers.

"And that," Maggie said when they finally separated, "is a very good reason to never, ever leave Pelican."

*

Bo walked Maggie and the pooches back to the cottage and, after a few more swoon-inducing kisses, left to pick up Xander. Maggie was daydreaming about the romantic interlude when her cell rang. She pulled the phone out of her jeans pocket and saw the caller was Vanessa. "Hey, Nessa, what's up?"

"You gotta come over right away—the dead guy's wife is here, and she's all into your paintings, the ones Lia's been trying to help you sell." The words tumbled out of an excited Vanessa.

"On my way."

Maggie made it to Bon Bon in five minutes. Vanessa subtly pointed to Emme Charbonnet, who was studying a painting that depicted Bayou Beurre making its lazy way behind Crozat Plantation. It was one of Maggie's favorites. She was relieved at least some of her artwork had been safely ensconced at Bon Bon, thus avoiding damage from her studio fire.

She approached Steve Harmon's widow. "Hi, Emme." Maggie kept her greeting simple and generic. No sense referencing the family debacle she had witnessed at their Belle Vista encounter.

Emme turned around and smiled. "Hello. I hear these are your paintings. I love them."

"Thank you. That means a lot to me."

"Your style is fascinating. Realistic, but with a slight undercurrent of the surreal. And the occasional surprise if you look at a painting very closely. Like how there's the silhouette of a man hidden in this one." Emme pointed to a painting where Maggie had indeed sneaked in Bo's silhouette.

Maggie was about to respond when Vanessa, who had joined them, jumped in. "That's our Maggie; she's full of surprises." She took a closer look at the painting. "And I'm afraid I got a bad surprise for you, ma'am. This painting is mismarked. There's a zero missing."

Maggie clapped a hand over her mouth to suppress a gasp. "What are you doing?!" she mimed to Vanessa behind Emme's back. Nessa ignored her. "The store owner's expecting, so I'm sure it's one of those mistakes due to pregnancy brain," Nessa said.

"It wasn't a mistake, Emme," Maggie said. "Vanessa doesn't know; she's only been working here a day." *And may not survive to work a second one.*

Emme pondered the painting. "No, I think she's right. Your work does seem underpriced."

Maggie's jaw dropped. Before she could say a word, Vanessa once again jumped in. "Poor Lia. She's expecting triplets and had complications. She had to be put on bed rest."

"That must be hard on her," Emme responded. "You know what? I'll take both these paintings at the adjusted price. And since I'm not paying an art adviser's commission, I'd like to add the amount of it to the sale as a baby gift to the owner."

"Well, isn't that the most generous thing." Vanessa flashed Maggie a triumphant grin. "I'll wrap them for you. Maggie, you mind watching the front of store for me?"

"You sold two of my paintings. I'll do anything for you."

The three women laughed, and Vanessa disappeared into the workroom with the paintings, leaving Maggie and Emme alone. "Thank you so much," Maggie said.

"No thanks necessary. I'm thrilled to support a talented local artist. Unlike my late husband, I don't need an 'expert' to tell me what I like."

"Good for you," Maggie said. But she wondered if Chris had any idea that his days on the Charbonnet-Harmon payroll were numbered.

Vanessa returned with the paintings and finished the sale. Emme's phone pinged, and she checked it. "That's Dan. He's outside. I had him drop me in town so he could go back to Belle Vista and talk to his son. He never stops trying to make that relationship work."

"I hope it went well," Maggie said.

"I doubt it," Emme responded with a wry smile. She took her paintings, nodded to both women, and left the store.

As soon as they were sure Emme was gone, Maggie and Vanessa shared a gleeful hug. "Nessa, you're the one who deserves commission," Maggie said. "And I owe you a big old apology for doubting you."

"That's okay. If there's one thing I've learned from hanging out with Quentin's richy rich friends, it's that the more expensive a thing is, the more valuable they think it is."

"I'm going to celebrate the sale with a class at DanceBod. How about you close up the shop and come with me? It's quitting time, anyway."

Vanessa, who had yet to shed much baby weight from her already zaftig figure, was skeptical. "Thanks, but since Ru's got the baby, Quentie's taking me out to dinner. Besides, who celebrates with exercise? That's more like punishing yourself." She popped a dark chocolate caramel in her mouth for emphasis.

"All right, but I'm going to find another way to thank you."

"Your friendship is thanks enough, Maggie. And I feel like we *are* friends now."

"We are, Nessa," said Maggie, whose past relationship with her ex-coworker had been contentious. "We definitely are."

After picking out a few chocolates to bring home to her parents and Gran', Maggie walked over to DanceBod. When she entered the dance studio, she found Sandy setting up for the next class. "You missed LatinBod," the instructor said.

"That wasn't an accident. I'm terrible at Latin dance. I look like I'm elbowing people out of the way at a Black Friday sale."

"Well, I think you'll like BalletBod. It's geared more toward toning than dancing."

"Perfect."

"I'm glad you came by. I wanted to talk to you." Sandy glanced around the room and then moved closer to Maggie. "That officer, Ru Durand, told me he knew about my past relationship with Steve Harmon. But he said he'd keep it between us for as long as he can."

"Really?" *Good call, Bo. You know your cousin Rufus.*

"I'd heard some bad things about him, but I think he's really nice."

"Sometimes people change," was Maggie's diplomatic answer. But she had to admit that in Ru's case, this seemed true.

The studio door opened, and half a dozen people came in. Among them was Bea Boxler. Maggie and Bea exchanged smiles of acknowledgment, and Maggie saw an opportunity to maneuver Belle Vista's manager into a situation where she might reveal a little more about the complicated life of her late boss. "Are you busy after class?" she asked. "If not, do you want to go over to Junie's and grab a bite?"

"Yes. I'd like that," Bea said. She then went to the ballet barre and did a few stretches, one of which involved an arabesque that would have been at home in any professional dance company. *Her boarding school education must have included a heavy dose of dance training*, Maggie thought as she did a few desultory stretches herself, including a halfhearted attempt to touch her toes.

The class flew by, and after freshening up, Maggie and Bea walked over to Junie's. JJ, clad in Christmas-green sequins, greeted them both with hugs and insisted on comping their first round of drinks.

"So," Maggie began as they sipped their glasses of Chardonnay, "that scene between Harrison and his dad was disturbing." *Lead with innocuous gossip.*

"Harrison was devoted to Mr. Harmon, who took it upon himself to be a father figure to the boy after his actual father went to jail." Bea ran a finger through the moisture that had collected on the outside of her glass. "Normally an employee of Harrison's caliber wouldn't last very long, but his uncle had his back, as the expression goes."

"That surprises me. From my experience with Mr. Harmon, he was very tough on people. He certainly was on us."

"Mr. Harmon was the kind of man who needed fans more than friends or even family. And Harrison was nothing if not a fan." Bea didn't bother to hide her disdain for the idea. *Wow, she really can't stand Harrison*, Maggie thought.

JJ appeared with two steaming bowls of jambalaya. "Here you go, lovely ladies. If you need them, there are three levels of hot sauce on the table: medium, hot, and sound an alarm because your mouth is on fire!" He winked and walked away.

Bea lifted a small forkful to her lips. "It's delicious. And exactly the right level of spice." She began to eat the jambalaya with a gusto belying her slim frame.

"It's a misconception that Cajun food has to be spicy," Maggie said. "It's supposed to be flavorful, but not superhot. In fact, there are jambalaya cook-offs where contestants are disqualified if their dish is too spicy."

"That would have made Steve happy. He forbade spicy entrées on the menus of any properties where he had a say. He once accidentally bit into a hot pepper on vacation in Puerto Vallarta. I'll never forget the look on his face."

Bea chuckled, and Maggie smiled to indicate an appreciation of the story. But her acute visual sense had picked up a look on Bea's face when she shared it. This was a memory of a shared, special moment. *And Bea called him Steve. Not "Mr. Harmon."* Maggie was more convinced than ever that Bea Boxler had had a clandestine relationship with her late boss. And she was determined to uncover exactly what that relationship was.

Chapter Twenty

Maggie had to put snooping on hold when she received panicked texts from both Nessa and Ione. A swarm of holiday shoppers had descended on Lia's stores, and the women were desperate for help.

Maggie spent the rest of the day and late into the evening running between Bon Bon and Fais Dough Dough, and by the time she returned home, she was bleary-eyed with fatigue. She decided delving into Bea's past could wait until the morning and fell into bed. Sleep came easily—and with it a dream. Magnolia Marie Doucet sat in the front parlor of a post–Civil War Doucet Plantation, embroidering a sampler as her husband tried to teach his stepson, Georges, his sums. General Cabot showed extraordinary patience with the boy, whose temper flared until it exploded. Georges shouted curse words, threw over the table, and stomped out of the room.

"The son is not the father," his mother, her face creased with sadness, said to a woman sitting next to her with a sigh.

The woman was Maggie.

The dream was fresh on Maggie's mind when she woke in the morning. "I've been having weird dreams," she told her grand-mère after pouring a bowl of cereal and sitting down at the shotgun cottage's small café table in the kitchen. "The same person keeps showing up in them: Magnolia Marie Doucet."

"I was wondering when you'd hear from her," Gran' said. She pulled off a small piece of her chocolate muffin. "Eventually most Doucet and even a few of us Crozat women do, because our families are so intertwined."

"Really?" Maggie frowned at her grandmother. "You never thought to mention this before?"

Gran' shrugged. "It's not my business to interfere."

"That's a nice, cryptic answer," Maggie said. "I feel like she's trying to tell me something."

"I've found that she leads more than tells."

"Hmm. Anything else you want to share? So I can maybe be prepared?"

"For what? There's no saying we'd have the same experience. Everyone's journey is their own." Gran' finished the last bite of her muffin and put the plate in the sink. "I'm going for a brisk walk. I need to get my endorphins going if I have to face another day of trying to reach an actual human being at Trippee.com. I'm determined to make them remove those awful reviews. Mr. O'Day tried to delete them but was unsuccessful."

Gran' left, and Maggie pulled out her tablet and typed "Bea Boxler" into a search engine. The first item on the list was the general manager's Belle Vista bio. Bea wasn't lying about her background. She'd been raised in Switzerland and had attended the kind of European boarding school that served as a way station for überwealthy girls marking time until they were old enough to marry men equally moneyed. Bea's rich-working-girl path wasn't completely illogical. Managing luxury hostelries was a good way to meet the elite.

So far the search only confirmed what Maggie already knew. She tried another tack and tapped on "images," hoping it might yield a visual clue. The screen filled with photos of Bea at a variety of ages in the company of a stunning blonde woman. Maggie clicked on an image and read the caption below it. "German supermodel Sayfrid Gerner is in Paris for Fashion Week, along with look-alike daughter, Bea Boxler." *Gerner, Gerner*, she thought. *Why does that name sound so familiar?*

Maggie replaced her search with a new one for "Sayfrid Gerner" and was rewarded with page after page of hits. Sayfrid ticked off all the lifestyle boxes of the supermodels that Maggie read about in tabloids during her visits to the Bayou Beauty Hair Salon: rock star boyfriends, short-lived marriages, and more than one rehab stint. *No wonder poor Bea was shunted off to boarding school*, Maggie mused. *Her mother was a dysfunctional narcissist.* She called up a tabloid headline that screamed, "Supermodel Dies of Overdose!" Sayfrid Gerner's dramatic life had an equally dramatic ending, leaving behind a lonely teenaged daughter. Maggie had a sudden inspiration. What if Bea wasn't Harmon's mistress? What if she was actually his daughter? She perused links to Sayfrid's life and found articles detailing her tumultuous relationship with Tor Boxler, the bass player in a British rock group who was supposedly Bea's father. Maggie wondered if "supposedly" was the operative word.

She continued scrolling through the decades-old images, which included the last known photo of druggy rocker Tor before he plummeted to his death trying to jump into a pool from the roof of a two-story house. She stopped at an old black-and-white shot from the *New York Post*'s page-six gossip column. Sayfrid was emerging from a club with a man. The caption read, "Supermodel Sayfrid Gerner and unidentified companion visit Danceteria." Maggie enlarged the photo to confirm her suspicion: the "unidentified companion" was a much younger Steve Harmon. And suddenly Maggie realized why the name "Gerner" sounded so familiar. She shuffled through a stack of papers on her desk and found an article her friend Lulu had printed out for her. It was the puff piece announcing Belle Vista had been folded into one of Steve Harmon's many companies: the Gerner Group.

Maggie was distracted from her Internet detecting by her mother's appearance at the door. "Sorry to bother you, chère, but it's your turn to man the stand," Ninette said. "I've got baskets of treats all ready for you to sell, including little bags of white chocolate candy cane bark that I decorated with red and green ribbons. I also put together a basket for Lia and Kyle that I want to run over to them."

Maggie put her tablet on sleep mode. "My bad; I lost track of time," she said, giving Ninette a kiss on the cheek. "I'm obsessed with trying to figure out who killed our guest."

"No apologies needed, darlin' daughter," Ninette said. She wrapped an arm round Maggie's waist. "We certainly don't want to be known as the B and B where guests come to an untimely end. We'll either attract no guests or ghouls."

"I think we've come up with this year's Halloween weekend special. 'The Macabre Murders of Crozat Plantation.'"

"Your grand-mère's already got a whole weekend planned around that exact theme."

"No! I was totally kidding."

"Talk to her. I'm not in a position to rule out any idea that might bring in business."

Maggie followed her mother back to the manor house kitchen, where she collected the day's assortment of pastries and treats to sell. She wheeled them over to the levee stand along with a carafe of coffee and set up shop. The bonfires were almost completed, their shapes stark against the backdrop of levee and sky. Maggie gazed across the road to Crozat and noticed a gaudy addition to the plantation's refined holiday decorations. On the roof of the manor house, Santa led a team of glowing red crawfish pulling his sleigh. Instead of toys, Santa's sleigh was filled with a variety of neon-sculptured liquor bottles. Maggie smiled. Saucy Santa making an appearance meant Tug was back to his old self.

A Pelican PD patrol car pulled up to the stand and parked. Rufus and Bo got out. Bo was in uniform; Rufus was not. "Perske still has you on desk duty?" Maggie asked her boyfriend, who gave a tightlipped nod. His cousin slapped him on the back.

"Ain't so bad," Rufus said. "I hear the ladies think there's nothing like a man in uniform. Right, Magnolia?" He once again raised his eyebrows up and down like a vaudeville comedian, and Bo punched him in the arm, which led to a good-natured tussle.

"If you kids are done, I have some interesting information," Maggie said.

"I'm listening," Bo said, and he released Rufus from a headlock.

"Bea Boxler wasn't just Steve Harmon's employee. They shared a past." Maggie detailed what she had uncovered. "I thought they might have had an affair, but now I think there's a chance that she's his daughter. She was born around the time he was beginning his career, which was built on seducing investors into entrusting him with their fortunes. You can see how he'd want to cover up an indiscretion that resulted in an illegitimate child."

"Nice work. She's on the list." Rufus helped himself to a muffin. "Let's recap our suspects. We got this Bea chick. Then there's the Charbonnet-Harmon clan, which would be Emme, the dead guy's widow, and his brother-in-law, Philip. There's that Tannis chick and your guests, the O'Days."

"I notice Sandy's not on the list," Maggie pointed out.

"I got a feeling about her. Like you do with this doof." He poked Bo, who grabbed his arm and held it behind his back. "Ow! Uncle."

Bo laughed and released him. Then he grew serious. "You did leave out one name. Chris Harper."

"Maggie's ex?" Ru said. "Interesting. Why do you think he'd kill his employer?"

"You've got a feeling about Sandy? I've got one about that guy. A bad one. And it doesn't have anything to do with him being your ex, Maggie."

She wasn't sure about that but chose not to voice her doubts. "I'm not defending him because he's my ex," Maggie said, "but the feeling I get is that Chris desperately needs this job, so I can't imagine he'd kill Harmon. Especially since the job has a clock on it now that his patron is gone." She told the men about her exchange with Emme at Bon Bon and the woman's dismissive attitude toward the art adviser. "So if there's anyone who wanted Steve Harmon alive, it's Chris."

"Ooo, your girlfriend's making excuses for her ex, cuz." Ru poked Bo again and then jumped out of the way. "I'd be worried."

"I'm not."

"And you shouldn't be." But seeing a hint of worry in her boyfriend's eyes, Maggie grabbed Bo and kissed him hard to prove her point.

Ru gave a wolf whistle. "You know, the Belle Vista bonfire's big enough to fit two if y'all wanna get busy. Just make sure you finish before they torch the thing."

Bo reluctantly separated from Maggie. "We gotta get to the station. I'll call you later. Ru'll check into Bea Boxler's history with Harmon. I don't have to tell you not to mention this to anyone."

"You sure don't." Maggie had learned through experience that there was no one more dangerous than a killer driven to hide a crime.

Bo and Rufus took off, and Maggie poured herself a cup of coffee. Morning fog, so common to winter in south Louisiana, lay low over the river. The chill it usually brought was tempered by unseasonably warm temperatures, so Maggie shed her hoodie. A nondescript sedan sporting magnets that advertised Belle Vista pulled up to the stand, and Harrison got out. He was dressed in a suit but looked tired and slightly disheveled. Mud stained the bottom of his pants. Maggie poured a cup of coffee and handed it to him. "Hey, there. I'm guessing you need this. It's on the house."

"I do. Thanks." Harrison took a few swigs of the coffee. "I was at my uncle's funeral this morning. I didn't want to stick around for the stupid socializing part." Harrison took another gulp of coffee. He picked up a coconut pecan bar, and Maggie waved away his money. "I'm sorry for how I behaved at BV. It's just that . . . my father spent four years in jail when I was in high school. Great ammunition for bullies." He gave a mirthless laugh. "My mom divorced him and moved to California with my brother and sister. Uncle Steve said I could stay with him and Aunt Emme, so I did. He's, like, my *real* father. *Was* like. I keep forgetting and doing that."

"It's natural." There was silence as Maggie debated what direction to take with the conversation. "I get that your father very much wants a relationship with you, Harrison. And I did read somewhere he wasn't really guilty. He went to jail to protect other people. Like your uncle."

"Yeah, right," Harrison scoffed. "That's total BS his lawyer made up to try to get him off. It didn't work. Uncle Steve was amazing. He taught me the business. He was grooming me to take it over someday. I wanted to change my last name to Harmon, but Aunt Emme thought it would be, I don't know, weird. So I took my mom's name. Anyone but my father's." He practically spit the last sentence.

"I hate to speak ill of the dead." *But I'm going to, so good luck to me*, Maggie thought to herself. "Harrison, your uncle was hardly perfect. Even we had some issues with him." *To put it so very mildly.*

"Oh, he was a psychopath." The young man's tone was almost blithe. "But so's half of Wall Street. I worked for Uncle Steve's hedge fund company until he wanted me down here at BV, and I saw it for myself with those guys. They say you find the most psychopaths in two places: jail and the Street."

Maggie had run into enough wizards of Wall Street during her years in New York to know that what Harrison said was probably true. She decided to steer the conversation in another direction. "Was Bea at the funeral? I mean, she must have been, considering he was her boss."

Harrison stiffened. He unwrapped his pecan bar but stared at it instead of taking a bite. Maggie sensed it was a way of avoiding eye contact with her. "Yeah. She was there."

"Is it me," Maggie said, affecting the gossipy tone she used when she was digging for information, "or did she not like your uncle very much?"

This got Harrison to look up from his pastry. "I think she hated him." Harrison spoke in a whisper, although the two-lane road was empty and the hum of ships on the river prevented any sound from traveling to the top of the levee, where a few locals continued to work on their bonfires. "And not the 'I hate my boss' kind of hate. There was something else going on. Something superdark." Harrison paused. He looked young and vulnerable. "Sometimes it scared me."

Despite the warm air, Maggie got a chill. She feared for Harrison . . . and for the Charbonnets as well, if Bea had some kind of vendetta against the family.

Maggie's phone pinged a text. "Sorry, I'll be quick," she said and took out her phone to read a message from Gaynell: "Get to DanceBod. King Cake kidnapped. Might be by murderer."

Chapter
Twenty-One

Maggie explained the situation to Harrison, who wished her luck finding the dog and left with three more coconut pecan bars. She called her mother, and Ninette took over the stand so Maggie could get to DanceBod as fast as possible.

All the regulars were at the studio, including Ione and Gaynell. Rufus held the sobbing Sandy in his arms, and for a brief minute, Maggie wondered if the police officer had set the whole thing up as a way to worm himself into the dance instructor's heart. She dismissed the thought, reminding herself that Rufus had changed. "They found a note that the kidnapper left," Gaynell told Maggie.

"It was nasty," Ione said. "It said something like, 'Your dog's alive, but you have to find him. Consider this a warning to stop spreading stories about Steve Harmon.'"

"Any clues about where King Cake might be?"

Both women shook their heads. "We've looked all over town," Gaynell said. "Nuthin'. I feel terrible for Sandy. She's so attached to him."

"She tried to keep the story quiet," Maggie said. "One of the dancers from Classy Lady must have heard about Harmon's death and started blabbing about what happened between him and Sandy."

"I heard about it when I was getting my hair cut," Gaynell shared.

"And people were gossiping about it in the checkout line at the grocery," Ione said. "There are no secrets in a small town."

"This is bad," Gaynell fretted. "With it being winter, if that pup stays out too long, he could succumb to the elements."

Rufus whistled to get everyone's attention. "Okay, folks, Chief Perske refused to make this a high-priority case, so we're on our own. I've got a squad car, so at least I can look for the little guy as part of my rounds. I'm gonna divide the area into four quadrants and split y'all up between them. I'm assigning a group leader to each quadrant, and we'll communicate by text."

Maggie, Gaynell, and Ione volunteered to be group leaders, and Rufus assigned each a quadrant. "Maggie, you take Doucet," he said. "There might be some connection to it in the kidnapper's mind since that's where Harmon was offed."

"Smart thinking, Ru."

"I'll come with you," Sandy said. Her eyes were puffy, and her face red from crying. Maggie felt for the dancer. She could tell King Cake was more than a pet. His unconditional love helped heal the emotional wounds created by Sandy's dark former career. Maggie thought of the animal brood that the Crozats tended to. She couldn't imagine losing one of them, especially her beloved basset hound, Gopher.

She had a sudden brainstorm.

"Gopher," she exclaimed. "He's a scent hound. Sandy, get me anything that would have King Cake's scent on it, like a blanket or a chew toy."

Sandy darted to her office and returned with a worn blanket and stuffed alligator. "He wraps himself with the blanket when he's cold and sleeps with his head on the alligator. It's his baby."

Sandy burst into tears and buried herself in Ru's arms again. "I swear," he said with clenched teeth, "when I find whoever did this . . ." He didn't have to finish his sentence. The look on Rufus Durand's face was enough to make the group actually fear for the fate of the dognapper once the officer got his hands on him—or her.

*

"How could anyone do something so cruel?" Sandy asked plaintively as Maggie drove them to Crozat so she could retrieve Gopher. "It's a rhetorical question. I don't think there's a real answer. I just don't understand it."

"Because you're a good person," Maggie responded. "Some people aren't. Sometimes they're born wrong. Sometimes they're too damaged to make the right choice." She pulled into the long driveway lined by oaks leading to the front of the manor house. Maggie had called ahead to Tug, who was waiting for them on the veranda with Gopher on a leash. He brought the dog to them, and Gopher eagerly leaped into the car, planting himself between the two women. "If there's sniffing to be done, Gopher's the dog to do it," he said. "He'll track down your boy."

"Thank you, sir." Sandy erupted into more tears. Gopher gave a deep, consoling bark and licked her cheek. She hugged the hound and kept her arms around him as Maggie took off for their mission.

By the time Maggie, Sandy, and Gopher reached Doucet, a group of volunteers was waiting for them. The plantation had yet to open for the day, so the search party was able to spread out over the plantation's grounds without fear of disturbing visitors. Maggie bent down in front of Gopher and held King Cake's blanket and toy under his nose. "You can do it, boy, I know you can."

Gopher barked as if in agreement and then began walking, nose to the ground. Maggie gave his leash a lot of slack, allowing him more freedom to follow the scent. He led her into the woods behind the manor house toward the ruins of the plantation's sugar mill. Gopher picked up his pace, and the two began jogging through the thick overgrowth, Maggie trying to dodge low-hanging branches as they went. She was only semisuccessful, and after a few minutes, her arms were covered with scratches.

She was beginning to feel like she was on a fool's errand when she heard a faint bark. "Gopher, wait," she said and gently tugged on his leash. They came to a halt, and for a moment, the only sound was Gopher's panting. And then the faint barking began again, this time with urgency. Gopher barked back and shot off toward the sugar mill ruins, dragging Maggie with him. They jumped over shattered bricks from the mill's broken walls. And there, resting haphazardly on a dirt mound, was King Cake in a crate. Maggie texted Sandy two triumphant words: "Found him!"

Sandy's reunion with her cherished pooch was euphoric, her joy seconded by Rufus and the search parties that reconvened on Doucet's front lawn. "I can't thank y'all enough," she told everyone. "And Gopher most of all. He's a hero. I'm buying him steak for the rest of his days."

"Not necessary," Maggie said with a laugh. "Much as he'd love that, it would probably shorten his life pretty fast."

"Well, at least one mystery around here is solved, after a fashion," Rufus said.

Sandy took his hand. "If it weren't for you, it might not have been. Thank you for caring."

"It's my job. And then some." Rufus gave Sandy a sly smile, and she blushed. Then he grew serious. "I still want to nail the SOB who did this. Whoever it is has a date with my chokehold."

Despite the morning's drama, Maggie had enough time to go home and shower before returning to Doucet for work. She parked and trudged back to the cottage. Her heart stopped when she saw Gran' slumped over her tablet keyboard. She rushed to her, but before she got there, the octogenarian popped her head up. "It's just form e-mail after form response from Trippee," Gran' moaned. "I survived

Katrina and the second Great Depression. I survived laying your grandfather, the love of my life, to rest. But if this madness continues, Magnolia, I swear Trippee.com will be the death of me. Anyway, enough about that evil website. Did you find that poor girl's doggy?"

"Yes, they've been reunited, and he seems fine."

"Who would do such a terrible thing?"

"Sandy asked that exact question. And I don't have an answer. It might be someone who genuinely liked Harmon, which is a pretty small pool of suspects. Besides Dan Levy, Tannis and Harrison are the only two I can think of. I don't know if Tannis has an alibi, but Harrison was at his uncle's funeral. Or . . . it could be Steve's murderer trying to throw the investigation off course."

"Well, much as I'd love to theorize with you, I'd best return to the miserable task at hand."

Gran' whimpered and turned back to the computer. Maggie gave her grandmother's shoulders a light massage. "I think you need a break from that stupid site. Before I was distracted by the King Cake debacle, I found out Bea Boxler's mother was a supermodel who once dated Steve Harmon. Would you do me a favor and see if you can find out anything else about their relationship?"

Gran' instantly perked up. "Yes, ma'am."

As Maggie got ready, she heard the computer-simulated clacking of typewriter keys coming from Gran's tablet and smiled to herself. She'd managed to both distract her grand-mère and use the older woman's love of the Internet to her advantage. Maggie finished applying her makeup and picked up her cell. She had one phone call to make. She dialed the number for Belle Vista and asked to be transferred to Harrison, who didn't bother to hide his surprise at hearing from her. "It's about our conversation this morning," she told him. "I know this is none of my business, but I think you should leave Belle Vista. Take a sick day or a vacation day. After what you've been through, I'm sure no one will wonder why. I've got a very weird feeling that won't go away."

"Thanks," Harrison said, "but I'd be letting my uncle down if I bailed. I owe it to him to stay here and do my job."

Still worried, she told Harrison to keep her posted and ended the call. Maggie's instincts were telling her that something was very wrong in the Harmon-Charbonnet universe. Since these instincts had helped catch killers and once saved her grand-mère from a murderous psychopath, she'd learned to trust them. But Harrison had sidelined her, and it was time to get to work.

As soon as Maggie arrived at Doucet, Gaynell pulled her aside. "As if today hasn't already been crazy enough, you would not believe what Tannis is doing," she hissed, furious. "Since her Doucet sugar daddy's gone, she's parading other rich people through here to see if they might take his place."

Little Earlie, who was loitering nearby, sidled up to the women. "What's up?"

"It seems Tannis wants to sell Doucet to the highest bidder," said Maggie, who was even angrier about the situation than Gaynell, "which was not my family's intention when we donated it to the state. My greats wanted to preserve its history and share its past, good and bad, with the public."

"I gotta say, selling isn't the worst idea in the world," Little Earlie said. "Rich people got the money to pour into an old place like this."

"Until it's not making money and they unload it," Maggie said. "Or if it stays nonprofit, but they don't need a tax deduction anymore."

Gaynell poked Maggie in the ribs to silence her. Tannis, back to her immaculately dressed business self, marched toward them. "You're not being paid to stand around having girl talk," she snapped. "Little Earlie excepted, natch." She graced him with a flirty smile, which he returned. Then Tannis continued to march on, her balance occasionally thrown off when one of her stiletto heels bumped up against a pebble on the decomposed granite path.

As soon as Tannis was out of earshot, an irritated Maggie turned to Earlie. "Every time I start to like you, you do something like hook up with that pain in the pricey do-me pumps," she told the *Penny Clipper* publisher and editor.

Little Earlie pulled himself to his full height, which almost put him at eyeline with the five-foot-four Maggie. "My personal life is none of your busybody business. Now if you'll excuse me, I have tours to lead, as do you." Earlie turned and marched off after Tannis.

"Maybe I should take an auto repair class and help Chret out at the garage," Gaynell muttered. "It'd beat this place these days." She slumped off to meet her tour group, and after releasing a deep sigh, Maggie followed her friend.

*

Maggie finished her last tour and was changing out of her costume when Gran' called. "I thought you'd want the results of my research project. It seems Mr. Harmon and Sayfrid Gerner didn't begin their affair until *after* Bea was born. I've checked a myriad of sites, and all mention approximately the same year."

"Oh," Maggie said, disappointed her instincts hadn't come through for her. "That rules out the Harmon-is-Bea's-father angle."

"I'm afraid so. But I did make an interesting discovery in a piece from a German magazine, thanks to one of those marvelous free translation sites. According to the article, Sayfrid didn't die of an accidental overdose. She committed suicide because she was despondent over the end of a relationship—with a married man."

Maggie contemplated this new twist. "So Bea was orphaned as a teenager, and years later she takes a job with the man who may have driven her mother to take her own life."

"That does not strike me as a coincidence."

"Me neither. Great work, Gran'. Thank you."

"You're welcome. And now, God help me, it's back to Trippee."

Maggie had a sudden flash of an idea. "Wait, Gran', can you make a note of the exact day Bea's mother died?"

"Will do, chère. Oh, and I spoke to our darling Lia. She's feeling much better, which is a great relief to all of us. Triplets. Isn't that something?"

Gran' chuckled as she signed off. Maggie dialed the Pelican police headquarters, and Cal Vichet answered the call.

"They're not here," he responded after Maggie asked for Bo or Rufus. "They were called to an accident at the river curve." The curve was a stretch of river road notorious for wrecks.

"I don't want to bother them on the job. Can you have either one call me as soon as they get back to the station?"

"Sure, but it may be a while. It looks like the kid from Belle Vista, the one whose uncle was murdered, got run off the road."

Chapter Twenty-Two

Maggie got to the hospital as fast as she could. She found Bo and Rufus drinking sodas in the waiting room. "Cal told me what happened," she said. "How's Harrison?"

"Bruised and shaken up," Bo said.

"Would it be okay if I talked to him?"

"Doctor didn't have a problem with us talking to him, so I don't see why you can't," Rufus said. "Go for it."

Maggie followed Bo's instructions to Harrison's room on the hospital's first floor and peeked inside. "Harrison?" she said softly.

"Hey," he responded in a weak voice. "Come on in."

Maggie stepped into the room. She was relieved to see his injuries appeared superficial. He had a large bruise under his left eye and a butterfly bandage adhered to his forehead. There were a few other contusions and scratches on his arms but no casts anywhere. He had dodged broken bones. "I wanted to check on you," she told him. "How do you feel?"

"Like I was hit by a car." Harrison gave a small laugh. "Which I wasn't. I was forced off the road by one into the gully below the levee. I'm lucky my car didn't flip over. I'd be dead meat."

"Did you see anything that could help identify the other car?"

"Nope. Like I told the cops, it came out of nowhere. That curve's a big blind spot."

"It really is. Does your family know what happened?"

"Yeah, the cops called my father. He wanted to come get me tomorrow when they let me out of here, but that ain't happening. I'm getting a rental car."

"Are you sure? I think it—"

Harrison held up his hand. "Sorry, ma'am, but I don't care what you think. Please stop trying to push me into some stupid 'and they all lived happily ever after' thing with my father. It's really none of your business."

"Ouch. That's the second time someone's told me that today."

"Well, maybe you should listen to people. You're kind of a pain in the butt. But," Harrison backtracked, "a nice one."

Maggie laughed. "Thank you. 'Kind of.' I won't bother you again. Feel free to bother *me* if you need to."

"Got it."

Maggie left Harrison and went down the hallway to the nurse's station. She had one other visit to make. She asked the nurse on duty to look up a room number for her, then took the elevator up one floor and found room 213. Lia, looking bored, lay in bed flipping through a magazine. Maggie cleared her throat, and Lia looked up. She instantly brightened. "Mags!" she said and threw her arms wide open.

Maggie went to her, and the women hugged. "I needed this," Maggie said. She mimed weeping. "I just got called 'ma'am.'"

"Oh, no," Lia said, patting her cousin sympathetically on the back. "Nothing hurts like the first time you go from 'miss' to 'ma'am.'"

"When are they releasing you from the hospital?"

"In a day or two. And then I have to take it real easy. Mostly bed rest. A couple of hours where I can do simple stuff, but that's it. Triplets, Maggie. Can you believe that?"

"No, I cannot. We'll all help out. Mama's already cooked up enough food to practically take you through the holidays. And Nessa's doing a great job minding Bon Bon."

"Too good," Lia joked. "Kyle's so impressed by her sales figures, I'm not sure he'll want me back at the store."

Maggie laughed. Then she grew sober. "I worry about you." She pointed to her cousin's stomach. "And them."

"Don't. We'll be fine." She hesitated for a moment. "Mags . . . before all this happened"—Lia waved her hands over her torso—"Chris came into the store to buy candy. He took a phone call, and it sounded like he was talking about money he owed, a loan or something. He kept saying that he'd pay it off in a couple of weeks and he'd never sell the loft. I thought you should know in case you still share anything with him."

"Thanks, sweetie," Maggie said. "I appreciate you looking out for me. But I cut that cord completely. The only thing I share with Chris is memories. Some good, some not so good."

"That's a relief. He sounded panicked."

"What's going on with Chris is his to manage. I'm passed done. Anyway, enough about him. We need to talk about your baby shower."

"Well," Lia said, "I was thinking maybe an LSU theme." The two women burst out laughing. They had endured an LSU-themed wedding-that-wasn't when Vanessa left Rufus at the altar.

The women chatted a little longer, then sensing Lia was growing tired, Maggie kissed her cousin on the cheek and said good night. She took the escalator down to the ER waiting room. Bo and Rufus were no longer there, but she caught up to them in the parking lot and relayed what Lia had told her about Chris's telephone conversation.

"We know," Rufus said.

"You do?"

"Don't sound so surprised. We may not have your famous 'instincts,' but we *are* professionally trained law enforcement officials."

"Yes. My bad."

"We didn't tell you—" Bo began.

"—because you know too much already," Rufus cut in.

Bo glared at him. "You mind? Anyway, that's part of it. The other part is . . . we weren't sure you were completely estranged from Chris."

"He is a definite person of interest," Rufus said. "Feel free to mention that to him, by the way. Nervous criminals make mistakes, which makes our job way easier."

The two men got into Bo's patrol car and took off. Maggie stood in the parking lot for a minute, trying to sort through her feelings. She was hurt but couldn't be angry at Bo for not trusting her. It was time to face the truth. She'd felt sick to her stomach when Lia revealed the conversation she overheard. Whether this was caused by a dormant affection for Chris or for the beloved loft they had once shared didn't matter. Despite what she said to Lia, the cord connecting her and Chris may have been frayed and down to its last thread, but it wasn't cut completely.

Maggie's phone pinged a text from Gaynell. It read, "DanceBod?"

She texted back, "Yes!!!! Will do anything to get out of my head!! Even LatinBod!!"

*

Since the class on the schedule was BollyBod, Maggie's fellow dancers were spared her clumsy samba steps. Sandy followed through with her warning that the routines would be high-impact cardio, and when the class was done, Maggie and Gaynell collapsed on benches, panting.

"I bet those routines got you out of your head," Gaynell said between pants.

"My only thought was, 'If I have an undisclosed heart condition, this is the class that'll activate it,'" Maggie replied.

She held up the towel that she'd used to wipe sweat off her face. "This is wet enough to wring out."

Whitney, Bo's ex, approached them. She'd also taken the class, but in typical Whitney fashion, looked as fresh post-workout as when she'd walked into the studio. "That was a nice little session," she said, popping a mint into her mouth.

"Little?!" Gaynell and Maggie chorused. "How are you not a puddle?" Maggie added.

"I was a cheerleader in college. We trained ourselves not to perspire. Makes your makeup run." Whitney took a seat next to Maggie. "I was so sorry to hear about your art studio fire."

"Thanks. I miss teaching Xander. As soon as I find a temporary space, you'll be the first person I call."

"Wonderful. Ooo, you just reminded me. Xander finished a painting. I want to show it to you. It's in the car. I'll go get it."

"I'll walk out with you," Gaynell said. Whitney popped up and jogged out the door. Gaynell rolled her eyes and mouthed, "How does she do it?" to Maggie. Then she followed after Whitney.

Sandy appeared in front of Maggie. "Did I hear you need studio space?" Maggie nodded. "Follow me."

Maggie did as instructed, following Sandy down a narrow hall that opened onto a back alley. A small addition jutted out from the DanceBod building, and Sandy led Maggie inside. She found herself in an old wood-paneled office with a linoleum floor, windows on three sides, and a skylight. "I love it," she enthused. "It'll make a perfect studio until mine is repaired. How much can I pay you for rent?"

"Nothing."

"No, seriously."

"I am serious. I got such an amazing deal on this place, I can afford to be generous."

"It had been empty forever before you moved in. I never did know who owned it."

"A man out of Baton Rouge. He died, and his son took over the business. But he overextended and had to sell off a bunch of buildings at bargain prices. That's the father and son over there."

Sandy pointed to a dusty black-and-white photo in a dollar store frame hanging on a wall. A handsome man brimming with self-confidence posed next to a man who looked like a tenth-generation copy of him. "The son is not the father," Maggie murmured.

"Excuse me?"

"Nothing. I'll take it. And I'll find some way to thank you."

"Not necessary. It's my way of thanking you and Gopher for finding my little boy. And it'll be nice having the company. It gets lonely here sometimes, just me and King Cake."

"Well, I know a certain gentleman who'd like to fix that."

Maggie flashed an impish grin, and Sandy blushed. "Oh, you stop," she admonished. "But," she added softly, "I might not mind that."

Maggie smiled to herself. *Rufus Durand, your lucky number just came up.*

Sandy stayed behind to lock up the office, and Maggie returned to the studio, where Whitney was waiting for her. "Look," Whitney said. "Xander tried a different approach this time."

She handed her a painting. Maggie recognized it as the portrait of puppy Jasmine that Bo had shown her on his phone. Xander had completed it, but the happy energy the painting originally radiated was overwhelmed by a chaotic, abstract background. "What is this?" Maggie gestured to the mishmash of shapes and colors.

"He added a more contemporary touch to the painting."

"Who told him to do that?"

"No one."

Maggie knew Whitney was lying. "Chris did, didn't he?" Maggie said, furious.

"Okay, fine, yes. Chris is blown away by Xander's talent, and he thought this would make his work even more powerful."

"Xander is seven. His work doesn't need to be 'powerful.' It needs to be *fun*. And from his heart."

Whitney snatched the painting back. "Chris was right. He told me not to tell you. He said you wouldn't understand."

"Did he say collectors gravitate more toward abstract art these days?" Whitney didn't respond, and Maggie had her answer. "So he's still trying to convince you to let him market your son." She took a deep breath to calm herself. "Whitney, you know how much I love Xander. I just want to protect him."

"Are you saying I *don't*? I'm his mother, for God's sake!"

"I know. But I'm worried Chris is playing you."

"Oh, so you think I'm some gullible, naïve victim."

"Not at all. I think you're a wonderful, loving mother who would do anything for her son. But Chris has changed since we were together. Something's wrong with him. I don't think he's a good person anymore."

"You know what, Maggie?" Whitney hissed. "I don't care what you think. What happens to my son is between me and his father, and you have no say in it, and you wouldn't even if you were Xander's stepmom, which you're not and probably never will be. You can forget about those art lessons. I'm going to a find a new teacher for Xander. We're done with you."

Whitney tucked her son's painting under her arm and slammed out the front door of the dance studio, leaving behind a devastated Maggie.

Chapter
Twenty-Three

For a moment, Maggie stood rooted to the floor, frozen by Whitney's attack. Then she slowly walked out of the studio. She sat on the sidewalk curb and tried to regroup. She had a sudden, almost desperate longing to talk to Father Prit. She missed his warmth and kindness. But he was in Rome, "@VaticanCity," as he tweeted, eagerly awaiting Midnight Mass with Pope Francis.

Maggie pulled out her cell phone and angrily punched in a number. "Hey," Chris answered. He sounded surprised to hear from her.

"Leave. Xander. Alone." Maggie spat out each word.

"Oh, that's what this is about. I warned Whitney."

"You mean you warned Whitney not to talk to anyone who might discourage her from ruining her son's life."

"Or save him from being trapped in a hick backwoods Southern town." Now Chris was angry.

"Chris . . ." Maggie fought to keep her temper. "I know you're hurting for money."

"You think that's what this is about? Wrong, Maggie. There was a clause in my contract with Steve guaranteeing me a payout in the event of termination. He may have been the one terminated, but it still counts."

"Do the police know this?" Chris was silent. "Do the police know this?" Maggie repeated.

"Why do you keep asking me that?"

"They know you were having money problems. And they're looking into it."

"They think I killed Steve?" There was disbelief in his voice. "Do you?"

Now Maggie was silent.

"You do. Wow."

"I didn't, Chris. But I'm starting to wonder."

"You know what? Just go to—" Furious, Chris then ended the call without even bothering to finish the sentence.

Maggie put away her phone and stared into space, overwhelmed by the one-two punch of her confrontations with Whitney and Chris.

"Seems like somebody besides me could use a nightcap."

Maggie looked up to find Philip Charbonnet. She was surprised to see him outside the comfortable confines of his New Orleans life. "Hello."

"Sorry if I startled you," he said. "Care to join me at one of Pelican's quaint establishments?" he asked.

Charbonnet held out a hand. Maggie debated. The man was loathsome. But he could also provide some valuable insight into the machinations of his twisted family. She took his hand, and he pulled her to her feet. "Let's go to Junie's," she said with her best fake smile. "Full of local color."

"I enjoy that. In extremely small doses."

Maggie led him down the street and into Junie's, where JJ raised an eyebrow when they entered together. She steered Charbonnet toward the restaurant owner. "JJ, this is Philip Charbonnet. He's the brother-in-law of our late guest, Steve Harmon."

She placed a hint of emphasis on the last sentence, and JJ's eyebrow went down. "Ah," he said. "Welcome to Junie's, sir. And please accept my condolences."

JJ extended a manicured hand to the visitor. Charbonnet eyed it with distaste but gave it a light shake. "Thank you. I'll take a bourbon, neat. Magnolia?"

"The same, thank you." Maggie scouted the restaurant and spotted an isolated table in a dark corner. "Let's sit there," she told Charbonnet, who followed her to it. JJ brought them their drinks, and Maggie's ersatz date handed the proprietor a credit card without even looking at him.

"What brings you back to Pelican?" Maggie asked. "Do the police have any new information on your brother-in-law's murder?" She knew pretty much all the information Pelican PD had, thanks to Bo and Rufus, but it seemed like a good conversation starter.

"Sadly, progress is slow, but that's to be expected from a small-town police force. I assume we'll have to bring in the FBI." Charbonnet seemed in no hurry to do so. "I was actually in the area meeting with the staff at Belle Vista to assure them their jobs were safe. For the moment. But more importantly, I wanted to see you."

"Me?" Maggie found this discomfiting.

"Yes. Your parents told me you were at some dance class, so I waited outside until you were done. I assume you'll be sharing your conversation with our art adviser with local authorities. One wouldn't want to withhold information in a murder investigation."

Charbonnet hadn't mentioned overhearing Maggie's argument with Chris when she first brought up Harmon's murder. He tossed it in unexpectedly, hoping to throw her off guard for some reason. "Why were you looking for me?" she deflected.

Charbonnet took a sip of his drink, savored it, and then swallowed. "I've been thinking about you since we met." Maggie was about to jump in and dissuade the man of any romantic intentions when he continued, "Your mother's a Doucet, and your father's a Crozat. Quite a pedigree."

"If you care about those things. Which I don't."

"Your bloodline is a very impressive collection of Creole and Cajun antecedents, with the exception of that Yankee general and whatever miscegenation produced your cousin Lia's side of the family."

Much as she'd love to let loose on the revolting man, Maggie managed to contain herself. "If you'd like to enjoy my company tonight, I'd recommend not insulting my loved ones, especially in such deeply offensive terms."

Charbonnet held up his hand. "Calm down, chère. I'm not judging, merely stating a fact. I imagine it's hard to find a bloodline in this state that doesn't sport a drop of color, including my illustrious family. Which brings me to my point. I noticed one leaf missing from your family tree: Charbonnet."

Maggie somehow managed to keep herself from gasping with horror at what the boulevardier was intimating. "Well, I guess we'll have to live with that bare branch."

"Not necessarily." Charbonnet flashed a lazy smile of entitlement. Maggie studied him. He was clinging to what was left of his looks like a man holding onto a cliff with one finger as he dangled over a precipice. She had the feeling that his was the kind of decay that would inch along before making a hard turn into total dissipation.

She forced her attention back to the conversation. Charbonnet was pontificating on his family's ancestral history. "So if we did conjoin in matrimony, the mix of our bloodlines would give us rather a superpower of heritage."

"Excuse me . . . but are you *proposing*?"

"I'm presenting an offer that would benefit us both."

"Ah, so what you're talking about is less marriage than merger."

"I assure you that you'll be impressed by other aspects of a relationship."

She recoiled, but he smirked and continued. "Despite the fact that it's the twenty-first century, much of New Orleans's networking revolves around Mardi Gras krewes like Rex and Comus. I'm fortunate enough to belong to several of these organizations, but without offspring, the Charbonnet name can only get me so far. During the season, there are dozens of parties a week, yet I only receive a few courtesy invitations. This week alone, I received only one token invite. A child with Charbonnet-Doucet-Crozat lineage would instantly bump me up the social ladder. And you with me, needless to say."

"So you're suggesting we marry and reproduce."

"Yes. And as quickly as possible."

"Mr. Charbonnet," Maggie said, choosing her words carefully and speaking slowly to prevent exploding with rage, "I'll give you the benefit of the doubt and assume your repugnant fantasies are unintentionally insulting. But I've put up with them long enough. There's no way on earth, in the universe, in the solar system, in this or any other galaxy, I would ever consider 'conjoining' with you. I have negative infinity interest in you and your 'bloodline,' and I don't appreciate being evaluated like a shar-pei at a dog show. I'm thrilled to say I have a boyfriend who I'm very much in love with. And by the way," she couldn't resist adding, "he's a Durand."

"Ah, so it is important to you after all. One can only rationalize so much, can one?" Maggie fumed, mad at herself for allowing the reprobate the last word. "Well, I had to float a trial balloon. Now that it's been popped, we can move on to my alternate topic. Stay away from my family. I see how you look at Dan and Emme—as if hearts and song-birds are swirling around their heads. He's a felon, and she's a Charbonnet. Even if he hadn't spent time in the big house, as they call it, it's a match I will personally doom."

"Goodness, if you can do that, you certainly don't need my 'bloodline' for superpowers," Maggie said, her voice laced with sarcasm. "Your sister Emme is a strong woman who can make her own decisions."

"Let's hope they're the right ones. And if she happens to get in touch with you because she bumps up against a spate of indecision, I'd advise you to cut the conversation short."

"Or?"

Charbonnet, now distracted by a text, didn't respond. "Oh, my God," he murmured.

He seemed genuinely distressed, and Maggie was taken aback by the man's sudden vulnerability. "What's wrong?"

He ran his hands through the hair receding from his forehead. "I need to get back to Belle Vista immediately." He pushed back his chair and got up so fast, he lost his balance. Maggie reached out to help him, but he grabbed the edge of the table and steadied himself. "My apologies," he said and hurried out the front door, pushing past JJ on his way out.

"What was *that?*" JJ asked.

"No idea," Maggie said. "He turned into an almost-human being and left most of his drink. I have a feeling neither of those things happens too often."

"He also left his credit card." JJ held it up. "Which, bee-tee-dubs, was declined."

"Why am I not surprised? No worries, JJ, I'll pick up the tab."

"You most certainly won't. But what do I do with this?" JJ waved the card around. "The only thing it's good for right now is jimmying open a door, but it's not my place to cut it up."

"I'll run it up to BV for him," Maggie said, taking the card. "It'll give me an excuse to see what's going on over there." A sudden scream of police sirens drowned out their conversation. The sirens faded in volume but remained constant as the squad cars headed away from the village center. "And if those sirens are any indication, it's pretty serious."

*

Maggie arrived at Belle Vista to find squad cars, an ambulance, and the dreaded coroner's van blocking the resort's driveway. She parked on the side of the road and, as she headed to the main house, saw guests and staff members huddling together on the front lawn. Some guests looked shocked, others merely curious. Several staffers were fighting to control their emotions and remain professional. She approached a guest in Bermuda shorts who was using the evacuation as a chance to have a cigarette. "What's going on?" she asked.

"Somebody died," he said, then blew out a few smoke rings.

"Who?"

"Don't know. Someone who worked here. But it must be hinky if all these cops are here."

Maggie's stomach lurched. *Harrison.* She looked around for a familiar face and saw the maître d' from her lunch with

Bea at the café. "Thank you," she told the smoker and hurried over to the maître d'. "Hi," she began, "I don't know if you remember me—"

"Yes, you're Ms. Boxler's friend." The man took her hands and held them tightly. His eyes filled with tears. "I am so terribly sorry."

Maggie was bewildered. "For what?"

"Oh, you don't know what's happened." Distressed, the man squeezed her hands tighter. "It's Bea. Ms. Boxler. She committed suicide."

Chapter Twenty-Four

Maggie was dumbstruck. "Suicide?"

"Yes. It's a total shock to everyone. We have a wedding booked for New Year's Eve, and I went over the menu with her only a few hours ago. She'd been invited to attend as a guest as well, and she showed me a picture of her dress. I've been talking to other staffers, and not one of us saw a hint of depression. But you never really know what's going on with people, do you?"

"No, you don't."

The maître d' wandered off to commiserate with his fellow employees. Maggie stood by herself, still in shock. Had her vaunted visual acuity failed her? Had she missed anything that indicated a state of despair? If so, the guilt would haunt her. Sayfrid Gerner had killed herself. Now the daughter had followed her mother's lead. Maggie replayed every interaction she'd had with Bea in her mind, searching for a clue to the woman's mental state. Not one moment pointed to Bea taking her own life.

Maggie saw Chief Perske marshalling the Belle Vista guests and employees into small, orderly groups. The Pelican PD mobile evidence van lumbered into the driveway. *Why would they need the van for a suicide?* she wondered. Rufus rounded a corner of the manor house, deep in conversation with Artie Belloise, and Maggie went to him, making sure to avoid the unpleasant Perske. "I heard about Bea. What happened?"

"There was an incident," Rufus said stiffly, motioning ever so slightly with his head toward Artie.

Artie snorted. "You don't have to put on some dumb-cluck show of protocol for me, Ru. Maggie's pretty much Pelican PD family. You can tell her."

Rufus glanced at Perske, saw the chief had his back to him, and relaxed. "All righty. This Bea Boxler woman apparently committed suicide. I say apparently because if this was a suicide, I'll swallow a hot pepper whole."

"I did that once on a dare at the police academy," Artie said. "Fair near burned a hole in my stomach lining."

"Wait." Maggie held up her hand as she tried to process the latest turn of events. "Ru, are you saying Bea didn't kill herself? She was murdered?"

"Without going into details—mostly because it's late, I'm tired, and this whole thing's putting a cramp in my plans to see if Sandy's up for a nightcap—it's looking that way."

Maggie grimaced. Her head was starting to pound. "So whoever killed Steve Harmon probably killed Bea too. I'm embarrassed by how way off I was. I really thought Bea might have killed Harmon because he drove her mother to suicide."

"Score one for Maggie," Artie exclaimed.

"Huh?"

"She is—was?—a suspect," Rufus said. "We found binders of articles about him in her bedroom and a shrine to her late mother in her closet. It fits the pattern of a revenge killing by someone unbalanced. And the knife Boxler used to 'stab herself' has the same kind of thin blade that sent Harmon to the hereafter."

"Ru, you didn't think I could drag Harmon's body into Doucet. What makes you think Bea could? Unless . . ."

"She had help." Rufus finished Maggie's sentence. "It's as much a possibility as anything else in this crazy case."

"Did you find a suicide note?"

"No. Which is also suspicious. If you're carrying a grudge that long, seems like you'd want to take credit for the kill. Plus, stabbing yourself to death is tricky. You'd think she'd take an easier way out."

"Juliet did it."

"Juliet who?" Rufus asked, scowling. "We got another murder now? I'll never get home tonight."

"No, Juliet in *Romeo and Juliet.* 'This is thy sheath; there rest and let me die.'"

"Now *that* would have made a good suicide note. Pretty and right on point."

It occurred to Maggie that Bo wasn't at the crime scene. "Where's Bo? I know he's not off tonight."

"On desk duty. You forget that he's still a 'suspect.'" Rufus glared at Perske, who appeared to be barking an order at a glum Cal Vichet.

"If you prove Bea murdered Steve Harmon and the timeline shows Bo was on duty when Bea was murdered—assuming she *was* murdered—then Bo won't be a suspect anymore." Knowing these were big hurdles to jump, Maggie tried to quell her excitement. But for the first time in days, she felt a glimmer of optimism, despite the unsettling circumstances.

"All that is true," Rufus acknowledged. "And it still leaves us with a murderer out there."

"Then there are people who might still be in danger. I'll see y'all later. I need to find someone."

Maggie rushed across Belle Vista's front lawn, stumbling on the occasional rut that the grass disguised. She found Harrison sitting on the front steps of the mansion by himself. "You heard?" he asked Maggie.

"Yes."

"The police interviewed me. It's like they don't believe Bea offed herself." Maggie saw the boy was shaking. She sat down next to him and put an arm around his shoulder. "This may be mean to say, but she wasn't a very nice person," Harrison continued. "I mean, her dying sucks and all, but she was kind of mean to me. She'd shoot down all my ideas and treat me like I was only here because of Uncle Steve. I don't know why the police think she didn't commit suicide. She probably had all this guilt from killing my uncle."

"Harrison, you've experienced a lot of trauma in the last couple of days. Are you sure you should stay at Belle Vista?"

"I couldn't even if I wanted to. The police are making us move everyone to one of our other properties so they can investigate. What a mess."

"Are you going with them? Do you want to come back to Crozat with me?"

"I called Emme and my dad. They're on their way to help out. Uncle Steve owned a boutique hotel in Lafayette, so we're moving people there for the night. But thank you." Harrison stood up and took a minute to calm down. "I better go see if the police need me."

Harrison gave her a wan smile. As he trudged toward Chief Perske, Maggie realized she'd never heard him call Dan Levy "Dad" before.

*

After a final check-in with Rufus, Maggie remembered the errand that had brought her to Belle Vista in the first place and went hunting for Philip Charbonnet. She found him nursing a scotch in the resort's dark, empty café. "Well, hello there," he said. "Forgive me if I don't get up. I'm grieving the loss of a lover."

"I didn't know."

"Few did . . . if anyone. The irony is, my sister thought her husband was the one having an affair with Bea. It was the rare time that she was wrong about his misadventures."

"You have my sympathies. And I have your credit card." Maggie placed it on the table in front of Philip.

"Ah, much thanks. I wouldn't get too far without it."

You won't get too far with *it*, Maggie thought. "Again, I'm sorry for your loss."

"Of course, it appears my inamorata is the one who put a knife to my brother-in-law," Philip said. "So there's that. Anyway, job number one now is finding a new general manager. Young Turk Harrison thinks he's the heir apparent, but at this point in his stunted development, that's laughable. If you'd like a step up from your little establishment, feel free to apply for the position. For the right inducement, I'd be happy to provide a recommendation."

Charbonnet, restored to his former smarminess, leered at her. "Pass," Maggie said, disgusted by the man. "And you owe JJ for your drink." She pointed to the credit card. "That thing's useless."

Maggie stalked out of the café to her car. She couldn't get away from the morbid scene and the offensive Philip Charbonnet fast enough. But instead of going home, she drove to Pelican police headquarters. She walked into the lobby, where Bo was behind the reception desk looking miserable. He came to life the minute he saw Maggie. "Hey," he said, then got up and came to her. He pulled Maggie into a corner of the room and kissed her. She lingered in his arms until he reluctantly pulled away. "I know Perske checks the security camera when I'm on duty."

"Which doesn't cover this corner of the room, I'm guessing."

"Nope." Bo grinned. "That's why we call it the Kissin' Corner."

"Cute."

Bo returned to his position behind the desk. Mindful of the security camera, Maggie stayed on the opposite side of it. "I was up at Belle Vista. Rufus thinks Bea Boxler killed Steve Harmon, but he doesn't think she took her own life. He's convinced someone killed her and then arranged the scene to make it look like she committed suicide. I also found out that she was having an affair with Philip Charbonnet, which would personally drive *me* to suicide."

"You know more than I do," Bo said, his tone tinged with bitterness.

"But if she's proven to be Harmon's killer, you're not a suspect anymore. Perske will have to reinstate you as a detective."

"That would be nice," Bo said, "but I trust him less than a tin nickel. I wonder what Bea Boxler got out of a relationship with Philip Charbonnet."

"The latest gossip on her target, Steve Harmon. Information that could have aided her plans for revenge. She certainly didn't get any financial benefit from it. Charbonnet shanghaied me into having a drink with him, and when JJ ran his credit card, it was declined. Not a great way to impress a girl you basically proposed to."

"*Proposed*?"

"Relax. It had nothing to do with me and everything to do with my ridiculous family lineage. Charbonnet's very old-world New Orleans that way, thinking the more 'names' he can throw out to business associates, the more doors he'll open. He's not wrong. It may be the only city left in the country where that can make a difference."

"Sorry, I'm still on the 'proposed' thing. There's been a lot of interest in my girl on the part of other guys lately. You can't blame me for being a little sensitive."

My girl. The two simple words from Bo sent a flush throughout her body. "If it makes you feel more secure, you're the only one of my beaus who's currently earning a steady living."

Bo burst out laughing. "Oh, chère, if you're dating me for my money, you are going to be very unhappy when you see my sad little Pelican PD paycheck." Bo turned his attention to the reception desk computer. "I want to take a closer look at this Charbonnet guy. Ru's been meaning to, but he keeps getting pulled away because we're understaffed. As long as I'm sitting around with my thumb up my you-know-what, I might as well make myself useful." Bo typed for a few minutes and then stared at the screen.

"Did you find something already?"

"Yes. A restraining order. Filed last year by an Alicia Guidry Charbonnet. Apparently your suitor has a nasty temper as well as an obsession with social pedigree."

"Well, he's an all-around catch, isn't he?" Maggie noticed the time on the old clock hanging on the wall behind Bo. "I better go. I've got an early shift at our bake stand in the morning. We're only a hundred dollars away from funding two porta-potties."

"Go, Team Crozat. I'm off tomorrow, so I'll come by in the morning to help finish your bonfire. But before you leave . . ."

Bo took Maggie's hand and led her out from behind the reception desk. "One last visit to the Kissin' Corner."

*

Maggie replayed Bo's kiss as she fell asleep and woke up to the same delicious memory. Her dreamy demeanor engendered amused looks between her mother and Gran' as the three women stocked her cooler with coffee and homemade breakfast pastries the next morning. When Bo showed up at the Crozat bonfire to help finish the log edifice, he noticed that Maggie was shivering because she'd left her hoodie at the house and lent her his worn leather jacket. She thought of the Christmas present that awaited him and smiled to herself. An hour later, Bo, Tug, Chret Bertrand, and the O'Days stacked the final logs on the bonfire. "I can't thank you enough for doing this," Maggie told Lindy and Tom as the small group celebrated completion with Maggie's coffee and crullers.

"We're the ones who should be thanking you for not booting us out on our keisters after we sabotaged you on Trippee," Tom said. "This is the least we can do."

"I owe you all," Tug said. "I truly thought this would be the first year Crozat didn't have a bonfire to light."

"Happy to do it," Chret said. "I'd best get to work now. We got a bunch of tune-ups scheduled for people getting ready to make the holiday drive to the relatives."

"And I'd better check in with the missus," Tug said. "I'm sure she's got a big old list of pre-Christmas errands for me to run."

Chret took off for his car, and Tug headed back to the manor house, leaving Maggie and Bo alone. Bo stared at the bonfire. "Did that thing have a lean to it yesterday?"

Maggie followed his gaze. "No. I don't think so. That's strange. I wonder—"

Before she could finish her thought, there was an ominous rumble. The bonfire suddenly collapsed, and Maggie's scream was drowned out by the roar of logs hurtling down the levee toward her.

Chapter
Twenty-Five

This must be what an earthquake sounds like, Maggie thought
as she ran from the torrent of lumber. She fell to her knees
and began to crawl, but Bo yanked her up and shoved her
out of the logs' path. She fell to the ground again and then
staggered to her feet. She saw the O'Days doing the same.
The last log crashed into the pile that had accumulated at the
foot of the levee. "Bo!" she cried out. She stumbled to the pile
of battered timber. Bo lay splayed out across it, unconscious.

Maggie desperately searched for a water bottle. The ava-
lanche had destroyed the stand and buried its products, but
she managed to extricate one that hadn't been crushed and
ran back to Bo. She heard voices calling from across the road
and saw Tug, Ninette, and Gran' racing from Crozat across
the road to the levee. Bo's eyelids fluttered just as the others
reached him.

"What happened?" Tug asked, short of breath from his quick dash to the levee.

"The bonfire collapsed. Don't ask me how. Call an ambulance; Bo might have a concussion."

"Already done," Ninette said. "I called the police too."

"And check on the O'Days."

"We're fine," Tom said. He and his wife had joined the group. "A few scrapes from falling as we tried to get out of the way, but we're more shaken up than anything."

"That was terrifying." Lindy clutched her heart. "We all could have been killed."

*

Sirens, at first faint, grew louder, confirming Ninette's statement that help was on the way. First to arrive was a Pelican PD squad car. Rufus and Chief Perske jumped out and climbed over logs to reach Maggie and Bo, who had regained consciousness but was groggy and incoherent. "These bonfires were an accident waiting to happen," Perske declared.

"Families have been building them for generations," Maggie shot back. "We know how to do them right. But I don't care about that now, I care about Bo."

Rufus, who had reached his cousin, carefully felt around Bo's head, causing him to wince. "Ooo, that ain't pretty," Rufus said, pointing to a contusion forming on Bo's temple. "But I'm more concerned about the bump in the back."

Bo pushed Rufus away. "I'm okay," he muttered.

"You're pretty much the opposite of okay, buddy," Rufus said.

The Pelican ambulance pulled up and parked by the side of the road. EMTs Cody Pugh and Regine Armitage unloaded a gurney and pushed it toward where Bo lay. "Head injury," Rufus told them. "Don't know what all else is going on."

Regine checked Bo's legs and arms while Cody examined Maggie. "I'm fine," she said. "A few cuts and scrapes."

"I can clean up your wounds."

"I can do that myself. Don't worry about me. Check on our guests, and then focus on Bo."

Cody strode over to the O'Days while Regine finished evaluating Bo's injuries. "Doesn't look like anything's broken," Regine said. "Some head trauma for sure. They can do a CT brain scan at the hospital."

Cody returned to them. "Your guests just need some ice for their bruises and probably a couple of stiff drinks. They're heading back to their room. Now let's tend to your boyfriend."

Bo fought Rufus and the EMTs as they tried lifting him onto the gurney. "I can do it myself," he insisted.

"Knock it off, you idiot," Rufus barked at him.

Maggie took her boyfriend's hand and squeezed it tightly. "You've already been a hero once today, chère. You saved my life. Let us take care of you now."

Bo gave a slight nod and didn't struggle when Cody and Regine snapped the gurney's safety restraints in place. They wheeled him to the ambulance. "I'm going with them," Maggie said.

"That'll have to wait," Chief Perske said. "I want to hear what happened while it's fresh on your mind."

Maggie started to balk, but Ninette stopped her. "The chief is right. If this wasn't an accident, you can't risk forgetting a single detail. The smallest thing might help catch whoever did it."

"Your mother and I will go to the hospital," Gran' said.

"Yes," Ninette said. "I'll drive."

"If we want to get there tomorrow, you can drive," Gran' said. "If we want to get there today, *I'll* drive."

The women took off. Perske headed to the top of the levee, where the base of the bonfire still stood intact. The others followed as he circled the base. A native of the state's northern half, the chief had no experience with bonfires, but he harrumphed and examined the base as if he did.

"There," Rufus and Tug said simultaneously, pointing to the bottom row of the bonfire, which faced the street. Both men bent down to get a closer look.

"Someone moved this one log just enough to make the whole thing unsteady," Tug said, pointing to a log sitting at an odd angle.

"Or maybe you or one of your helpers isn't the bonfire-building genius they claim to be," Perske rebutted.

Tug was about to reply, but Rufus jumped in. "There are three things every man in this town pretty much learns from birth. How to build a bonfire, boil crawfish, and jump-start a car. It's easier than looking for your keys sometimes. Anyways, I can speak to the Crozats' expertise. And I can assure you the first thing Tug here would've done is make sure the bonfire base is sturdy as a German hausfrau."

A Durand defending a Crozat? I should check the sky for flying pigs, Maggie thought. She was surprised and grateful for Ru's show of support. If there was solace to be found in the week's disasters and tragedies, it was the rapprochement between two families whose feud predated the Civil War.

Her father was on his hands and knees examining the bonfire's base. "Whoever did this had no way of knowing when it would fall. It could have killed or injured someone or just been destroyed."

"Making it more of a message than a weapon," Rufus mused.

"Could be another bonfire builder," Perske said. "I hear you locals get pretty competitive about these things."

"No way," Rufus instantly responded. Maggie could tell he didn't appreciate Perske's patronizing tone. "Any competition is pure fun and good natured. There's no prize except a feeling of pride when you have the biggest or loudest bonfire. The kids go nuts with excitement. I can't wait until I build my first bonfire with my little Charli."

Maggie was touched by the emotion in Rufus's voice. She was ashamed of herself for ever doubting fatherhood would change the man for the better. "Would you mind interviewing me now?" she asked Chief Perske. "I'd like to get to the hospital and make sure Bo's all right."

"Who was here first, you or your father?"

"My father," Maggie said with reluctance, knowing the contrary police chief would use this as an excuse for not honoring her request. But once again, Rufus leapt in.

"Chief, why don't you interview the dad, and I'll take the daughter? Kill two birds at the same time."

"Fine. It'll give us more time to check the base of every Pelican bonfire on the river. I don't trust the craftsmanship of these structures."

Rufus and Tug shared an eyeroll behind Perske's back, and then Rufus led Maggie back to the street, cussing out his temporary boss the whole way down the levee. He pulled out a small pad to take notes. "Okay, so walk me through your morning as it pertains to the bonfire."

"Honestly, there's not much to tell. I came out with my supplies around eight AM. My dad, Bo, and Chret Bertrand were already working on the bonfire. I sold coffee and pastries to a couple of regulars: Eula Banks, who works at the Hall of Records, and Lee Bertrand, who stopped by to say hi to Chret but I think was really hoping that Gran' was working the stand because they've been dating."

"Okay, more than I need to know yet nothing useful. Let's check into your famous instincts and ability to see stuff others miss. Anything?"

Maggie thought hard and then shook her head. "Sorry, Ru."

"Unless your father drops some kinda clue, we'll have to assume someone paid the bonfire a visit in the middle of the night." Rufus closed his notebook. "All righty, we're done. Go visit my cousin. And tell him to get his butt back here as soon as he's on his feet—I'm not doing some lame-o bonfire-building patrol on my own."

*

Bo smiled as soon as he saw Maggie peering into his hospital room. She came to his side and kissed him lightly on the lips. "This is the third time I've visited a loved one here this week," she said. "The head nurse greeted me by my first name."

"I like hearing I'm a 'loved one.'"

"Very loved." Maggie kissed him again, this time a little less gently. "How do you feel, chère?"

"Like I have a hangover from a bangin' frat party."

Maggie laughed. "Did the CT scan show any damage?"

"No fractures. I have a mild concussion. They're keeping me overnight, but I can go home in the morning. I'm supposed to have Xander tomorrow for Christmas Eve, but Whitney and I are going to switch things around so I have him Christmas Day instead. That way I can rest some and still come to the bonfires but not have to keep an eye on him the whole time."

"There's going to be one less bonfire on the levee. Ours was totaled. All that hard work . . . gone."

"Makes me furious. Any update on what happened?"

"Someone moved a log and compromised the structural integrity."

"Quick sidebar to say you sound sexy when you talk like an engineer."

"Thank you. I wish I could do it more often, but that's all I've got. Anyway, I saw nothing, I'm sure my dad saw nothing . . ."

"Neither did I."

"And the end result so far is that Perske's now making Ru and probably a few other officers check out every single bonfire to ensure they're safe. So if your doctor brings up the possibility of releasing you early, you might want to pretend your head still hurts."

"Hearing about that makes it hurt, so I won't be lying."

Maggie checked the time on her phone. "I need to get to work. Three for luck," she said and bent down to kiss him one last time. Bo pulled her toward him, and they became entwined in a heated embrace. "We have to stop," he murmured in her ear. "It can't be in a hospital room after an attempted murder."

"Or when you're nursing a couple of nasty lumps," They forced themselves to separate. "We'll wait," Maggie gently stroked Bo's thick, black hair. "I love you."

"I love you too."

Maggie took leave of Bo and headed for the elevator. The doors opened, and Whitney got out. As usual, her red-gold hair glimmered as if sprinkled with fairy dust. Whitney was one of the few human beings whose beauty could survive the unforgiving glare of fluorescent lighting. Under other circumstances, Maggie would have loved to paint the stunning woman's portrait. But given Whitney's status as Bo's ex-wife, it would be a bridge to a relationship neither woman was ready for.

"Hi, Whitney," Maggie said. Mindful that their last interaction had turned into a bitter fight, she kept her tone neutral.

"Hi," Whitney responded. "I talked to Bo on the phone but wanted to stop by and see him in person. I'm glad I ran into you." Maggie didn't respond, wary of what might come next. "Maggie, I'm so sorry for how nasty I was the last time I saw you. I've been obsessing about why you feel so strongly that Chris promoting Xander as an artist is a bad idea. And then Bo got injured, and I thought, what if it had been more serious and we were in New York or some other art place and couldn't get to him? What would that do to Xander?" Tears began to roll down Whitney's cheeks. "I could never, ever separate him from his daddy. I worry so much about what will happen to him when we're gone. I can't bear to think of him alone someday without love or family."

"Oh, Whitney." Maggie wrapped the woman in a warm hug. "That won't happen because *my* family will always be here for him and so will everyone else in Pelican. If he even chooses to stay here. And his talent won't desert him, it will only develop. I think he'll have a wonderful career when he's ready to handle it. Right now, Xander would be a flavor of the month, and he'd spend the rest of his life as an artist living that down. If you let him wait and grow personally and professionally, he'll have a happy, successful life. With lots and lots of love."

Whitney stepped out of Maggie's arms and wiped her eyes. "You're totally right. Zach and I both get it now. I told Chris under no circumstances is Xander going to New York or having his work shown there. We're going to let him be a kid."

"I'm so glad. When you think about it, we only spend this long as a kid"—Maggie held her hands about six inches apart—"and *this* long as adults"—she threw her arms wide open. "We should hold on to the short part as long as possible."

"Yes, I agree one hundred percent. After the holidays, let's make sure to get you and Xander together for an art class."

"I'd love that."

The women hugged again. And Maggie had a feeling she might be painting Whitney's portrait sooner than she expected.

*

Maggie was about to head to Doucet when she remembered she'd brought her costume home and would have to stop by the shotgun cottage to retrieve it. She texted Tannis that she was running ten minutes late and deleted the scolding message her boss texted back. Maggie got into the driver's seat but didn't move. She felt beaten down by the week. Dealing with murders, kidnappings, the attack on her studio, and on a lesser note, a boss she loathed—it was all too much.

On a whim, Maggie lowered the top on the car and then peeled out of the parking lot. She was whipped by the chilly December wind as she drove but found it bracing. Her head, which had felt like it was stuffed with soggy cotton, began to clear. She rounded the bend toward Crozat and slowed down. On top of the levee across from the plantation, a small army of people were hauling logs and stacking them carefully in the shape of a pyramid. Maggie parked the car, overwhelmed by what she saw.

Neighbors and guests had come together to help Tug rebuild the family's bonfire. She jumped out and hurried up the hillside. Marco Cornetta and Akira, a man from his tour group, were carrying logs to the site. "Hey, sweetie," he greeted her. "Look at me—I'm doing something physical for a change!"

"Marco, I don't know what to say."

"Please, you're doing me a favor. I'm so tired of the same old, same old on these tours. My 'groupies,' as I'm fond of calling them, are loving this. It's like a farm-stay holiday. Come on, Akira, let's get steppin'."

Marco and Akira marched off. A persistent yapping stole Maggie's attention. She walked around to another side of the bonfire and saw King Cake's head sticking out of his doggy carrier. She turned and found Ione and Sandy Sechrest hard at work. Both women waved away her appreciation for their efforts. "Stop it," Ione said while Sandy gave a vigorous nod. "You nagged Pelican PD so much that they had to admit there was zero evidence linking me to Steve Harmon's murder. If it wasn't for you, I'd probably be in jail right now, not getting paid at Fais Dough Dough to sell and eat delicious pastries."

"And you didn't judge me by my past, Maggie," Sandy said. "You supported me and brought friends to my studio. Friends who were there for me the minute King Cake went missing. I'll never forget that."

Maggie bit her lip. "If I stay another minute, I'll cry a flood, so I'm going now. Again, thank—"

"Don't thank us!" her friends and guests chorused. "Go!"

Which Maggie did.

*

The workday at Doucet proved to be unexpectedly pleasant. With Christmas Eve only twenty-four hours away, guests and coworkers were filled with the holiday spirit. Since Tannis had canceled the annual staff party due to her draconian fiscal restraints, Maggie and her friends threw their own potluck lunch celebration, complete with Secret Santas. No one had to fear pulling Tannis's name from the bag because it wasn't included. Ione's was, however, and Maggie had been thrilled to see her close friend's name on the slip of paper she pulled. Maggie received a small rectangular box from her Secret Santa, who serendipitously turned out to be Ione. Inside was a gift card from New Orleans's best art supply store.

The workday ended with a surprise appearance by the Peli-Carolers, a group of locals who came together once a year to sing a mix of traditional and quirky Cajun Christmas carols like "'Zat you, Santa Claus?" and "Santa's Second Line." They sang with the Doucet manor house as their backdrop, the elegant estate decked out in all its Christmas finery. After they completed their set to enthusiastic applause, Maggie wished her last tour group a happy holiday and retreated to the staff lounge to call Rufus and get an update on the investigations into Bea's murder and the bonfire collapse.

"New Orleans was a busy place last night because most of our suspects seem to have been there," he said when she reached him by cell phone. "Your ex, Chris, went down last night to meet with a lawyer first thing this morning because the widow Charbonnet's contesting some clause in his contract that would pay him out. Harrison took a break from BV to shack up with the Charbonnets, none of whom are answering my calls. Any one of those doofs could've zipped back up here in the middle of the night and messed with the bonfire. And then there are the locals, like your O'Day folks and that boss of yours if she got a body-moving assist from Little Earlie. I wouldn't mind putting that nosy reporter away for a while."

"I don't get that Earlie is so into Tannis that he'd help kill for her."

"Yeah, it's a reach. But it'd be fun to pick him up on suspicion just to put a scare in him. Anyway, the good news is that Perske finally gave up on trying to make a case against Bo. Try as he might, he couldn't find a way to justify Bo's messing with the bonfire and then being there to get conked out when it came down."

"So bottom line, no closer. Argh, this is so frustrating. Whoever killed Harmon and almost killed Bo can't get away with it."

"They won't. FYI, I paid a visit to our boy, and by the time I left, he was snoozing. You might want to wait until morning to check in with him."

"Will do. Thanks."

Maggie ended the call, took her purse, and stepped outside. She realized she was the only person left at the plantation. All guests and employees were gone. She had an idea.

She moved her car to a remote spot on the road that ran behind Doucet and then walked back to the plantation. She pulled the manor house key out of her purse and traipsed along the path to the front door, her way lit by the plantation's holiday lights. Tannis had wanted to turn them off at night as a cost-cutting measure but relented after local schoolchildren circulated a petition to keep the place glowing through New Year's Eve. Maggie let herself into the house, locked the door behind her for safety, and then entered the parlor, where she'd found Steve Harmon's body. She sat on the antique fainting couch that faced the family portrait she loved so much and stared into Magnolia Marie Doucet's eyes. "Talk to me, Magnolia," she said out loud. "Help me."

The son is not the father. The son is not the father . . .

Maggie woke up several hours later with this mantra running through her mind. It seemed to be the only message her ancestor wanted to send, and Maggie thought she knew why. Stiff from falling asleep on a one-hundred-and-fifty-year-old piece of furniture, she stretched and gave herself a shake to fully wake up. She peered at a carved black walnut Victorian clock on a side table that still worked after a century and a half and saw it was four AM.

The room was lit only by moonlight and the diffused glow from the outdoor holiday lights. Maggie waited a minute for her eyes to adjust. Then she stood up and was about to walk to the door when she heard a floorboard squeak in the bedroom above her. She froze in place. The sound came again, and this time she could identify it as footsteps.

Maggie was no longer alone in the house. And judging by what she was hearing, whoever else was in the house might not be alone either.

Chapter Twenty-Six

Maggie never understood why people in horror movies ignored common sense and put themselves in ridiculously dangerous situations. She had no intention of doing this herself, so her goal was to make it out of the Doucet manor house without being caught by the unwelcome visitors. She tiptoed out of the parlor and down the hallway. Months as a tour guide had taught her which of the home's old floorboards creaked, and she maneuvered around them. She heard giggling coming from upstairs, followed by what sounded like seductive murmuring. Whatever was going on sounded more like a hookup than a robbery. *At least they're busy getting busy*, Maggie thought as she opened the front door.

She passed the parking lot on the way to her car and noticed Little Earlie's PT Cruiser next to Tannis's BMW

Coupe, outing the two as the couple trysting in a Doucet bedroom. "Consorting with the enemy, huh, Little E?" she muttered, furious at the low-rent journalist. Much as she wanted to bust him, Maggie forced herself to focus on a much more important task. She was convinced she knew who had murdered Bea and tampered with the bonfire. Now it was a matter of convincing Pelican PD that her instincts were right.

Maggie slowly made her way down the old road. Dawn had yet to break, so it was still dark when she reached home, and she fumbled in her purse for her house key. She let herself into the cottage, careful not to wake her grand-mère, and sat down at the petite antique desk in the living room, taking a moment to turn on her laptop. An Internet search yielded nothing useful. There was so little, in fact, that she wondered if the lack of information was intentional.

Maggie checked the computer clock. It was five AM, too early to call Rufus. Her body tingled with fatigue. Figuring she'd be useless exhausted, she retreated to her room and slipped under the covers. As Maggie drifted off, it occurred to her that it was Christmas Eve.

*

Maggie's alarm clock went off two hours later, and she reached for her cell phone. She called Bo, but it went straight to voice mail. She left him a message to call her and texted the same request as insurance. Then she called Rufus, who answered on the first ring. "Happy, happy," he greeted her jovially. "I just put Charli in her 'Baby's First Christmas' onesie, and she's totally rockin' it. What's up?"

"I have a theory."

"Well, mercy me, you do?" Rufus feigned shock. "I used to find your theories superannoying, but they've grown on me. So shoot." Maggie shared her conjecture with him. She knew it was inspired by guesswork, not fact, so she was relieved when he responded, "I never thought I'd say this to a Crozat-slash-Doucet, but we are on the same page. We've already discovered some very interesting facts about said suspect that I'll share when Charli isn't fussing for a feeding. The coroner's report states that Bea's wound could only have been made by someone holding a knife in their left hand, and Bea was a righty, which pretty much proves our assumption that her death was no suicide. This dang case gripes me. For every murder we solve, another pops up. It's like whack-a-mole but with bodies. Anyhoo, I think it's safe to say that we have a person of interest. I'll let you know when we bring them in for questioning."

Maggie thanked Ru, and he signed off. For the first time since Steve Harmon arrived, bringing drama and death with him, Maggie felt a sense of relief. The case was in the hands of law enforcement. She could finally focus on the holiday.

She showered and put on jeans and a long-sleeved green T-shirt, topping off her look with a kitschy Christmas sweater that she'd found at a garage sale. The design was a riot of candy canes, kittens, and Christmas trees with little bells that jingled when she walked. Maggie hummed "Deck the Halls" as she headed over to the manor house, where she helped Gran' and her mother serve their guests a holiday breakfast. Ninette surprised no one by coming up with her own recipe for muffaletta frittata, which was accompanied by fresh biscuits, andouille sausage, and bananas foster coffee cake.

After breakfast, it was finally time to trim the B and B Christmas tree. "I made two dozen sugar cookies for ornaments, all decorated with a Louisiana theme," Ninette said. She revealed a large tray of frosted cookie streetcars, pelicans, alligators, and Mardi Gras masks to gasps of delight.

"They look so pretty *and* yummy," Sophie O'Day said. "Would it be okay if I maybe ate just one?"

Ninette smiled at the young girl. "Don't worry, sweetie; I made a whole other tray of cookies for eating. I'll leave them in the kitchen with a pitcher of milk for anyone who wants one."

Maggie and Gran' invited everyone to join them in the front parlor, where the imposing Douglas fir awaited its ornamentation. Ninette and Tug excused themselves so Tug could put the finishing touches on the bonfire and Ninette could prepare vats of gumbo and jambalaya for the B and B's bonfire viewing party. Marco and his tour group opted to assist Tug. "I'm getting actual biceps, Mags," Marco bragged, pulling up his shirt sleeve to show off a small muscle.

Tug and his volunteer crew took off for the levee while the O'Day family followed Maggie and Gran' into the parlor. "We've never been away from home at the holidays before,"

Lindy said as they began removing delicate glass ornaments from an old box. "But it's worth it to see the bonfires."

"We'll make sure it's as warm and cozy as a Christmas can be," Gran' assured her. She pulled out a faded children's shoebox. "Oh, my, look. 'Baby's First Ornament.' There must be half a dozen of them here."

"Yes, Mom went all in on 'Baby's First' paraphernalia." Maggie reached into the box and held up a ceramic white cherub. "I think I'll give this to Rufus for Charli."

"That's a lovely idea. It even looks a bit like her." Gran' eyed her granddaughter. "Could it be? Am I sensing a rapprochement with the Durands after a century and a half of feuding?"

"I've come to have a newfound respect—I admit, a little grudging—for Rufus." It occurred to Maggie that hours had passed without the promised confirmation from the police officer. She texted him, "Any luck re: suspect?" but received no response.

"Maggie, chère, can you get the stepladder so we can decorate the upper branches?" Gran' asked.

"Sure."

Maggie retrieved the ladder from the supply closet and set it up next to the tree. Tom climbed to the top, and the others handed him ornament after ornament until the upper branches sported as many as the lower half. He climbed down, and Maggie flipped a light switch, illuminating the majestic tree. Glass and glittery baubles sparkled under the glow of a thousand tiny white lights.

"It's the most beautiful tree I've ever seen," Allison O'Day said, dropping her jaded attitude. Her younger sister, Sophie, too awestruck to comment, simply nodded in agreement.

"I think we've earned ourselves a few of those sugar cookies in the kitchen," Gran' said. "Why don't y'all come with me?"

The O'Days chorused their enthusiasm and started to follow Gran' out of the parlor. "I'll be there in a few," Maggie told her grand-mère. "I want to check on Bo."

As soon as the decorating party cleared the room, Maggie scurried over to the sideboard in the dining room. She pulled out an armful of presents, carried them back to the parlor, and placed them under the tree. She repeated this task several times until the family's hand-embroidered heirloom tree skirt was covered with gifts. After playing Santa, she relaxed for a minute on the dark-green velvet daybed and then called Bo. "Polar Express here, ready to pick you up at the hospital and transport you to your holiday destination of choice."

Bo laughed. "Too late. My ex gets props for remarrying well. Zach picked me up this morning and brought me back to their house so I can hang out with Xander while I rest. We're in the middle of watching *Rudolph the Red-Nosed Reindeer* for the second time this morning. I'm guessing there'll be at least four more viewings before the bonfires."

"Okay, chère, I'll leave you to *Rudolph*. Text me when you get to the bonfires tonight."

"Have you looked outside? It's ugly."

"I haven't been paying attention. But not to worry, they'll only postpone if there's a big storm."

"Here's hoping that doesn't happen. Xander would be heartbroken."

"I'm guessing his dad would be too."

"A little," Bo acknowledged. "I am a bonfire virgin. We didn't have them up in Shreveport, and remember, it's not just Xander's first Christmas in Pelican—it's mine."

Maggie heard cheers and applause coming from outside. "There's some whooping going on. I'd better see what's up. Love you."

"Love you too."

Maggie threw on her black hoodie and left the manor house for the levee, where two workers were offloading portable toilets from a truck. "We have achieved porta-potties," Tug called to her. "*Laissez les bon temps rouler!*"

Marco held up his phone. "I have a zydeco playlist." He tapped in a few numbers, and an infectious tune began to play, instigating an impromptu dance party. Maggie watched, amused. She didn't want to dampen the holiday spirit by pointing out that the sky was blanketed with glowering black and gray rain clouds, so she said a silent prayer that any storm would arrive after the bonfires.

Ninette stepped out on the veranda holding a heavy antique bell. "Lunch for anyone who wants it," she called to the revelers. She rang the bell, which let out a few sonorous bongs, and people drifted back to the house.

"It's lunchtime already?" Maggie asked her mother.

"Yes. It's almost one o'clock, chère."

Ninette stepped back inside, and Maggie checked her phone again. Still nothing from Rufus. *Okay, now I'm nervous*, Maggie thought. She debated briefly and then punched in his telephone number. He answered immediately. "Hey. Sorry I haven't called. But our P of I appears to have gone AWOL. We put out an ATL."

"I was with you until the end."

"An Attempt to Locate. Until we do that, be careful, Maggie. If our suspicions are correct, we're talking about someone seriously deranged."

Maggie put her phone away. The conversation had escalated her nerves rather than quell them. The front door opened behind her a crack, and Gran' stuck her head out. "Come eat before everything is gone, chère. Your mother's oyster po' boys are a huge hit. I think Akira's on his third."

Maggie followed her grandmother inside. Her stomach might be twisted in apprehensive knots, but it was also rumbling. And like all Pelican natives, Maggie knew nothing helped elevate a mood like some fine Cajun cooking.

*

Maggie spent the rest of the afternoon assisting her mother in the kitchen as Ninette organized the food for the festivities with the timing of a military chef. Meanwhile, Tug, Chret Bertrand, and off-duty Pelican PD officers Artie and Cal set up the family's party tent on the Crozat front lawn. The family's Christmas Eve bonfire party was legendary, drawing hundreds of locals and visitors. Gaynell and her band, the Gator Girls, launched into a string of zydeco versions of Christmas songs as soon as they set up their equipment, and within minutes the tent's dance floor was filled with couples dancing to the infectious rhythms.

By six o'clock, the stretch of road fronting Crozat was so packed with eager observers it was reduced to a single, very slow lane. A light drizzle, one step above a mist, began to fall. "Don't worry, it'd have to be a full-on storm for me to shut this shindig down," Mayor Claude Beaufils assured Maggie, a bowl of Ninette's seafood gumbo in one hand and a bottle of Abita beer in the other.

"Glad to hear that," Maggie responded politely, her attention elsewhere. The mayor wandered off, and Maggie circled the crowd, looking for anything or anyone suspicious. Little Earlie and Tannis were building themselves hefty plates of food at the buffet, but Maggie ignored them, still mad at the pipsqueak wannabe media mogul for hooking up with her detested boss. She passed Vanessa and Quentin MacIlhoney on the dance floor. Gaynell and the Gator Girls switched to a Cajun dance number, and the couple nimbly two-stepped, infant Charli happily bouncing up and down in the top-of-the-line baby carrier her stepfather wore strapped to his chest.

"You Crozats sure know how to throw a party," Quentin called to her as he gave his bride-to-be a twirl. "You ever need a defense attorney, I'm all yours at an extremely reduced hourly rate."

"Thanks for the offer, Quentin, but here's hoping I never have to take you up on it."

Maggie continued her search but found nothing that merited concern. She helped her mother carry a large bourbon pecan bread pudding to the dessert table. "Dad wants us to meet him at the front of the house," Ninette said after they deposited the pudding, which was instantly set upon by hungry revelers. "He's got some kind of surprise."

The two women wended their way through the growing crowd to where Tug stood on the lawn in front of the manor house veranda. "Wait until you see this," he said with childlike enthusiasm. "I found it online and figured what with all we've been through, we deserved something special."

Tug plugged a cord into an outdoor socket, and large red letters that spelled "Happy Cajun Christmas" came to life. Maggie, Ninette, and the partygoers burst into applause. Maggie noticed that Whitney and Zach had arrived, along with Xander, who was staring at the display with fascination. "Merry Christmas Eve," she greeted them.

"Merry to you too," Whitney said. "Bo'll be here ASAP. He got called into work at the last minute. Pretty much everyone else is working the bonfires."

"Thanks for letting me know," Maggie said. She hoped Whitney was right and Bo showed up soon. Having him nearby would help relieve her growing anxiety. "Xander, the pups and kittens could use some petting, especially Jasmine. But be quick, sweetie. They're going to light the bonfires soon."

The young boy instantly began jogging toward the house with his mother and stepfather on his heels. Maggie heard Ninette calling and went to her mother, who was filling a paper cup with coffee from a carafe. "Your father's gone up to the bonfire with a few others to get ready for the lighting.

Would you bring him this coffee? He could catch the worst kind of winter cold from this weather."

Maggie took the coffee cup and tromped through the damp grass toward the levee. She passed Gran' and Lee, who had set up folding chairs at a prime viewing spot. They huddled under Lee's large umbrella. "It's dark as pitch out here," Gran' complained. "This road isn't well lit to begin with, and it's made even darker by this cussed mist and the clouds blocking the stars."

"I like this weather," Lee said. "It's right good for snuggling."

He rested his head on Gran's shoulder. She sighed theatrically but didn't push him away. Maggie suppressed a grin and continued on her way. She struggled to get through the crowd, which had grown tenfold in the last half hour, and finally made it to the foot of the levee. She started to traipse up the hillside but lost her balance and slid back down.

"Need a hand, Maggie?"

She squinted, trying to identify the shadowy figure offering assistance. A hand reached out and yanked Maggie to her feet. She found herself face-to-face with Harrison Fenner.

"I think you and your buddies have been looking for me," he said. "But awesome luck, I found you first. Well, lucky for me. For you? Not so much."

Chapter
Twenty-Seven

Maggie tried to pull away from him, but Harrison held tight to her wrist with his right hand. Maggie saw that he held a gun in his left. "Harrison, I have no idea what you're talking about. I need to get this coffee to my father."

"Sorry. Not gonna happen."

Maggie, heart pumping with fear, tried another tack. "You're obviously pretty upset. Can you at least let me go so we can talk about it?"

"Uh, that would be no. Props for a nice try, though."

Fear made Maggie perspire. The sweat mingled with the light rain and dripped into her eyes, stinging them. She struggled again to release herself, but Harrison yanked her arm behind her, causing Maggie to wince with pain. "Stop that," he ordered. "It's superannoying."

"Ten, nine, eight, seven, six . . ." came a chant from the crowd. The countdown to the lighting of the bonfires had begun. Maggie prayed that the bright glow from the flames would illuminate her dire situation and bring about a rescue. "Five, four, three, two, one!"

There was a whoosh and then the snap and pop of fire-crackers. A distant bonfire burst into flames. But the ones nearest Maggie stayed dark, too damp from the rain. Maggie could distinguish the outlines of bonfire builders trying to ignite their masterpieces. But no saving light came.

"Hey, do me a favor and ditch the coffee," Harrison said. "And not on me, or boom boom." Harrison mimed shooting. Maggie hesitated and then did as she was instructed. She tossed the coffee cup and with it her plan to throw it at him, creating a distraction that would allow her to run for safety.

Harrison, confident that he was in control, became chatty. "Even though it's superdark, I see the way you're looking at me right now. I know that look. I've seen it when people all of a sudden start being scared of me. I saw it in your eyes for a flicker of a second on the steps of BV the night Bea Boxler died. There was a question in your eyes too. Could he? Did he? I could tell you weren't sure, but the fact that it even occurred to you I might have killed her was no good. With her gone, I was the acting general manager. I finally had the position I wanted. The position I deserved. But there you were, snooping around."

A nearby bonfire suddenly exploded into flames, setting off the dozens of firecracker strands that covered it. The brief flash of light provided by the bonfire disappeared under a cloud of smoke and soot. Ash fell on Maggie, combining with the rain and perspiration to create a grimy coating. Between the roar of flames and relentless explosion of fireworks, the noise was deafening. Maggie knew screaming wasn't an option. No one would hear her, and it might push Harrison into using the pistol he had trained on her. So she kept quiet, hoping if she lulled Harrison into complacency, it would give her an opportunity to break free.

"The interesting thing is," Harrison continued, "I never saw that scaredy-cat look in Uncle Steve's eyes. He always thought he was so much smarter and better than everyone else. But I bet he wouldn't have figured out how to get the bonfire to collapse. I was pretty proud of myself for that. I was always really good at Jenga. I knew exactly what piece to move so the tower would either stay upright or fall down."

He let go of Maggie's wrist and gestured with his gun for her to start walking. They climbed the levee with his gun to her back. "Don't even think about trying to get away," he warned her. "Uncle Steve made all his execs learn how to shoot. He sometimes based bonuses on your target practice scores. I got *really* good bonuses."

They reached the top of the levee, and Maggie paused. One bonfire after another burst into flames. The Crozats' was the last to go, and Maggie could hear her family and friends cheer. "It really is a festive occasion," Harrison said. "I was looking forward to it."

He frowned at Maggie as if missing the event was her fault. "Uh . . . sorry?" she responded, stupefied by his attitude.

Harrison poked her in the back with his gun. "Keep moving."

"Where?"

Harrison pointed toward the river. "That way."

Maggie carefully negotiated the wet hillside, but she couldn't stop herself from slipping and falling a few times. "You're wearing the wrong shoes for this," Harrison admonished her.

"If I'd known I was going to be kidnapped, I would've worn hiking boots," she responded, adding with a mutter, "with switchblade toes."

"Heard that. Wasn't funny."

They finally reached the river's edge. Maggie felt numb with fear. "So what are you going to do? Shoot me and dump my body in the water?"

"Eventually. But first, a boat ride."

Harrison prodded her toward an old boat with an ancient motor attached to its stern. Labeling it a rust bucket would have been a compliment. Maggie feared for both their lives in the beat-up dinghy. She couldn't imagine it bucking the forceful currents of the Mighty Mississip.

"Welcome to the *SS Good-Bye Maggie*," Harrison said, grinning at his mordant joke. "I had a great idea for doing river tours from Belle Vista. In a better boat, natch, but this is all I can afford right now. But isn't that a good idea?"

"It's a great idea." *Maybe if I flatter him, he'll let me go*, Maggie thought. She knew this was a reach but was desperate for any kind of plan.

"Uncle Steve shot it down. Said the insurance premium would be too high. I thought once he was dead, Bea would go for it, but she was all, 'Your uncle was right; it's too expensive to insure.' Idiots."

"Being rejected by your idol must have been hard," Maggie said, mustering up a sympathetic tone, hoping to soften Harrison. A spasm of emotion crossed his face, and for a moment she thought the tactic might have worked. Then he shrugged.

"Just makes him as big a loser as my father. Hop on board."

Maggie did as she was told, and Harrison followed after her. She clutched the side of the small boat as it rocked back and forth. "Let me guess. Your plan is to head down the river a few miles, shoot me, and then toss me over. The current is so strong, it could carry me to the ocean. They might never find my body."

"Yes, exactly. Look at you, so smart."

"I know the river. I grew up next to it."

Harrison picked up a long, heavy rope. "I have to put my gun down to get the engine started, so I need to tie you up." He grabbed Maggie's hands before she could make a move away from him and wound the rope around them. He tied it off and gave her a shove. She fell on her back, and Harrison began tying her feet together with another piece of rope.

"You're the smart one, Harrison," Maggie said. "It sounds like neither your uncle nor Bea really appreciated what you could bring to Belle Vista."

"I know, right?" Harrison sounded aggrieved. "Bea never respected me or my talents. You should have seen the performance evaluation she wrote about me. It was a bunch of lies. Okay, so sometimes I took a little cash when I needed it or yelled at a guest when they were asking for stupid stuff like extra towels. But I *was* the owner's nephew, so it's like the money was mine. And it cost money to wash those towels. I was doing BV a favor. But what really ticked me off is when she said Uncle Steve only sent me down here because he thought I couldn't hack the investment banking business. Turned out to be true. Wow, was that a bummer."

"Is that why you helped . . . bring about his demise?" Maggie posed the question delicately, hoping it wouldn't cause him to blow.

"Oh, I didn't. I loved Uncle Steve. Well, until he turned on me. Stupid Bea's the one who offed him. I just helped her cover it up."

"When you think about it, she did you a favor," Maggie said. "It removed one obstacle to you running Belle Vista."

"Well, yeah, except there was still Bea." He smirked and added, "Until there wasn't." Harrison finished tying up Maggie and gave the ropes a tug. "Excellent. We're in good shape here. Now let's hit the river."

Harrison turned his attention to the motorboat engine. He yanked on a cord to engage it but nothing happened. He cursed and tried again. The engine sputtered for a minute and died. As Harrison futzed with the engine, Maggie came to a potentially lifesaving realization. Steve Harmon's nephew might claim to be a sharpshooter, but he'd clearly never been a Boy Scout. His knots were weak, and he'd left enough slack in the rope for Maggie, with some effort, to wriggle her hands free. She reached down and untied her legs as quickly as possible. The noise from the bonfire celebrations was her friend, masking the sound of her sneaking up behind Harrison. There was nothing on the boat that she could use to knock him out, so she simply grabbed his gun and threw it in the water. Then she jumped out of the boat onto the shore. The rocking caused by her leap got Harrison's attention. He yelled a stream of profanity as he jumped out of the boat after her and gave chase.

Maggie slipped and slid as she ran from Harrison. She fell to her knees and clawed her way up the hill. Lightning flashed, and the clouds unleashed a hard, steady rain. She reached the top of the levee, where the earth was compacted into a dirt road, and sprinted through a thick haze of soot and rain toward the Crozat bonfire. She blessed Sandy and DanceBod. No one could hear her screaming for help, but frequent classes had given her increased stamina and agility. Maggie easily kept a fast pace and leapt over bumps while Harrison, who was clearly no athlete, stumbled as he tried to keep up with her.

She finally reached the Crozat bonfire, now a fierce blaze that even the rain couldn't dampen. She saw her father halfway down the levee offering beer to bystanders and yelled to him. Another strand of firecrackers erupted, trapping Maggie in a smoke cloud. A hand reached out and grabbed her arm. Maggie turned and came face-to-face with her would-be captor. She remembered a move from Hip-HopBod and threw all her strength into leaping into the air and spinning. She landed on one foot and kickboxed Harrison with the other. Taken by surprise, he lost his balance, falling backward into the bonfire with a scream. As Maggie watched in horror, the fire illuminated Harrison's face, making him resemble less a man than a fiery, homicidal gargoyle.

Chapter Twenty-Eight

As Maggie dragged her attacker out of the fire by his feet, there was a flash of lightning and more rain poured down on them. The cloudburst stopped as quickly as it began, dampening the fire and saving Harrison's life but not preventing him from receiving severe burns. Tug and other partygoers realized what was happening and ran to her. Suddenly, the bonfire collapsed. Tug grabbed a fire extinguisher and aimed it at the flaming logs rolling toward revelers, who screamed and stumbled in a desperate dash away from the blazing wood.

"Call an ambulance for Harrison," Maggie yelled, collapsing on the ground next to him. "And the police. Harrison killed Bea Boxler and just tried to kill me too."

"Already done," said Little Earlie, who was by Tug's side. "Ambulance and police were here to begin with, in case of an accident. That's them coming up the levee."

Maggie saw EMTs Cody and Regine making their way up the hillside with a stretcher. Behind them were Rufus and Artie Belloise, moving as fast as the spare tires around their middles would let them. Cal Vichet loped up the hill after Ru and Artie. Tug tossed aside the fire extinguisher and went to his daughter. He helped Maggie to her feet just as Rufus and Artie reached them. "We were right, Ru," Maggie said, using her jacket sleeve to wipe grime off her face.

"Harrison, huh?" He walked over to the EMTs. "He gonna live?"

"Yeah," Cody said. "But the next few months are gonna be painful." He and Rene lifted Harrison, now conscious and groaning, onto the stretcher.

"Artie, go with the ambulance and guard the suspect," Rufus said.

The official business was interrupted by Tannis Greer, who'd managed to make her way up the steep levee despite her cocktail attire. "Little Earlie Waddell, you are the worst date *ever*," she snapped at him, furious. "I'm still waiting on the drink you said you were going to get me, like, a half hour ago."

"You're gonna have to wait a lot longer," Little Earlie said. He addressed the officers. "While you're arresting people, you might want to take her into custody. I found out why she's so het up on selling Doucet. She's been taking bribes from developers."

"What?!" Tannis screeched. "He's lying because I said I was thinking of breaking up with him."

"Actually, the only reason I 'dated' you was because I got to wondering how someone on your salary could afford such fancy clothes and a fancy car. I had a feeling something bad was going on, and I was right. I took a ton of notes whenever I was around one of your 'business meetings.' I shared them with the executive board, and they filed charges against you. The executive board has filed charges to have you arrested for fraud."

"Wha—you—I—" Tannis sputtered. Then a look of panic crossed her face, and she took off running down the levee. However, her expensive pumps were not designed for anything except showing off toe cleavage, so she lost her balance, fell, and began rolling down the hill like a beer bottle.

"I'll get her," Cal Vichet said. "With all this arresting, I'm barely getting to see the dang bonfires." He sighed and set off after Tannis.

"Little Earlie, forgive me for thinking you'd traded your morals for a hot blonde," Maggie said.

"I'm not *that* desperate. Well, a little, maybe. But I do try to keep my standards a skosh above rock bottom."

Tug put his arm around his daughter's shoulder. "Let's get you home and into a hot shower. Then we can talk the rest of the night away."

"Sounds wonderful, Dad."

Maggie, Tug, and Little Earlie hiked down the hillside. In the dark, Maggie saw the outline of a man striding up to meet them. "Bo," she cried out and ran to him. She slipped and slid her way down the hill until she literally fell into his arms.

"Thank God you're okay," he said, holding Maggie close to him. They clung to each other for a moment, and then he released her. "We need to talk." He stepped away from the others and motioned for Maggie to follow him. "I'm sorry I couldn't get here faster, but with so many officers on bonfire duty, I got pulled onto another case." Bo paused. "A warrant went out for Chris's arrest. He's alleged to have stolen and then tried to sell a painting from Belle Vista."

Maggie took a moment to process this ugly turn, and then it hit her. "The Audubon print at Belle Vista," Maggie said dully. "I was right. It's authentic."

"Yes, and apparently worth a fortune. Anyway, we picked him up at St. Pierre Parish Airfield. He was about to take off in Harmon's plane."

Maggie nodded. "Harmon taught him how to fly."

Her voice broke on the word "fly," and Bo took her in his arms again. "I'm sorry."

"He's not who he was, Bo. He's just not."

"I know."

Tug approached the couple. "Y'all up for trying to salvage some of tonight? It is Christmas Eve."

"Yes," Maggie said. "But the first stop is church."

Chapter
Twenty-Nine

Somehow, despite the evening's mayhem, Maggie made it to the nine PM mass at St. Theresa's. So did her friends, family, and guests. Visiting priest Father Jerome, well aware he was a ringer for beloved Father Prit, kept the mass light and quick. Maggie said a silent prayer for Chris. She hoped that somehow he'd find his way back to being the man she once loved.

By ten PM, everyone was gathered under the Crozat party tent, enjoying a potluck buffet as they waited for a special showing of the Midnight Mass broadcast from the Vatican. The Crozats had used extra proceeds from their bake sales to rent a blow-up screen. A playlist of Christmas carols mixed with traditional Cajun tunes provided background music. *Only in Pelican is there a Midnight Mass after-party*, Maggie thought with affection.

The tent was filled with people she cared deeply about, or could at least tolerate. Little Earlie and Ione were hanging out together. Ione was grateful to the journalist for exposing Tannis, and he was happy to celebrate the emergency phone call from Doucet's executive board restoring Ione to her position as Doucet's general manager. "The descendant of enslaved people running a plantation," Ione mused. "I've always wondered how my ancestors would react to that. Would they see it as ironic or as some kind of vindication? Anyway, Earlie, I don't know how you figured out what that Tannis was up to, but I owe you for it."

"You don't, and it wasn't too hard. No one's driving a Beamer on that salary."

"That is the God's honest truth," Ione chortled.

As Maggie made the rounds of guests, she noted a prodigious amount of hand-holding. Gaynell and Chret hadn't let go of each other all night. Lee had managed to intertwine his calloused fingers with Gran's soft, delicate ones. Whitney and Zach each held one of Xander's small hands. And Sandy held Ru's big mitt with one hand while the other clung to King Cake's lead. Maggie was happy to see that the O'Days and Marco's tour group were having a great time as well, although she didn't spot Marco in the crowd. Bo had gone home to shower and change after his encounter with Chris but was due back shortly. The only loved ones missing were Kyle and Lia, who was still on bed rest, but Maggie planned on visiting them Christmas Day, armed with a hot meal and baby presents.

Ninette came toward her daughter. She was wearing a red sweater with dark-green pants and her Christmas apron. Since Maggie's mother was so rarely without an apron, for years her family had given her ornately decorated "holiday" aprons as a joke. This one sported jingle bells, along with a sequined Santa. "There's someone to see you," Ninette said.

"Really?" Maggie responded, intrigued. "I thought everyone I knew was here."

Ninette raised an eyebrow and gestured with her head toward the tent's opening, where Emme Charbonnet Harmon stood. Maggie raised an eyebrow as well and went to the widow.

"My apologies for disturbing your party," Emme said.

"You're not disturbing a thing. In fact, we'd love to have you join us. Is Dan here?"

"He's in the car. We're on our way back to New Orleans from the hospital. We met with Harrison and his lawyer."

"This must be so hard on Dan. And you, of course."

"It's really only hard on me because it's hard on Dan. But his other son is flying in from California to be with him. And he's got me." A strand of hair had escaped Emme's black velvet headband. She tucked it back in place. "Having experienced my mother and brother—and I'm sorry for that—I thought you'd appreciate a small update on their situation. To help out my mother financially, Steve bought the family manse using a reverse mortgage arrangement years ago. That's run out, so I own the house now. I'm putting it on the market right after the holidays. Mother will be relocated to an assisted living facility."

"And Philip?"

"He's on his own. He'll actually have to—gasp!—get a job. So if you were considering commingling your bloodlines—"

Maggie held up her hand. "Oh, stop right there. *So* not happening."

Emme smiled. "I didn't think so. You seem bright and capable, qualities that would doom my brother's chances with you." She glanced behind her. Maggie could see Dan in the driver's seat of the car, resting his head against the steering wheel. "I better go. But thank you. Hideous as it is to lose a husband and learn a nephew is a murderer, it's better to have answers. And I know you were part of that."

"Good luck, Emme. And I'm not sure if this is appropriate or not, but . . . Merry Christmas."

"That's not my holiday anymore. It's my mother's. I'm converting to Judaism." The expression on Emme's face was happy yet also slightly malicious. "So mazel tov, Maggie. Good luck to you."

Emme departed, and Maggie made a beeline to the liquor table. JJ, dressed in a silk caftan covered with a design of holiday ornaments, reached under the table and pulled out a chilled bottle of champagne. "Private stash," he stage-whispered, holding a finger to his lips.

"I promise not to tell if you promise to keep pouring," Maggie said. JJ winked at her, and she kissed him on the cheek.

Her friends had all convened at a large table. Gaynell motioned her over. "We want to know how y'all figured out Harrison was the murderer."

"He didn't murder Steve Harmon," Rufus said, correcting her. "We have evidence that would make a solid case against Bea Boxler, if she was still among us. Her knife was confirmed as the murder weapon. We also found a key to Doucet among her belongings. Harmon had one as well, and she sneaked off with it to make a copy at Colombe Hardware. Emile Bouchard verified making it for her, as well as selling her an accelerant that matched what was used to start the fire at the art studio. Apparently Maggie's reputation as an amateur detective made her nervous. It's a little insulting that my detecting skills didn't inspire her to torch me, but I'll get over it."

"I was a way easier target, Ru. You're too intimidating."

"Nice, Magnolia. Thank you for that," Rufus said. He tipped an imaginary hat to her. "What also helped us tag Boxler as the culprit was an interesting discovery that Maggie and her Gran' made."

"Bea began working for Harmon on the day that marked the ten-year anniversary of her mother's suicide," Maggie said. "And killed him on the twentieth anniversary of her death. It was a plan that must have festered inside of her for years. We—" Maggie stopped herself. "I can say 'we,' Rufus?"

"Yeah, but don't make a habit of it."

"Noted. Anyway, we think when Harrison discovered Bea's plot, not only did he do nothing to stop her, he helped transport Harmon's body from Belle Vista where she killed him to Doucet."

"We—and by this we I mean the actual Pelican PD—picked up evidence of blood splatter in her car that we matched to the victim," Rufus said.

"But I thought Harrison idolized his uncle." Ione put her hands on her head and shook it back and forth. "It's all so messed up."

"That's because Harrison is 'messed up,' mentally and emotionally. Gran' once said something about Philip Charbonnet that kept coming back to me: 'The son is not the father.' I was looking at Magnolia Marie Doucet's portrait one day and noticed how the artist portrayed her second husband, General Cabot, as being very protective of his stepson." Maggie chose not to include Magnolia Marie's appearances in her dreams. "Steve Harmon didn't have sons. But he had a nephew: Harrison. And what if the nephew was not the uncle? As I got to know Harrison, I began getting a sense that he wasn't quite right. He had major anger issues and was self-involved to the point of being a narcissist. And it occurred to me the only person who ever mentioned that Harrison was in line for the throne was Harrison himself."

"Steve Harmon was one of those business dudes who had an employee whose only job was to hide or get rid of negative stories about him or his family," Rufus shared. "But when Bo was stuck on desk duty, he used the time to drill down on the Internet and found some interesting facts about our suspect. Court records of assault charges brought against him as early as prep school. He spent a year at a Connecticut facility for troubled teens after he tried stabbing a teacher with a letter opener for giving him a bad grade."

Maggie picked up the story. "I think at first Steve Harmon probably saw Harrison as a kid from a troubled background who was acting out. Who knows, maybe he felt a glimmer of guilt after Harrison's dad took the fall for him in an insider trading case and went to jail. He may have also thought Harrison's aggression would make him a success on Wall Street. But Harrison's deviant behavior was only that. It didn't go hand and hand with some kind of business brilliance. Once Harmon realized this, he sent him down here. Harrison's not stupid. He knew his uncle had shunted him aside. And the flip side of adoration is hatred. But he was desperately conflicted. That's why he punished Sandy by kidnapping King Cake. He was furious that she shared how his uncle had assaulted her."

"I can talk smack about my people, but you can't," Ione said.

"Exactly. He stopped by our bake stand the morning of the kidnapping and said he was on the way back from Harmon's funeral. But I noticed big splotches of mud on the bottom of his pants and on his jacket. It made me suspicious."

"Gotta love that artist's eagle eye of yours," Rufus said, nodding with approval.

"When he signed credit card receipts for baked goods, I also happened to notice he was a lefty. I usually pick up on that because I'm a lefty too."

"Magnolia Marie Crozat, we finally have something in common," Rufus said. "Lefty fist bump."

He made a fist with his left hand that Maggie bumped with hers. "The coroner determined Bea was stabbed by a lefty, so there was that. And when I was with him at Belle Vista the night Bea died, he somehow knew that she was the prime suspect in Harmon's murder. I asked Ru if there was any chance this information leaked out from Pelican PD—"

"No way, no how," Rufus interrupted. "We might only follow the rules we like in Louisiana, but that don't mean we'd blab about a suspect before we had proof. Harrison drugged Boxler before he stabbed her. We're assuming he probably drugged her more than once so he could do some snooping in her room, which is how he figured out what she was up to. Saw her hate shrine to his uncle and the knife and put things together."

"Harrison knew Harmon would never reinstate him in his New York financial operations," Maggie said. "But he thought that with his uncle and eventually Bea out of the way, he'd at least be able to claim Belle Vista for himself."

"But who ran him off the road?" Gaynell asked. "Or, wait—did he do that to himself to make it look he was being targeted by the murderer?"

"Oh, man, don't tell me we got another amateur detective," Rufus grumbled. "But yeah, that's exactly what happened. There was no evidence of another car on the patch of road when he was there. Plus if he had truly been run off the road, his injuries would have been a whole lot worse. I've seen some accidents when people lost control on that curve, and all I'll say is that the results ain't pretty."

"Well, I'm glad y'all nailed him before the holidays," Gaynell said. "Knowing we don't have to run around in a panic because a murderer is on the loose is a nice Christmas present."

"Speaking of presents," Ione nudged Maggie, "your handsome man is here."

Maggie looked toward the tent opening to see Bo. He had the sheen of a fresh shower, and his still-damp ebony hair was slicked back, which seemed to articulate the angles of his high cheekbones. He wore a crisp white shirt and black sport coat over jeans, along with the cowboy boots Maggie remembered from their recent trip to Texas to investigate a previous murder. *Gran' was right about the male model thing*, Maggie thought. She could sense the eyes of every unmarried woman—and a few who sported wedding rings—in the room gravitate toward him and was suddenly overwhelmed with insecurity.

Bo spotted Maggie. His face lit up. She went to him, and he gave her a kiss that made all self-doubt evaporate. "How do you feel?" she asked.

"A little woozy, but aside from that, pretty good. Especially right now."

His hand caressed Maggie's back. "Wow, my knees are actually buckling," she said. "I'm this close to passing out from desire right here in the middle of this tent."

Bo released her with a chuckle. She led him to her table, where hugs and holiday greetings were exchanged. "Maggie, chère, come here," Gran' called to her. "Wait until you see this."

"I'll be right back," Maggie told Bo, then hurried to her grandmother. "Is everything okay?"

"Oh, darlin', it's better than okay. Look." Gran' handed Maggie her tablet, which was opened to the Trippee.com website. "All our negative reviews are finally gone. They've been replaced by raves from Marco, everyone in his group, and each individual member of the O'Day family."

"It's a Christmas miracle, Gran'."

"Indeed it is, chère."

"I'll thank our guests. They're all here, except for Marco. But he must be somewhere around."

"Isn't that him by the entrance to the tent? Oh. Oh . . ." Gran' put her hand on her heart.

"Gran', what?" Maggie asked, worried.

Gran' ignored her. Instead she ran to the tent entrance as quickly as her winter-white patent leather pumps would carry her. She threw herself into the arms of a tall, redheaded man who was a reflection of his identical twin, Tug Crozat.

"Uncle Tig," Maggie cried out and dashed to him. Her parents were already there, and all the Crozats vied for hugs from the effervescent man.

Marco stood proudly by Tig's side. "A little holiday gift for you Crozats." He smiled affectionately at Tig. "And for me too."

"Marco let me know what y'all have been through," Tig said. "I had to come."

"Brother, my brother," Tug said, his voice husky. "I have missed that thick head of yours."

"I think you mean thick head of *hair*, brother," Tig teased, tousling his twin's thinning locks. "Where's my gorgeous niece?"

"Not sure who that might be, but I'm right here, Uncle Tig."

Maggie let her Tig bury her in a bear hug. "I've missed you in New York, chère," he said, squeezing her tightly. "You need to know that the way you fought back against Steve Harmon's take-over really impressed my general managers. If you ever want to move up in the organization, let me know. I'll make sure there's an art studio wherever you go."

"Hey, no poaching my kid," Tug said, faking a glare at his brother.

"Whoa, both of you," Maggie said. "My New Year's resolution is to make art my top priority again. Much as I love Crozat—and all of you—that's what fills my soul. But for now, I think we need to put business aside and focus on the holiday."

"Yes, there's so much catching up to do," Gran' said. "I'll make you a plate, Tig." She bit her lip, overcome with emotion. "Oh, sweet boy. You here . . . tonight. It could bring a tear to a glass eye."

Tig gave his mother a hug that lifted her off her feet. "Crying is no way to celebrate Christmas Eve."

"Oh, man, I almost forgot." Tug hastened over to the giant screen and whistled to get everyone's attention. "It's minutes to midnight, y'all," he announced. "They're about to rebroadcast the Vatican Midnight Mass." He pushed a button on a remote, bringing the screen to life and with it, St. Peter's Basilica.

The crowd in the Crozats' tent, like the one in the Basilica, was hushed. "The screen is so big, I feel like I could walk right into that mass," Gaynell whispered.

A camera panned the papal audience. Everyone in the tent watched for a glimpse of Pelican's own Father Prit. "There!" Lee Bertrand shouted.

The camera caught the priest in profile, but he turned around as if he heard Lee call out. The Pelicaners whooped and cheered as the procession of cardinals, bishops, and prelates marched solemnly down the Basilica's aisle, followed by the pope himself. Tears rolled down Father Prit's cheeks. "He's so moved, he's crying," Ione said, wiping tears from her own eyes. Father Prit then surreptitiously held out his cell phone and took a picture of himself with the promenade of religious leaders in the background. "Did he just take a selfie? I sure hope the pope didn't see that."

There was a chorus of text pings, including one from Maggie's cell phone. "It's from Vanessa," she told her friends. "She's asking us to come to the road."

"I know, we all got the same message," Little Earlie said.

Maggie's crew trooped out of the tent to the road fronting Crozat, followed by most of the other partygoers. "Do I hear music?" she asked.

"I know I do," Bo said.

The sound grew louder. Around the bend came a massive tractor trailer festooned with a blaze of Christmas decorations, pulling a float decorated like the North Pole. "It's the

Christmas Caroling Truck," someone in the crowd yelled. The Peli-Carolers, dressed in their Dickensian garb, waved from the back of the float, and a half dozen Cajun musicians waved from the front. Vanessa and Quentin MacIlhoney, dressed as Mr. and Mrs. Claus, sat in two quasi thrones in front of Santa's house. "Hey, Maggie," Quentin called to her, "this is a little thank-you present for landing me three clients in one day—Harrison Fenner, Tannis Greer, and Chris Harper. Merry Christmas, y'all!"

"Merry Christmas!" the crowd yelled back.

With that, the musicians broke into an up-tempo rendition of a Cajun classic, "Christmas on the Bayou," inspiring the crowd to dance as they sang along. Bo took Maggie's hand. "I've got something for you, and I don't want to wait until tomorrow. Come."

Bo led Maggie to his car. He opened the passenger's-side door and took out a flat, rectangular box tied with a red satin ribbon. "Merry Christmas, chère," he said, handing her the box.

Maggie undid the ribbon and opened the box. Resting on cotton was an assortment of the highest quality sable paintbrushes. "They're perfect." She stroked the brushes' soft bristles. "I love them."

"Look under the cotton."

Maggie did as Bo told her and gasped. She pulled a gold chain from the bottom of the box. Dangling from it was a charm shaped like a painter's palette, with each color of the palette a different gemstone. "Oh, Bo," she said, a catch in her throat. "It's the most beautiful necklace I've ever seen."

"I found it when we were in New Orleans. It's like the universe sent me on that trip to find the necklace. Let me put it on you."

Maggie lifted her hair, and Bo fastened the clasp around her neck. She stooped down and admired the charm in the car's sideview mirror. "I'm in love. With the necklace *and* you." She stood up and kissed him. "Now it's my turn."

She raced to the shotgun cottage and pulled the box holding Bo's gift out from under her bed. She ran back to him, stumbling as she tried not to lose her grip on the bulky bundle. "Merry Christmas to *you*, chère," she said, thrusting it into his arms. "The universe was speaking to both of us in New Orleans."

Bo opened the box and pulled out the black leather jacket. "Wow," he said, gaping at it. He opened the trunk door of his SUV and tossed the box inside. Then he pulled off his sport coat and threw that in as well. He put on the new jacket and leaned against the car, striking a pose. "How do I look?"

"Like a male model."

Bo chortled. "I don't think so. But to quote someone I love very much, it's 'perfect.'" He relaxed his pose, reached for Maggie, and pulled her to him. They embraced as the partygoers segued into a boisterous rendition of "Jambalaya."

"That's a whole lotta hootin' and hollerin'." Maggie laughed.

"We'll have a better view of all the fun from the levee," he said.

Bo and Maggie crossed to the levee and climbed to its crown. Maggie gazed down at the river, where a tugboat festooned with white lights nudged a barge down the Mississippi. Then she turned her attention to the festivities in front of Crozat. The carolers below began singing a French version of "The First Noel," accompanied by the Cajun musicians. Gradually the party guests joined in. *"Aujourd'hui le Roi des Cieux au milieu de la nuit voulut naître chez nous de la Vierge Marie,"* they sang. Bo put his arms around Maggie's waist. He bent down, and his lips brushed her neck. "Come home with me," he whispered. "It's time."

Maggie couldn't find the breath to speak, so she simply nodded and rested her head on Bo's shoulder. She closed her eyes and imagined where she might be in New York on Christmas Eve. An elegant cocktail party in Brooklyn perhaps, overlooking a glittering Manhattan skyline and the Empire State Building bathed in green and red lights. It would have been beautiful. And nowhere near as magical as Christmas Eve in Pelican, Louisiana. Her home. Where she belonged.

And where on Christmas morning, she would wake up next to the man with whom she dreamed of spending the rest of her life.

Shrimp Remoulade

Shrimp remoulade is a popular New Orleans appetizer that is served cold. Some restaurants like the legendary Galatoire's offer it on a bed of lettuce. Ninette Crozat likes to serve it to her guests atop a pitted avocado half. It's a delicious and easy dish to make.

Ingredients

Note: It's important to finely mince all ingredients that require it.

3 minced hardboiled eggs

3 minced scallions

2 minced celery ribs

½ cup minced fresh parsley

3 tbsp. minced dill pickle

1¾ cups vegetable oil

⅔ cup stone ground mustard (or Creole
  mustard, if it's available)

2 tbsp. horseradish

3 tbsp. lemon juice

1 tbsp. paprika

½ tsp. salt

½ tsp. sugar

2 lbs. cold shrimp, peeled and deveined

Instructions

Mix together all the ingredients, *except for the shrimp*. Chill for at least half an hour.

When you're ready to serve the dish, halve 4–5 avocados and remove the pits. Distribute the shrimp evenly over the avocados, and then top each serving with cold remoulade sauce. (Leftover sauce can be transferred to a jar and stored in the refrigerator for several weeks.)

Serves 8–10.

Muffaletta Frittata

The muffaletta sandwich originated with New Orleans's Italian immigrants. The sandwich consists of a variety of Italian cold cuts covered with olive salad on a round loaf of Sicilian sesame bread. Ninette's dish is inspired by this unique sandwich. You can serve it for breakfast, but it also makes a great lunch meal when accompanied by a salad.

Ingredients

1 cup diced hard salami
¼ cup grated Parmesan cheese
2 tbsp. chopped pepperoncini salad peppers
1 (2.25 oz.) can sliced black olives, drained
¼ cup sliced green olives, drained
4 oz. provolone cheese, diced
1 celery rib, finely chopped
½ red bell pepper, finely chopped
1 tbsp. olive oil
2 tbsp. cooking sherry

1 tbsp. red wine vinegar
¼ cup chopped fresh parsley
6 eggs
1½ cups egg whites
¼ tsp. salt
¼ tsp. pepper

Instructions

Preheat the oven to 375 degrees.

Stir together the first twelve ingredients (everything except the eggs, salt, and pepper) in a medium mixing bowl. Cover and chill between one to twenty-four hours.

When ready to prepare the dish, grease a 13″ × 9″ pan with olive oil. In a separate medium mixing bowl, beat the eggs, egg whites, salt, and pepper. Spoon the muffaletta mixture into the eggs, and stir them together. Pour this mixture into the greased pan, making sure the ingredients are evenly distributed.

Bake for 15–20 minutes until the eggs are firm.

Serves 8.

Holiday Brandy
Pain Perdu

Pain perdu translates to "lost bread." It's the Louisiana equivalent of French toast. Ninette's version of the dish is baked, not pan-fried. If you prefer your pain perdu alcohol-free, substitute another ½ cup of half-and-half cream for the brandy.

Ingredients

1 loaf French bread, cut diagonally in thick slices
    that can cover the bottom of a 10″ × 9″ pan
8 eggs
2 cups milk
1 cup half-and-half cream
½ cup brandy
2 tsp. vanilla extract
¼ tsp. ground cinnamon

¾ cup butter
1⅓ cups dark brown sugar
3 tbsp. light corn syrup

Instructions

Butter a 13″ × 9″ baking dish. Arrange the slices of bread in the bottom. In a large bowl, beat together the eggs, milk, cream, vanilla, brandy, and cinnamon. Pour over the bread slices, cover, and refrigerate overnight.

When ready to bake, preheat the oven to 350 degrees. In a small saucepan, combine butter, brown sugar, and corn syrup; heat until bubbling. Pour over the bread and egg mixture.

Bake uncovered for 40 minutes.

Let cool slightly, and then dust with powdered sugar.

Serves 12.

Coconut Pecan Bars

Enjoy the Crozat family's twist on a popular Southern dessert. It's not as sweet as your typical pecan pie, which is a plus for a lot of people. If you'd like it sweeter, try adding ⅓ cup more corn syrup or a full cup of brown sugar. I'm a big fan of fiddling with recipes, as are the Crozats!

Ingredients

Crust

1¾ cups all-purpose flour
¾ cup butter, softened (you can save a few calories by used reduced-calorie butter or margarine)
⅓ cup sugar
⅓ cup unsalted coarsely chopped pecans

Filling

4 large egg whites, lightly beaten
⅓ cup light corn syrup
⅔ cup dark brown sugar, firmly packed

6 tbsp. butter (or reduced-calorie), melted

1 tsp. rum or vanilla flavoring (baker's choice)

⅛ tsp. salt

¾ cup unsalted coarsely chopped pecans

1 cup shredded coconut

Instructions

Heat oven to 350 degrees.

For the crust: Combine 1¾ cups flour, the butter, and the sugar in a mixing bowl. Beat at slow, then medium speed, scraping the sides often, until the mixture resembles coarse crumbs. Stir in ⅓ cup pecans. Press the crust mixture evenly onto the bottom of an ungreased 13″ × 9″ baking pan. Bake for 18–22 minutes or until the edges are very light golden brown.

For the filling: Mix together the egg whites, corn syrup, melted butter, brown sugar, salt, and rum or vanilla flavoring. Stir in the chopped pecans and shredded coconut. Pour the mixture over the baked crust, and return the bars to the oven. Bake for twenty minutes or until the filling is firm and no longer wobbles.

Remove the pan from the oven, and let it cool completely before cutting. If there are any leftovers, I like to store them in the freezer. They get deliciously chewy.

Makes 8, 16, or 24 bars, depending how you cut them.

Spicy Cajun Sugar Cookies

This is the recipe that Ninette uses to make the cookies that the Crozats snack on and use to decorate their Christmas tree. It's got a unique kick to it, thanks to a special ingredient.

Ingredients

Cookies

1 cup (2 sticks) butter
1 cup sugar
2 large eggs
1 tbsp. vanilla extract
3 cups flour
1 tsp. cinnamon
½ tsp. cayenne pepper
½ tsp. baking soda

½ tsp. salt
Cookie cutters

Frosting
Boxed royal icing mix (available at craft stores)

Instructions

For the cookies: Cream the butter, then add the sugar and beat until it's fluffy. Beat in the eggs and vanilla. In a separate bowl, combine all the dry ingredients. Stir the dry ingredients into the butter and sugar mixture. Mix together until well combined. Chill the dough for a minimum of two hours or overnight.

Preheat your oven to 350 degrees. Roll out the cookie dough to ¼-inch thickness *on a well-floured board*. Cut the dough with the cookie cutters, and place the unbaked cookies on an ungreased cookie tray. (If the dough sticks to the rolling pin, add more flour to the board.) Use a chopstick to make a hole at the top of the cookies if you want to hang them on your tree. Make the hole bigger than you think it may need to be because the cookies will expand when they cook.

Bake for 5–8 minutes or until they're golden brown around the edges. *Let cool completely.*

For the frosting: Once the cookies have cooled, follow the directions on the icing box to make the icing. (Royal icing hardens quickly, so you don't want to make it too soon.) If you want to make colored icing, separate it into different bowls and mix the desired color into each bowl.

Ice the cookies, and let the icing harden. If you're using the cookies as decorations, add a loop of string or ribbon to hang them.

Makes approximately two dozen cookies.

Note: Two recipes mentioned in A Cajun Christmas Killing *can be found in previous Cajun Country Mystery novels. The recipe for Bourbon Pecan Bread Pudding is in* Plantation Shudders *and the recipe for Bananas Foster Coffee Cake is in* Body on the Bayou.

A Lagniappe About A Cajun Christmas Killing

"Lagniappe" is a Louisiana term that means "a little something extra." For me, it's a way of sharing some personal anecdotes about the wonderful region that inspired my Cajun Country Mystery series.

The bonfires on the Mississippi levee are an extraordinary Christmas tradition that I recommend everyone experience at least once in their lifetime.

Families, friends, and even coworkers spend weeks between Thanksgiving and Christmas Eve building the bonfires. As I write in this book, most are pyramids of logs stacked upward of thirty feet. Some people get whimsical and build bonfires shaped like a plantation home, or they rope together stacks of cane reed that snap, crackle, and pop when lit. During a recent visit, I even saw a bonfire shaped like a pirate ship. Many of the bonfires are laced with strands of firecrackers that add a noisy festivity when the bonfires are lit at seven PM on Christmas Eve. The river roads on both sides of the Mississippi are lined with enthusiastic onlookers who alternate between viewing the bonfires and celebrating at potluck parties packed with delicious homemade Cajun dishes. Bonfires are built up and down the Mississippi on both sides of the river, but the highest concentration is found in St. James Parish, around Gramercy (where we partied), Lutcher, and Paulina.

The origin of this tradition is murky. Some trace it all the way back to ancient Europe, where bonfires celebrated the end of a harvest. Others say that in previous centuries the bonfires were a way of guiding boats up the tricky Mississippi River during the holidays. But the most popular explanation of the bonfires on the levee is that they guide Papa Noel's way to the homes of Cajun children on Christmas Eve.

My dream of experiencing the levee bonfires finally came true thanks to a contest sponsored by the River Parishes Tourist Commission. The fabulous prize included a B and B stay, gift cards, swag, and most importantly, a chance to view the bonfires from a private party at a home on the East River Road. The weather was bad on Christmas Eve, and the bonfires were touch and go up until the last minute. My husband, daughter, and I said silent prayers that the event would take place as scheduled and not be postponed until New Year's Eve when we'd no longer be in town. Luckily, despite a persistent drizzle, the celebration was on.

Our hosts were an extended family of adult Cajun siblings who join forces every year to throw a legendary party. Guests may bring sides and desserts, but the family provides the main courses—a variety of jambalayas and gumbos that were hands down the best versions of these dishes I've ever eaten. A cry went up from the crowd when the first bonfire was lit, and fireworks exploded from a location down by the river. One by one, the bonfires burst into flames, setting off the firecrackers. I ran from one to another like a kid, getting soaking wet and covered in ash. The smoke haze became so thick, I couldn't see the person next to me as I slipped and stumbled on the wet levee grass. I shared every aspect of this adventure with Maggie Crozat—including the shower I had to take before attending Christmas Eve Mass. It was one of the most exciting events of my life.

*

I wanted to share something else with you inspired by a real-life incident. Recently, my daughter and I toured Laura, a Creole plantation on the West River Road. The tour guide told a story about how the family that built the manor house managed to skirt some laws imposed by American rule after the 1804 Louisiana Purchase. "In Louisiana," she said with a sly wink in a husky smoker's voice, "we only follow the rules we like." In a few words, the tour guide summed up a quirky attitude specific to Louisiana. I loved this line so much I gave those exact words to sometime-police chief Rufus Durand.

While we're on the subject of Laura, if you're considering a visit to Plantation Country, I recommend touring both a

Creole and an American plantation. Laura and Oak Alley are two of several that offer in-depth tours of the former; for the latter, plan a visit to a plantation like Houmas House or Nottoway. You'll come away with a greater understanding of the differences between the two cultures. And don't leave the area without visiting Whitney, the only plantation in Louisiana focused solely on slavery. The tour may be heart-wrenching, but it's essential.

Acknowledgments

DanceBod, the dance fitness studio in *A Cajun Christmas Killing*, was inspired by a real-life program called Dance It Out created by Billy Blanks Jr. I want to thank Tricia McNatt, Rae Toledo Latsch, Tristin Rupp, Marita De Lara Sobel, Victoria Genisce, and Emma Berdie Donson for their fabulous—and obviously inspirational—routines.

Reveille New Orleans Hotel was inspired by two wonderful French Quarter hostelries, Hotel Mazarin and Le Marais. They're both part of the New Orleans Collection, which transforms historic properties into five-star lodgings. I created Tig and Preferred Properties before I'd ever heard of the New Orleans Collection, and it made me so happy to know that there's a company that actual does what I fictionalized. A thank-you to Laura Fanguy and Tara DiPascal for all their help regarding the hospitality industry.

Beaucoup thanks to the awesome Jo Banner and Visit New Orleans Plantation Country for gifting us with the most wonderful way to watch the levee bonfires. And an equally big "merci" to Denise Hymel and the Roussel family for throwing a bonfire party that my family and I will never, ever forget.

Thanks to Ernie Back for his invaluable help with the business aspects of the story. A shout-out as always to my indefatigable agent, Doug Grad, and to Matt Martz, Sarah Poppe, and Heather Boak, the extraordinary team at Crooked Lane Books; also to the superterrific Dana Kaye and Julia Borcherts at Kaye Publicity. Mindy Schneider, Kathy McCullough, and Kate Shein—GoWalk rules! As does chicksonthecase.com and my fab fellow chicks Lisa Q. Mathews, Kellye Garrett, and Mariella Krause. Sandy Sechrest and Tom and Marie O'Day, thank you for your generosity at the Malice Domestic Convention, and I hope you enjoy being in print.

Thanks to all the friends who've supported me throughout this fabulous journey, with big hugs for my pals of umpteen years, Nancy Adler, Laurie Graff, and Von Rae Wood. And infinite thanks to my mom, my bros, and especially my husband, Jerry, and daughter, Eliza. Jer says that since I started my mystery series, he sees me more than he does when I work on television sitcoms, but he talks to me less because I'm always writing. Thanks for being so patient and keeping your sense of humor. Right now I'm writing I love you!